I0610412

The Chase Continues

A Novel of Suspense

Marc E. Overlock

Marc E. Overlock Books are available for order through
_____ Press

"This is a work of fiction. Names, characters, places and
incidents either are products of the author's imagination or
are used fictitiously. Any resemblance to actual events or
locales or persons, living or dead, is entirely coincidental."

Marc E. Overlock

Visit my website at www.MarcEOverlock.com

Printed in the United States of America
First Printing: November 2016
Published by Sojourn Publishing, LLC

ISBN-10: 1-62747-409-9
ISBN-13: 978-1-62747-409-2
eBook ISBN: 978-1-62747-023-0

For Wendy, again and always.

Though I walk in the shadow of the valley of death
I shall fear no evil.
Thy rod and thy staff they comfort me.
Psalm 23

SEQUEL NOVEL CHARACTERS

Name	Age	Comment / Characteristics
Jared Aloysius	76	Pinehurst Nursing Home resident. In love with Amy Quinn, the receptionist.
Mrs. Lacey Anttonen	68	Witness to first kidnapping in progress.
Mr. Collin Anttonen	68	Witness to first kidnapping in progress.
Roy Argulara	23	Law Intern at the law firm of Pellatino, Degrazio and Gomez.
Dr. Ian Baker	49	Chief of the Intensive Care Unit, Burbank Hospital.
Ms. Barbara Bennett	50	Pinehurst Nursing Home Administrator.
Mack Bistowish	46	Judge Melanson's Court Officer.
Axel Block	30	Amy Quinn's boyfriend.
Kristen Brigham	29	Fitchburg Sentinel Reporter.
Dan Brodie	39	Ship Welder at General Dynamics; gambling addict.

Velma (Koskinen) Brodie	38	Dr. Rebovitz's receptionist/transcriptionist. Tells Rican Rangers about Jeremy's mind-reading gift.
Gerald Callahan	29	Fitchburg Police Officer—guard at Edgerly Elementary School.
Connie Calhoun	48	Foreman on the General Dynamics shipyard.
Ezequiel Camacho	28	Burbank Hospital mechanic.
Juan Candelaria	40	José's Orchard Tenant Farmer.
Mia Candelaria	40	Wife of Juan, and José's Orchard Tenant Farmer.
Jayden Casiano	22	Ambulance Driver for the Rican Rangers.
Josephine Collier	5	Classmate of Jeremy's in Edgerly's accelerated kindergarten class.
Julia Condon	52	Librarian—Fitchburg Public Library. Helps José with hospital emergency response research.
Dr. Hercules Copoulos	48	Jeremy Hergenroeder's family doctor.
Nathan Cotter	58	Alexandria Hergenroeder's father; road crew boss for Massachusetts Dept. of Public Works.

Kurt Crider	42	Moderator of Rollstone Congregational Church.
Benita Cruz, RN	27	ICU Nurse—taking care of Ricardo at Burbank Hospital.
Cedro Cruz	12	Benita Cruz's brother. New member of Rican Rangers.
Mrs. Maria Fernanda Cruz	48	Mother of Benita Cruz.
Linda Dunn	35	Office Secretary, Rollstone Congregational Church.
Tammy Fiandaca	32	Tammy Fiandaca, JD, Boston Assistant DA. Finished second in her law class at Boston College in 1963.
Rafael Figueroa	23	Male nurse orientee at Burbank Hospital. Possible Rican Ranger.
Becky Filcher	13	7th grade student whose bike Jeremy steals.
Bill Fontaine	40	Organist, Rollstone Congregational Church.
Anna Franklin	38	Director, Human Resources Department— Burbank Hospital.

Mark Gallagher	29	Karate / Judo instructor. Owns the Karate studio next to Rollstone Church. Vietnam Vet; former MP.
Joe Garibaldi	38	Boston Globe crime beat reporter.
Duane Gurk	5	Classmate of Jeremy's in Edgerly's accelerated kindergarten class.
Pablo Gomez	48	José's criminal defense attorney. With the law firm of Pellatino, Degrazio and Gomez.
Caesar Gutiérrez	33	José's deceased father.
Daniella Gutiérrez	62	José's grandmother.
José Gutiérrez	35	Rican Ranger Leader / El Jefe.
Pilar Gutiérrez	29	José's cousin; Rican Ranger #3. One of Jeremy's first kidnappers.
Ricardo Gutiérrez	36	José's cousin; Rican Ranger #2. Huge guy; no neck. One of Jeremy's first kidnappers.
Jeremy Nathan Hergenroeder	5	Main character. Reads people's minds.
Alexandria Hergenroeder	29	Jeremy's mother and David Hergenroeder's wife.

Rev. David Hergenroeder	31	Minister at Rollstone Congregational Church. Jeremy's Dad.
Phillip Hergenroeder	55	David Hergenroeder's father. Builds houses for a living.
Frank Hirschfeld	56	Burbank Hospital's Director of Facilities.
Sgt. Finch Hudson	43	Fitchburg Police Desk Sergeant.
Christopher Johnson	30	Fitchburg Assistant District Attorney General.
Evelyn Kendall	34	Jimmy and Lori's mother; next door neighbor to the Hergenroeders.
Jimmy Kendall	5	Jeremy's neighbor and best friend. Also a student in Edgerly's accelerated kindergarten class.
Lori Kendall	9	Jimmy's sister and neighbor to Jeremy. Jeremy has a crush on her.
Sean Kirkpatrick	51	Mayor of Fitchburg, Massachusetts.
Missy Klondike	27	ER nurse at Fitchburg's Burbank Hospital.
Ben Knight	62	Fitchburg Fire Department Chief.

Marian Koshgarian	33	Fitchburg librarian—children's section. Helps Jeremy find books to read.
Tildemon (Tildy) LaFleur	37	Brothel owner; client of Pablo Gomez.
Vic Langston	39	Mass. State Policeman; works at State Police Barracks in Foxborough where José is taken after his arrest.
Paula Lovejoy	37	5th Grade Teacher at Edgerly Elementary School. Called police after Jeremy's first kidnapping.
Kathy Lundberg	5	Classmate of Jeremy's in Edgerly's accelerated kindergarten class.
Hector Madera	25	Rican Ranger Truck Driver—helps José at the orchard hideout.
Trixie McLoughlin	44	Bar maid tipster for Det. McNamara. Warns him about Rican Ranger infiltration into local trucking firms.

Det. Rodney McNamara	40	Fitchburg Police Detective. Third generation police officer. Wiley student of game theory before it became part of the public lexicon. Been married 15 years.
Agnes McNamara	38	Det. McNamara's wife.
Rod McNamara, Jr.	17	Twin son of Det. McNamara. Takes Ray Peterson's auto mechanics class.
Conor McNamara	17	Twin son of Det. McNamara. Takes Ray Peterson's auto mechanics class.
Col. Edward McPherson	55	Retired Army Colonel; Korean War Veteran; Rollstone Congregational Church member; Son Truman died in Vietnam.
Frankie	19	Truman McPherson's Teddy Bear.
Mrs. Lily McPherson	53	Wife of Col. McPherson.
Pinky McPherson	6	Col. McPherson's pet Doberman.
Truman McPherson	20	Col. McPherson's son. Killed in Vietnam War.

Winifred Meagher, RN	47	Dean at Greenfield Community College. Oversees nursing students.
Gianna Mercado	23	Niece of José Gutiérrez and Rican Ranger Pilot.
Charles "Chuck" Melanson	49	Judge, Boston Superior Court.
Julio Mendez	17	Fitchburg High School Mechanics Student.
John Miller	42	Burbank Hospital facilities department mechanic.
Penny Montgomery	27	Rican Ranger hired prostitute—fake girlfriend of Judge Chuck Melanson.
Ms. Helen Murphy, Prof.	38	Professor at Fitchburg State Teacher's College. Main teacher for Jeremy's advanced kindergarten class.
Kelly Owens		Receptionist for José's criminal defense firm, Pellatino, Degrazio and Gomez.
Ray Peterson	51	Fitchburg High School Shop Teacher—Auto Mechanics.
Gloria Petri	59	Burbank Hospital's Volunteer Receptionist/Greeter.

Wicksham Petri	57	Deceased husband of Gloria Petri, the volunteer greeter at Burbank Hospital.
Solomon Purdy	52	Boston's District Attorney General.
Amy Quinn	29	Pinehurst Nursing Home receptionist.
Dr. Azriel Rebovitz	42	Jeremy's treating psychiatrist; 6'5" tall; German émigré; Jewish.
Eva Rebovitz	67	Dr. Rebovitz's mother; German émigré; Jewish. Room 109 at Pinehurst.
Luis Ortiz de la Renta	25	Rican Ranger Truck Driver—helps José at the orchard hideout.
Tilsbury Ringgold	50	Sheriff—Ashburnham, Massachusetts.
Andy Ryan	32	Fitchburg Police Officer—one of the guards at Edgerly Elementary School.
Dominick Sangria	37	Shipyard welder and colleague of Dan Brodie. Hooked Dan up with José for a loan. José is Dominick's Uncle.

Dr. Chelsey Sneed	44	ER physician at Fitchburg's Burbank Hospital.
Artie Smithson	39	Burbank Hospital mechanic.
Granny Steele (Cotter)	56	Alexandria Hergenroeder's mother. Her cousin Grace was a "seer."
Rebecca Sullivan	8	Disabled daughter of Rick Sullivan. Suffered brain damage at birth.
Rick Sullivan	42	Shop Steward for the Industrial Union of Marine and Shipbuilding Workers of America; Local 8650.
Sondra Taylor	33	Office Secretary at Edgerly Elementary School.
William Testarossa	36	Policeman guarding Ricardo Gutiérrez in Burbank Hospital ICU.
Wendy Thomas	5	Classmate of Jeremy's in Edgerly's accelerated kindergarten class.
Roger Tomlinson	45	Rollstone Sexton
Tim Tolliver	52	Fitchburg Police Chief
Josiah Van Buren, Ed.D.	55	President of Greenfield Community College.
Parma Ventura, RN, MBA, MPH	49	Chief Nursing Officer, Burbank Hospital.

PREFACE

Welcome to the second novel in the *Chase* trilogy. This is the continuing story of five-year-old Jeremy Hergenroeder whose mind reading gift caught the attention of a local mob in his hometown of Fitchburg, Massachusetts. The year is 1968. Jeremy's parents, David and Alexandria, got worried that the voices he apparently was hearing in his head were a clear sign of early onset schizophrenia. Thinking that they should get him to a doctor and fast they managed to get a next day appointment with child psychiatrist Dr. Azriel Rebovitz. Dr. R, as Jeremy came to call him, figured out in about 15 minutes what the problem was—no problem at all, other than how to keep Jeremy's gift a secret. Like all good doctors, he dictated his chart notes right after the visit—and at that moment the secret got out.

I urge you to read the first novel in this trilogy entitled, *The Chase Is On*. Family and friends, every one of them biased, tell me it's a good read. Many of them also asked me, "What happens next, Marc?" So, this is Part 2. If you cannot get immediate access to the first book, fear not for I have written this sequel on the assumption that I can get you up to speed as the next phase of the chase unfolds. Wish me luck.

Enjoy!

PROLOGUE

Tuesday December 12, 1967—12:30 p.m.
Benita Cruz Comes of Age
Greenfield, Massachusetts

"Line up against the wall! Right now!" Winifred Meagher hollered to the 17 women in her charge. The women jumped to attention and rushed to get in line, all in the proper order just as they'd practiced the day before under Meagher's watchful eye.

Benita Cruz, almost RN, angled to the second spot in the line of fellow nursing students about to get their diplomas. "I'd never thought it possible to get a four year degree in just eighteen months," she whispered to no one.

The 17 students had been the guinea pigs in Greenfield Community College's brand new, *accelerated* nursing program, right beside the Berkshire Mountains, some two hours west of Benita's home town of Fitchburg. In that year and a half they'd digested and regurgitated enough medical science to choke even the brightest of medical students. Yet, as they embarked on their careers, they would never quite measure up to those same MDs, even though they did most of the healing work. Their Dean, Mrs. Meagher, age 47, stood a startling six foot, two inches tall. A long time RN herself, she'd never cottoned to any doctor's arrogance, and could haze them right back should they challenge her knowledge base. She'd served for 15 years as the school's hard driving nursing coach. Every student knew to watch out for her black bouffant hairdo in a crowd. When they'd see her coming, they'd duck around a corner or into the shadows to avoid her intimidating glare. It is said that nurses eat their young. Meagher never went hungry.

Josiah Van Buren, Ed.D, GCC's President, beamed as if each new nurse was family. Benita Cruz, salutatorian, was about to realize her lifelong ambition. As a Girl Scout, she had read about the exploits, not of the mother of nursing, Florence Nightingale, but Walt Whitman, the great American poet. Whitman had served as a nurse in various Army hospitals during the Civil War. By accident she had stumbled on his poem entitled 'The Great Army of the Sick' and sat transfixed as she read each verse. At that moment as she neared her 13th birthday, she felt God calling her to be a nurse.

Five years later, just weeks before her Fitchburg High School graduation, Benita asked her mother for help with the college's tuition. Mrs. Maria Fernanda Cruz responded by shaking her head in shame.

"You know, Benita, I would hand you the world if it was mine to give. Between my waitressing and seamstress work, we barely make ends meet as it is. Why don't you get a job and save for a couple years? You'll get the money together. I know you will. You can live here until you are ready to head to Greenfield."

"But Momma, the $250 scholarship they gave me has a deadline. I must accept by July 1st. Surely we can scrounge up the other $500!" Benita exclaimed, knowing the family had but $60 in the cookie jar. And that was for emergencies.

After Maria Fernanda whispered to a dear friend about her daughter's financial plight, word percolated through the Fitchburg, Massachusetts' grape vine. Poverty had dashed Benita's dream. Within minutes of hearing the tragic news, José Gutiérrez, de facto CEO of the Rican Rangers, a local Puerto Rican underworld organization, rang the Cruz's doorbell. Maria Fernanda answered the door. She knew of José and his Rangers and welcomed him into her living room.

Speaking in Spanish, José said, "Mrs. Cruz, I beg your forgiveness, and apologize for bothering you. I will only stay a minute. I have just now heard of Miss Benita's wish to go to nursing school. Why should a bright young girl in our community *not* go to college? I have met with my Rican Ranger leadership and we would welcome her application for an RR scholarship. Naturally, it would be more than the $500 I have heard she needs. Are there not the costs of books, room and board, laundry fees and, what of a nursing uniform or two? We cannot have Miss Benita walking the halls of Greenfield Hospital in street clothes, no? The patients and doctors would laugh at her!"

"I cannot ask your favor José. You are too kind. Benita will work and save for the money she needs. In a few years, she can pursue her dream and be indebted to no one."

"Perhaps you misunderstood me, Mrs. Cruz. Our organization offers scholarships. We do not provide college loans. Imagine us—trying to track down graduates for loan payments. We have not the offices to handle the paperwork. So silly are you, no?"

Maria Fernanda considered José's offer again in a new light. "Benita!" she called from the living room. "Please come down from your room and welcome *our* guest!"

Benita came bounding down the stairs. "What is it Momma. Who is our…?"

José stood to greet her. "Miss Benita. Allow me to introduce myself. I am José Gutiérrez. I head up a local social organization called the Rican Rangers. Being a fellow Puerto Rican, I offer you our congratulations on your acceptance to nursing school. I, of course, have heard of your tuition issue. Surely you know of our organization and the support we provide to all local families of Puerto Rican origin, yes?"

"Of course, Mr., ahh, Gutiérrez. You are well thought of in the neighborhood."

"As I was explaining to your Mamma, we were surprised that you did not apply with us for an RR scholarship. So, I am here to encourage you to do so and to do so quickly. Is a deadline not approaching?"

"Oh my God, Momma! Why did you not tell me of this option?"

Before Maria Fernanda could answer, José intervened, "Your Momma is too proud and too hard a worker to ask anyone for help. I came here today to humbly beg her to allow us to support your nursing career. Will you object?"

Benita looked at her mother for an answer.

"Mr. Gutiérrez," Maria Fernanda responded, "of course, we will be pleased to accept your gracious offer. But how can we ever repay you?"

"Let me remind both of you," José leaned in, "this is a scholarship, not a loan. It is for the full term, not just the first year. You need never repay us. But perhaps someday, Benita, you will return to our Fitchburg community and help our children and elders with their infirmities, no? That would be payment enough for me and the Rican Rangers. It is all we can ask."

The next day, José sent the full tuition with Benita's signed letter of acceptance to Greenfield, and Benita spent the rest of the summer working at a nursing home cleaning bedpans and learning the basics of long-term care. Once at school, Benita studied hard. She never partied like many of the other girls on Friday or Saturday nights. They made fun of her as a nerd until they saw her name on the Dean's List and started asking her for tutoring assistance. She enjoyed teaching her 'colleagues' and eventually finished as salutatorian of her graduating class.

A few weeks before Meagher lined up her students for graduation, fortune again came knocking on Benita's doorstep. Ms. Anna Franklin, the Human Resources Director for Burbank Hospital in Fitchburg, had consulted with the school's career placement office and learned of Benita's aptitude and grades. Ms. Franklin wrote Benita a letter inviting her for an interview. Thrilled, she jumped at the chance to 'go back home' and received a job offer one week before graduation. The nursing department would start her on one of the medical-surgical units where patients ended up after surgery. It would be a stressful gig, but she knew she could dig in and eventually impress her future supervisor as a real asset.

"It is my pleasure," Dr. Van Buren began, "to present these students with their degrees in nursing. This, ladies, is the first step in a journey of healing, for there are hundreds, no thousands, of patients today and tomorrow who will look to you as their first line of defense against all manner of dread disease, injury and disability. For it is in your hands, not the doctors with whom you will work, that the delivery of care is primary and constant. Doctors, whom we admire and respect, do not have the luxury to be omnipresent on hospital wings to attend to every patient need. That task falls upon each of you—for, as I understand it, every single one of you who are graduating today will be working at hospitals around the Bay State. Congratulations to each of you and thank you for going out tomorrow to serve!"

As Benita heard Van Buren call out her name, she proudly stepped toward the dais to accept her diploma, which had the designation, *Summa Cum Laude*. She shook Van Buren's hand and looked out at the crowd, finding her mother seated next to José Gutiérrez, who had not only made the trip, but had shuttled Maria Fernanda from Fitchburg.

As the glorious day wound down, José treated the three of them to dinner at a fancy restaurant nearby where he had made reservations weeks ago. The dinner was lovely, the company relaxed, and Benita found the whole evening magical. At the end, José offered a second blessing, asking Benita to keep his Ranger Corps in her thoughts and prayers and to come to their aid should they ever need some small health care service that she, and she alone, could provide.

"But of course, José, please call us anytime," her mother had responded, without understanding the true meaning of that promise.

Mrs. Cruz regarded José and decided to plunge ahead to find out what made him tick. "Señor José, please, help us understand who you are and why you have helped us so."

"Of course, Mrs. Cruz. Most people look at me and assume I am a simple *Latino* businessman. I strive to be the kind of guy you wouldn't notice at the gas station or the bank. Just taking care of business, *my business.* I worked extra hard in school, taking vocabulary seriously, especially after I realized the power of words. I decided in fifth grade that I'd never let anyone be able to talk above me. In business negotiations, I will play the fool, however, when necessary, but only when it suits me and only when it's part of my grander plan for success.

"You may know that some hoodlums murdered my father when I was a young boy—I saw the whole thing. Took me quite a while to get over the sight, but after that, I watched all those mobsters. I learned their ways, but did not practice their methods. I marveled at how every one of them fell off their wagons out of greed, or by doing the drugs they and their henchmen dealt on the street. Just a little snort—no biggie, *I ain't gonna get addicted or OD like my customers, hell no*, I'd hear them brag. Off they all went to the slammer and I moved in to take over the *legitimate* parts of their businesses, except for the drug portion of things. I met people's needs, but never by drugs. Period. This is how I built up my Rican Ranger corps. This is how I am able to help you and Senorita Benita.

"I always insisted that my Rangers study hard. Just like your daughter. Make the grades, not excuses. I insist that each Ranger report to me on a daily basis the results of their schoolwork. Every report card comes to me—even their parents see fit to include me and they, in turn, appreciate the financial support I give them to help with rent and home maintenance costs. I make sure their families, and you know this, never want during the holiday season for hams, turkeys and guacamole! My Rangers make house calls, delivering these gifts door to door."

José didn't say that this long-term support network ensured that local criminal court juries always had Ranger sympathizers in the pool just in case a José minion ran afoul of the law. *After all, if my team and I have helped someone's little Pedro, Maria or Diego to get good grades and a job that helps the family make ends meet...well, then, I don't have to get into the drug trade. I've already bought and paid for every jury that might face one of my Rangers!*

All Maria Fernanda could say after José's speech was, "Gracias!" Thereafter, Benita didn't think about José or the Rangers until she stumbled upon one of their own in the ICU. Then, she knew, her bill had come due.

CHAPTER 1

Fitchburg, Massachusetts—*Burbank Hospital Emergency Department*
Tuesday June 11, 1968—4:00 p.m.

"Well, nice to meet you Mr. Jeremy! And what brings you into *my* emergency room this fine Tuesday afternoon?" asked Missy Klondike, a smiling ER nurse who had just come on for the second shift.

Five-year-old Jeremy hesitated before answering. Like most minister's kids, or *theologian's offspring as* he'd heard his dad say, he studied people carefully before opening up. Unlike most "TO's," however, Jeremy had a special gift—mind reading, which he called 'feeling people's heads.' He focused on Ms. Klondike's thought channel and immediately realized she had not a clue what he had been through earlier that day. He looked down, avoiding eye contact, and whispered, "Ma'am, two men kidnapped me during recess today, and my dad and Colonel McPherson saved my life. They thought I should come to the hospital so you all could check me out. Make sure I'm OK."

Ms. Klondike caught her breath and gasped, "Oh my God." Aghast, she looked into Jeremy's emerald eyes and noticed how they sparkled in the harsh exam room lights.

"I'm sorry Ms. Klondike," Jeremy's father said as he stepped forward hoping to calm her down. "I'm Rev. David Hergenroeder. I'm the minister at Rollstone Congregational, down in the valley on Main Street. This is my wife, Jeremy's mother, Alex. Jeremy is quite forthright as you can see."

Missy nodded and acknowledged Alex with a sheepish grin. *Forthright,* she thought, *that's a big word for a five year old. Why would you talk above your child's head?* "Gosh Sir, I mean, Reverend. Didn't mean to use the Lord's name in vain. But I must tell you three," she said in hushed tone as she pulled the privacy curtain around the bed, "I think the kidnappers are three rooms over. I suppose you already know this information so I'm not breaching patient confidentiality. They came in screaming in pain. I'm not sure the ambulance drivers gave them any pain meds. Must have been worried first about stanching all that arterial bleeding. They both lost a lot of blood. One had his hand shot clean off *and* his knee looks like a shark tore into it pretty good. The other guy might never walk again— some walloping bullet shattered his femur. Hole the size of a small grapefruit for his troubles. The cops really took those guys to the mat."

"Ah, yeah, well, that wasn't the police," David burped out, and then thought mum's the word here. David took a deep breath, now realizing that this story might be one of those light-bending events that would forever change how he described his family life. He was used to overcoming huge obstacles—starting with contracting polio at the age of three. The kidnapping seemed equally paralytic to him all of a sudden. *What do I tell people from here on out? Do I tell people? What's that Mom used to say when nosy neighbors would ask intrusive questions? Oh yeah!* 'Why do you ask?' *Then, no matter what the neighbor said in response, Mom would just nod her head and say,* 'I see.'

Recovering from his momentary stupor, David sought to move things along saying, "Yeah, they caught us all off guard."

"We wondered when the ambulance brought them in if they were gangster types," Missy offered. "Ya know, once any gang member comes in with a gunshot wound, we're on high alert for rival gang members sneaking in to finish the job."

As diligent a nurse as she had become, Missy's first career vision had nothing to do with health care. Just about the time she graduated from nearby Leominster High School, the career of John Glenn caught her attention. She'd admired his bravery and quiet competence. The idea of becoming a space traveler got her juices flowing. But in the early 1960s, since NASA wasn't looking to put a woman on the moon, she'd gotten a reality check and declared nursing as her major. She attended "the" Ohio State University in Columbus, Ohio, and immersed herself in her biology and chemistry studies, earning top honors in her 1963 graduating class. Missy had dated a few medical students at OSU before realizing that most of them were pompous jerks who viewed nurses as slave labor—good only for cleaning bed pans and giving shots. At 27, however, after having spent the last five years at Burbank Hospital, she felt like her maternal clock might be ticking away too quickly and perhaps it was time to start dating again—*outside* the medical field. Her powers of concentration and sponge-like mind made her a sharp nurse. She often whispered to herself a patient's diagnosis long before the medical residents did, even though they'd had four more years of graduate schooling than she had.

Nothing substituted for bedside experience and that's why she'd loved ER work from the moment she'd interned at OSU's hospital after her freshman year.

"Dangit David!" Alex exclaimed, fearing the obvious. "I've had about all I can take today. Ms. Klondike, is Jeremy OK or not? I think we oughta get outta here and fast."

Since childhood, Alex had been all business. Everything she did required a plan of action—no musing or wasting idle time. She'd have made a great architect or engineer if she'd pursued her math aptitude. Instead, she'd fallen in love with David at a summer camp where they'd both worked. He'd saved her from a mother who'd never understood how to convey love and familial warmth. In her household growing up, nurturing was an alien concept.

Before Missy could answer Alex, the curtain pulled back and Hergenroeder family friend Col. Edward McPherson poked his blonde head in. "David, Alex...err, I'm sorry Nurse...what is your name? Klondike?" He'd eyeballed her nametag. "We've got a situation here."

"Sir, ah...Colonel, if you'd just give us..." Missy tried to respond just as Dr. Chelsey Sneed, the ER Director, stepped in. She looked at Missy and then Jeremy. "So, what's going on here? Why are *all* you people in here? Don't answer, it's not important. According to the chart, you must be David Hergenroeder and you must be, ahh, Mrs. Hergenroeder, correct? And, who are you, sir?" Sneed asked, eyeballing the Colonel.

"I'm a friend of the family, doctor. My name is Col. Ed McPherson. We go to church together at Rollstone Congregational. And, yes, this is Rev. Hergenroeder and his wife Alexandria." An astute judge of character, McPherson noted Sneed had quite a commanding presence. *This is her battlefield and all us adults are just in her way!* The Colonel was right—Sneed was a great ER Doctor precisely because she was incisive. Ambiguity did not factor into her thinking—get the patient diagnosed and treated. Quickly. For Dr. Sneed, all other considerations were secondary.

Picking up on the signals that time was of the essence, Dr. Sneed scanned the chart and found only Jeremy's name, rank and serial number. Missy had not yet checked the boy's vitals.

Taking advantage of the lull, Jeremy sat up in the bed and said, "I'm fine. Those guys didn't hurt me. We need to go. Now!" Jeremy wished he were with his Nanna in the woods adjacent to her home in Northboro, Massachusetts hunting tigers right now, or catching frogs in his Grandpa Phillip's fish pond. *Those were the days*, Jeremy thought to himself, as if he were an old man looking back fondly on his carefree youth. He felt Dr. Sneed's head and learned that she hadn't figured out the Gutiérrez gang had kidnapped him during his lunch recess.

Eyeing Jeremy, Dr. Sneed said, "What guys? You seem a bit agitated Jeremy. Are you OK, are you hurt?"

Missy stepped back from the bed to give Jeremy and Dr. Sneed some breathing room. "He's the kidnap victim, Dr. Sneed. Let me just take his vitals, OK? He looks fine to me and you hopefully can confirm my observation. We just need to make sure and then we can get these folks discharged before we have a gang situation erupt."

Missy angled past Dr. Sneed, slipped a blood pressure cuff over Jeremy's right arm and stuck a thermometer in his mouth. As Missy and Dr. Sneed watched the instruments, Jeremy felt the heads of Pilar and Ricardo Gutiérrez, the two kidnappers down the hall. They indeed were in bad shape, awaiting their triage exams. Both needed emergency surgery. Jeremy figured out they were worried about two things: whether they'd ever walk again and making sure they said nary a word to the hovering policemen, including Det. Rod McNamara, Jr., who'd been the lead investigator on his kidnapping and their arresting officer.

Dr. Sneed looked at the blood pressure read-out and the thermometer. "BPs fine and you are a perfect 98 degrees, Jeremy." Then she ran her hands over his arms and legs, took a bright flashlight and looked at his eyes, did a few reflex tests, examined his head for trauma and possible contusions, and then said, "I don't find any broken bones or evidence of concussion. Did those men hit you?"

"No, Ma'am. They just held me down in the back seat floor of their Cadillac. Oh, and then they did it again when they stole two more cars." Jeremy had a photographic memory and could recall, word for word, everything Pilar and Ricardo had said to him from the moment they grabbed him in the schoolyard. He'd never again view recess as simple playtime. Nor would his classmates, who had witnessed the scofflaws make off with their classmate and friend.

Dr. Sneed turned to Missy, "What do you think?"

"I don't see any obvious injuries. Still, this might be gang related—if the looks of those other two patients are any indication. We've had problems before with gangs taking revenge right here in our ER. I think we should sneak these four out the back—through the staff passageway," Missy said, pointing the way. Her bob style haircut, pert as ever, bounced as she gesticulated excitedly. Jeremy sat transfixed at her alluring beauty. He loved hanging out with girls in church school. They seemed so different and way cooler than his male friends did. What a wonder God had provided, Jeremy'd thought more than once. His Dad often explained that you could see God best in the wonder of nature and in the bounteous relationships the family had with other church folk and their neighbors.

Dr. Sneed pulled back the curtain just a hair and looked down the hallway. As she started to turn back into the room, she bumped heads with Col. McPherson, who also was scanning the ER for signs of danger.

"Sorry, Doc. Just my old military training kicking in. Too many times I served on point in World War II, leading patrols. My rule of thumb: never set foot in a patch that you haven't reconnoitered."

"I understand. I'm sending the two of them to surgery—we've done all we can for them here in the ER. I didn't see any obvious gang members lurking about, did you?"

"No Ma'am. I'm a bit worried about your parking lot—could be their *compadres* are waiting out there with baited breath. My gut tells me, however, the whole bunch of them are lying low since the Massachusetts State Police busted their leader, José Gutiérrez, earlier today. They call themselves, now get this, the Rican Rangers."

Jeremy piped up. "There's no one from that gang out in the parking lot Col. McPherson."

"Jesus H. Christ, how in the bloody blazes do you know that? Never mind, don't answer that question son."

Flummoxed and unused to losing control in *her* ER, Dr. Sneed interrupted, "Excuse me? I don't understand." As she looked at the gathered adults, no one made eye contact with her. Everyone had taken a sudden interest in the white tile flooring beneath their feet.

Finding only silence, she decided to press on. "What I don't get is what they wanted with Jeremy! Small town ministers aren't rich by any stretch of the imagination. Did they think your church would step up and pay some big ransom?"

Feeling Alex's eyes boring into him, David responded, "Look, I think it's time we headed home Doctor, unless you aren't ready to discharge Jeremy. We'll let the police work out all the what—fors. Is that OK with everyone? Please, my wife and I would really like to leave. We gotta get Jeremy somewhere safe."

Before Dr. Sneed could confirm the discharge, Det. Rod McNamara's head with its blazing red hair poked gently through the slit in the privacy curtain. "Sorry to intrude, but the Gutiérrez boys are about to get shunted off to the surgery. I've got a man out in the parking lot keeping an eye on things. You know, David and Alex, I'm a bit concerned about you going home. I'd like to put you all in protective custody. You know, for your own safety."

Now it was Alex's turn. "Wait just a doggone minute. We need to be at home to take stock. I don't want our family sitting in a jail cell. That's crazy!"

Caught off guard, Det. McNamara, who had helped break the Rican Ranger case, took a deep breath and said,

"Yes, of course, I understand. I certainly didn't mean that we'd house you all in the jail. What I meant was..."

"I've got a better idea," McPherson interrupted. "Why don't you all come out to the *ranch* in Ashburnham? Hell, no one would think to look for you there. I'll have Momma make us up a fine dinner, roast beast, mashed taters and, I believe, she somehow managed to snag some early corn on the cob from Florida. It was on sale at the Piggly Wiggly over in Cleghorn. What say you, Jeremy? I'd love for you to meet Pinky, my dog!"

"Awright! Can we Mom, pleeeeaasse?" Jeremy begged.

"Give us a minute, would you Doctor?" Det. McNamara asked.

Before Dr. Sneed could answer, the curtain swung back yet again and Hercules Copoulos, MD, Jeremy's family doctor, stuck *his* head into the cramped space.

"Dr. Copoulos, what are you doing here, not that it's not great to see you? Just not used to you making rounds in *my* ER," Sneed said without a hint of derision or sarcasm. She'd had a crush on him for several years and his Adonis like body didn't help tranquilize her passion. Ever the gentleman, he never acted on her obvious interest.

"Well, you're right. I was just making my rounds and one of the med-surg techs who is working a double shift happened to be down here when they brought in Jeremy. He mentioned something about a five-year-old kidnapping victim, and my curiosity got the better of me. I hoped the boy wasn't one of my patients, but lo and behold, they gave me his name at your nurse's station."

"Hi, Dr. Copoulos!" Jeremy said. "I don't need a shot, do I?" Jeremy often had difficulty feeling Dr. C's mind and he happily had come to understand that it meant Dr. C really did care about Jeremy's well-being out of a profound sense of love, the same calling Dr. C felt for all of his patients.

"That's not up to me, Jeremy," Dr. C responded. "You're Dr. Sneed's patient right now and she's the boss. How is he by the way, Dr. Sneed?"

Dr. Sneed reached out her hand to shake Jeremy's and, when he responded in kind, she announced, "I consider you healthy and well Jeremy. You are hereby discharged! Doctor's orders. Do I need to write a prescription commanding you to obey your parents?"

"No Ma'am." Jeremy said.

As Jeremy hopped off the gurney, Drs. Sneed and Copoulos, and Missy stepped out and headed for the nurse's station. Dr. Sneed wanted to get started on documenting in Jeremy's chart. Two hospital transporters were pushing the Gutiérrez boys, Pilar and Ricardo, up to the surgery, and Dr. Sneed noted with a new sense of disgust their moans of discomfort as they passed by. Little did she know that Pilar and Ricardo were José's top lieutenants in the Ranger Corps, or that, like a pro quarterback, they'd called an audible outside their chain of command when they'd rousted Jeremy from the schoolyard.

"Those two gentlemen look awfully banged up and where's that one fellow's left hand?" Dr. C asked no one in particular.

"Those two are the kidnappers, Hercules. They're the ones that got your patient to come here for a quick check of his vitals. Best I can tell they were on the losing end of a gun battle with the police."

"My, my! Glad to know Fitchburg's finest were up to the task!"

"Missy, before you run off, and Dr. C, I wanted to ask you both a question," Dr. Sneed said conspiratorially. "During my brief exam, I couldn't help but notice Jeremy's musculature. Did you notice Missy?"

"Not really. What do you mean? I was sort of distracted with the kidnapping issues," Missy offered, figuring she missed some crucial piece of diagnostic magic and Dr. Sneed was about to pounce on her obvious lack of skills.

"Of course. No, I'm not trying to catch you here in some mistake. I didn't want to say anything in front of his parents. Lord knows they've been through hell and back today. But Jeremy, I think, has a rare genetic condition. And I'm guessing, Dr. C, you would know for sure. I just read about it in a pediatric medical journal last month. Never dreamed I'd see it in practice. Some kid in Germany, they had pictures in the journal, looked like some sort of miniature Charles Atlas. I think he was Jeremy's age. Like Jeremy—about 60 pounds. Of course, they weighed him using kilos, so it would have been around 27 kilograms. Anyway, it's a muscle anomaly. The researchers called it, ah, *myostatin-related* something or other. All I really remember were the pictures of this German kid carrying his mother around the house as if she weighed ten pounds or something. If it's true for Jeremy, I bet he was a handful for those kidnappers. Strong as a little ox! I'm not going to document it in the chart, especially since we don't want to draw further attention to the youngster."

"Why yes, Chelsey, I have noticed his precocious physical development. Hadn't researched it, but sounds like you may be on to something. Bet those kidnappers indeed had all they could handle when they grabbed him," Dr. C offered up as the threesome parted ways.

Back at Jeremy's ER bedside, Det. McNamara advised the family: "As you'd suspect, Ricardo and Pilar aren't saying a word. We've already had some beat reporter from the *Fitchburg Sentinel* sniffing around the case, but all we gave her, Kristen Brigham's her name, was the notion that there'd been a kidnapping and the case resolved quickly. I don't think she bought it. She'd already found out that the State Police picked up José Gutiérrez, the ringleader for the Rican Rangers. They found him headed to Quincy, the shipyard, for some meet up with the shipbuilder's union steward, whom I'm not even sure knew José was coming. They're gonna hold him in Foxborough until his arraignment."

"You guys are amazing," David offered.

"I don't know about that. I put in a call to a friend with the state patrol and, apparently, they've had a separate investigation going on with these clowns. All I did was sweeten the Intel they had in their working file and off they went. You know it really was that elderly couple, the Antonnens, that saved the day. Right as they exited that McDonalds in Leominster they heard Jeremy screaming from the back of Ricardo's stolen car. Mrs. Antonnen figured out that Ricardo and Pilar were way out of their element with Jeremy in the back seat. Thank God Sgt. Finch took their call—he tried to pass them off to the Leominster Police, you know, since they were calling from

Leominster. I'm guessing the Ranger's plan involved taking Jeremy along to Quincy to do some sort of mind reading trick. I've put a call into my favorite assistant DA, Christopher Johnson, to start getting this case airtight. You may have read about him. Little pugnacious ball of fire he is. We've worked several cases together and I must say his advice is always spot on. He's working up the charges right now. And, just so you know, I was going to host you at my house, not the jail. Just for a bit until we could be sure the coast was clear."

"No need, Detective," McPherson said, strutting himself back into the conversation. "We'll just keep this as part of the church family. Me and Lily will host these fine folks. We'll keep you apprised. I've built a bit of a safe house, with Pinky on guard and all. It's all gated and such. We don't need to worry your wife, none." Pinky was the Colonel's Doberman, but with a full tail and his ears still intact. The dog had the run of the McPherson compound, north of Fitchburg in Ashburnham. Pinky loved his master, Ed, and looked upon him as the alpha wolf in his pack. Mrs. Lily McPherson followed Pinky in the pecking order, at least in Pinky's mind.

Alex intervened. "Well, I do appreciate all the offers of housing and board. I am speechless. If you think it's best, Detective, and Ms. Lily wouldn't mind, maybe we can stay with you all till Sunday, when David has to preach again."

"Speaking of preaching Rev. Hergenroeder, I'm going to have a plain clothes officer attending your church services for the next few weeks. Let's just keep that between us and your executive leadership. What do you call them—deacons?"

"Yes, that's right," David answered.

"That's good. Just so you don't start trying to recruit the officer to join the choir or something. And one more thing, Jeremy. I'm going to have two officers standing watch at Edgerly Elementary School to help keep the kids safe till school lets out for summer vacation and then afterwards for a time while you continue in that accelerated kindergarten class. Is that OK with you? How about you two: Rev. Hergenroeder? Mrs. Hergenroeder?" Fitchburg Teachers College had accepted Jeremy into a special pilot kindergarten class composed of students who tested out at a third grade level in reading and math. Jeremy beat them all with his fourth grade aptitudes, but he'd never let on with his classmates since he'd learned humility from his mother at the tender age of three. Alex had often told him that, *God don't cotton to braggarts and that means us, too!*

Alex spoke up. "That's OK by me. I'd feel safer and I don't want Jeremy falling behind his classmates. Do you David? Agree I mean?"

"Yes. I just feel like the last several days have rocked our whole world to its foundations. We really do need all the help we can get."

Just then, Dr. Sneed pulled the curtain back and said there was a psychiatrist here who wanted to see everyone. Jeremy looked up and could see Azriel Rebovitz, MD's head three inches above the curtain rod.

"Dr. R! Boy am I glad to see you. It worked, it worked!" Jeremy hollered before realizing he needed to hush.

Dr. R, as Jeremy called him, stepped into the crowded bedside circle. "*What* worked Jeremy?"

"You remember what Mr. Gallagher, my judo teacher, said to do? When I get into real trouble, just start hollering 'It's a good day to die!' I screamed it so loud in that McDonald's parking lot that the kidnappers didn't know what to do. And that nice lady heard me and called the police. *That's why I am still alive!* Mrs. Anttonen heard me because those kidnappers had the windows down. It was hot outside. She ran back into the McDonald's and called the police.

Having spied the giant Dr. R striding across her ER while doing Jeremy's chart, Dr. Sneed quickly followed him back to Jeremy's room and now stood speechless. Perplexed once again, she finally intoned, "OK, this is just way too much information. I've got other patients to see. Just thought it odd that a psychiatrist would show up at the ER. Not something we have every day Dr. Rebovitz, but I must say your pre-eminence for healing war veterans of their battle fatigue precedes you. I am honored to finally make your acquaintance. I will take my leave of you all. Call me if you need anything!"

Dr. R shook Dr. Sneed's hand and slipped her a business card, which announced child psychiatry as his specialty. "Please call me if I can ever be of assistance to you Dr. Sneed, or may I call you Chelsey? I should return the compliment—I hear nothing but praise from our peers about how you lead this ER."

"Of course, call me Chelsey. Thank you again for your graciousness," she said as she pulled back the curtain for privacy and headed off to the next patient. She wondered about the child psychiatry gig, not having heard that "Dr.

R" had switched to children after drinking in all of the war trauma from his veteran-patients.

"So it's decided then. You all are coming home to Ashburnham, yes?" Col. McPherson confirmed.

The Hergenroeders all nodded and Jeremy beamed.

"Okey-dokey, you all have my number, right?" asked Det. McNamara. "I'm going to make sure I've got a round-the-clock guard on those two clowns while they stay here. No breaking out of this hospital, no sir." Little did McNamara know how soon the Rangers would be back on the trail of the Hergenroeders.

CHAPTER 2

Tuesday June 11, 1968—Early Evening
Foxborough, Massachusetts
Rican Ranger Leader Gets His Phone Call

"**A** lright, you know the drill José. One call and you better make it your lawyer, Dude," barked state patrolman Vic Langston. Vic towered over José. Like virtually all "Staties," Vic stood well over six feet tall, the state minimum height at the time. He prided himself on weight lifting and could bench press 400 pounds, several times in a row. José eyeballed him thinking it would take several of his Rican Rangers *brandishing Billy clubs* to bring this guy to his knees. Vic also sported a butch style military hair cut—keeping it no longer than a half inch in length, except for the front "hedgerow" that stood up tall as you like.

"I'll step out so you can have some privacy. And that's not anything you'd have offered that five year old, huh? You're going down for this, big time, so wipe that frickin' smirk off your face. Now."

José erased the smirk, not even realizing he was smirking. As Vic closed the door, José called the firm he'd had on retainer for the last several years, *Pellatino, Degrazio and Gomez*. He'd literally picked up a Boston phone book one day and, as soon as he saw the Gomez name, he figured Mr. Gomez just might be bi-lingual, meaning there'd be an extra layer of confidentiality. Sure enough, he'd guessed right.

Kelly Owens, the receptionist, answered on the second ring, "Pellatino, Degrazio and Gomez, how may I help you?" She emphasized the "grazio" as if it was spelled "grits-ee-oh."

"Kelly, its José. I'm calling from jail. I must talk to Pablo Gomez now, and please don't put me on hold or nothin'. If I get cut off I don't get another call!"

"But I have to put you on hold to transfer the call, Mr. José. Mr. Gomez can't take this call at our front desk!" Kelly said incredulously.

"Got it! *Lo siento.* (Sorry.) Just put him on and fast."

"Well, he *is* with a client, but I'll run down the hall and see what I can do," Kelly said with some disgust. *Every client thinks their issue is the only emergency.*

Kelly knocked on Mr. Gomez's office door, sheepishly, fearing she'd set off his vengeful temper. One time he'd come into the office early to prep for a death penalty trial and let out a blood curdling scream when he realized his "shoe clerk," law intern Roy Argulara, hadn't picked up any of his starched shirts from the cleaners. Kelly had found him in his t-shirt standing with a purple face amidst a sea of shirt buttons—ripped off when he realized he had put on a dirty shirt. "I'll get to the cleaners right now Mr. Gomez!" she had said, not waiting for a reply. Ten minutes later she had him dressed and dispatched to the trial. That role fell under "other duties as assigned." In 1968, no God fearing receptionist would think twice about filling the boss's coffee cup or running an errand, including fetching the prior day's dry cleaning.

"Yeah, what is it? Gomez shouted.

"Ah, Mr. Gomez…"

"Open the goddamn door, will ya for Chrissakes?"

Kelly gingerly turned the knob and saw Gomez with the client she had escorted in earlier, escort being apropos since the client was the voluptuous madam, Tildemon Lafleur, who'd had the current appointment and who ran a local brothel. LaFleur, whom every john knew as "Tildy," sat atop Gomez's desk leaning toward him in an alluring manner. Gomez was ignoring her manipulation, even though he did find her attractive.

"Sir, ah, José is on the line. He says it's urgent and he only gets one call."

"Alright. Jesus Christ, what's he gone and done now? Ah, Tildy dear, do you mind stepping out with Kelly? She'll get you a cup of coffee." Gomez petted her on the butt and she cooed her delight as she slithered off the desktop to follow Kelly out the door.

"Yo, what's up José?"

"Listen, talk to me in Spanish. The walls have ears, I'm guessing!"

The pair switched to Español, much to the chagrin of Vic who was standing guard just outside the porous door.

"Listen, Gomez, I need you to bail me out, pronto. The state cops got me on trumped up charges of extortion, loan sharking, transporting stolen goods, and some other *caca*. Call that judge friend of yours—the Melanson guy we keep making all dem frosting payments to—that keeps his ex-wife in her furs. I want an immediate return on our salary supplements, plus I need that call girl, Penny, who he thinks is his girlfriend, to step up to the plate. Get her on the line and set it up. Poor judge thinks he's in love, again. Stupid ass can't afford his alimony payments. The hell kinda lawyer was he anyway? Now, get my ass out of the slammer. Also, I gotta know what's happening to my other Rangers, Pilar and Ricardo. They got busted. I think up in Fitchburg. At least that's what I'm guessing cause I ain't heard a peep outta dem. They're never far off the leash."

"Got it. So where'd they bust you?"

"Outside Quincy. On my way to the shipyard. And you ain't gonna believe the mind reading trick I ginned up. More on that later—but should be a help down the road. Anyway, they hauled my ass to their Foxborough barracks. Some major operation. Seems like they been watching me for a while. Do you think our Boston judge can *lend a hand*? I'll be ever so grateful! *Es muy importante*!"

"He's my next call—*but he ain't gonna be able to help* with the Fitchburg situation, ya know."

"I figured. Ya get me outta here and I can take care of that *problemo* real easy."

"OK, I'm on it. You behave in those barracks you hear? And for Chrissakes don't talk to nobody. I mean it. You think the Staties might be listening in? I can assure you they got moles all ready to sing your admissions of guilt. They'd happily trade your sorry ass for a few years off their sentences. So shut up. This is no time to brag about how much of a badass you are."

"I'm as silent as one a dem Trappist monks—ya know, the *novitiates*—the ones who don't get to talk for their first year in the monastery. The Abbott, see, gots to figure out if they can handle the pressure of keeping every thought to themselves. Most of them break, what I hear. Not me! *Adios* and get me outta here fast," José raged as he rang off.

Vic saw the call light go off above the doorframe and stalked back in. "Get everything taken care of José? Didn't get cut off now did we? No excuses right…one call only. I think you're getting arraigned tomorrow or the next day. Seems like you may have two sets of charges—one set from Fitchburg related to a kidnapping conspiracy that some badass DA name a Christopher Johnson has all ponied up. Just for you. I hear he's a bolt of lightning and juries just eat him up. Stalks the courtroom like a hungry grizzly on the prowl. Looks like you'll be getting a Boston trial as well. You can't win for losin'. What the hell did you see in that five year old, anyway? The press is going to have a party all over your sorry ass when this gets out. You all ready to face 12 Woolworth's shoppers in the jury box? Got a PR plan all prepped?"

José could feel bile rising in his throat. He struggled to contain it knowing that it would just feed Vic's appetite for more emotional torture. Instead of answering or glowering, he just nodded sheepishly feigning acceptance of Vic's interpretation of future events. A few moments after Vic returned him to his cell, José chuckled to himself realizing that, once he got out, he might just be able to turn the tables on this Statie. He'd have to make it look like the guy did something to off himself—*maybe we can stage a suicide, or an unavoidable accident on a slippery road. Off a bridge—swerved to avoid a puppy dog in the middle of the lane. A puppy I'd plant after the car took a tumble. Yes, the possibilities are endless. Go ahead Mr. Vic, keep feeding me!*

As Maria Fernanda and Benita had learned during their post-graduation dinner, José had lived a rough life indeed.

After his mother died of breast cancer when he was five, his father, Caesar, took over household duties and raised him with a watchful eye. But just when his peers had started feeling their oats as they reached age 13, José saw his father murdered. Stupid loan shark overplayed his intimidation routine on a 1960's version of a payday loan. The goon only meant to maim José's dad. Rather than cry in grief, José suddenly felt the hand of God telling him to hunker down and never, ever fall into anyone's debt. Growing up in the Puerto Rican ghetto of Fitchburg, he'd seen first-hand all the stupid PR on PR and black-on-black violence. For what? Drug deals gone bad or stupid arguments over nothing. Street smart by the age of 8, he took a separate measure that he had not told Maria or Benita. He studied how the white men across town rolled up cash from their factories and paper mills that sat on the banks of Fitchburg's Nashua River. He realized that they'd gotten there with schooling and *connections*. José applied himself at school, unlike his peers—who dared not laugh at him, else he'd break their jaws. His motto? Depend only on yourself—and blood kin. But spread the wealth and the spirit of hard work. And always, always, love your mamma! Or, in this case, if you didn't have a mother, love your grandmother!

By 14 he'd become the family's chief breadwinner, selling joints to the white boys for their lunch money. As some of them got hooked on the weed, he'd loan them joints and started making extra cash on the interest payments. Each joint cost a white boy $1.00, which in 1968 wasn't exactly chicken feed. He never cut the weed with oregano or some other spice like his stupid peer pushers did—quality reefer for the money. He banked major coin after just a few months. But he never sold weed to any of his kind. He'd beat them up if they dared ask.

In José's mind, leisure time was for losers. Work, work, work and look to the future. Plan, man! Instead of caffeine to help him stay awake to study, he'd lift weights. For some reason, he could get along on three or four hours of sleep a night. His simple pattern: lift weights, study for 90 minutes, lift weights, study for 90 minutes. All that weight lifting made his neck disappear and assured that school bullies gave him a wide berth.

"José, please go to bed," his grandma, Daniella, would implore from downstairs. "It's alright, *Abuelita* (Grandma), just studying up for this algebra exam. The weights help me focus!" His grandmother would shuffle back to bed, amazed at her first-born grandson's industriousness. Straight A's on every report card.

Vic would never find out any of these details. But after closing the cell door, Vic looked through the security window at José and sensed the room temperature and power differential somehow had changed. He turned and left, ordering the guard to keep a close watch on José. *I'll think up some new lines for tomorrow's fun. Get ready José.*

CHAPTER 3

Tuesday June 11, 1968—Early Evening
Lily McPherson Greets Her Guests

As they left the hospital, Col. McPherson called his wife Lily on his CB to advise her they were about to have guests, and to get the spare bedrooms ready. "Lily—do I need to pick up any groceries or is the larder fully stocked?"

"Silly man. You know we're always prepared. I have lasagna warming in the oven. Found that soft mozzarella you love so much. It's all slathered on top. I tried something new—put some fresh spinach in between a couple of the layers of noodles. I heard the recipe on WBZ a couple of days ago. You know, Dave Maynard's *Tried and True Secret Family Recipe* radio show that I like to listen to?"

"I know Mama! I love what you cook so I'm game to try anything. The Hergenroeders are used to fine cooking—thanks to all of those potluck suppers we have at the church. They get to sample everyone's finest recipes. This won't disappoint them in the least, especially after the day we've had. Oh my."

Jeremy got to ride with Ed in his wide body, 1963 Lincoln Continental, the kind with the back doors that opened forward. As they drove northwest towards Ashburnham, Ed glanced at Jeremy and marveled at this gifted child. He recalled hearing through the Rollstone Church grapevine that David and Alex had submitted an application for Jeremy with Fitchburg State Teachers College, which had advertised a special accelerated kindergarten class several months earlier. Jeremy's aptitude tests revealed that he could read and understand math concepts at a fourth grade level. When Ed congratulated Alex on her son's admission, she had told him that when Jeremy was a baby, she counted aloud one to ten as she touched each of his fingers and toes while she breast-fed him. Then she'd alternate with the alphabet. Jeremy could recite his ABCs and could count to 100 by the age of two. She bragged that David had been taking him to the library ever since he could walk and let him pick out books to explore. The children's librarian at Fitchburg's library, Miss Marian Koshgarian, had taken an immediate liking to Jeremy and always had a new book stashed away for him, awaiting his next visit. Jeremy's favorite book was *Tell Me Why,* which David had purchased as a present for Jeremy for birthday number four. The book had lots of science answers about dinosaurs, the stars, basic chemistry and the like. Jeremy gobbled up the book almost in the first week.

Ed wondered why, earlier that day, the Gutiérrez cousins, Pilar and Ricardo, had snatched Jeremy off the Edgerly Elementary School yard during the students' lunch recess. Word was they had hoped to use his mind reading gift to help their older cousin, José Gutiérrez, the Rican Rangers' CEO type, get an angle on some longshoremen at the dock area of Quincy, Massachusetts. The gang called themselves the Rican Rangers, seeing as how they were all Puerto Rican. Det. McNamara had told Ed that small town Fitchburg had proved a discrete location to run their illicit trucking and shipping operations—far from the prying eyes of the State Police, the FBI or the Boston area police.

Jeremy's mind drifted, too, as the caravan made its way north along Rindge Road. Earlier that day after the Gutiérrez arrest, Jeremy had felt McNamara's head and saw his old style home, the garage out back that housed some big bad red Ford pick-up truck, and his two teenage boys, Conor and Rod Jr. He figured out that those two high schoolers had helped their dad break open the case. The *Rican Rangers* really involved gang recruitment that started in junior high school and sometimes even earlier.

Det. McNamara got his hunch after hearing his boys talk about Rican Ranger graffiti in the Fitchburg High bathrooms, not to mention the Ranger students' diligence and "gunning" for every advantage with all of their teachers, straight A students every one of them. Plus as Rod Jr. said, "Man, they're always flush with cash, Dad. How they get the cash I'll never understand, since they must have to study morning, noon and night to get those straight A's!"

Rod Jr. and Conor both loved repairing cars and took every class that Fitchburg High School's auto mechanics instructor, Ray Peterson, offered. Ray appeared to be the befuddled professor type, glasses always about to fall off his nose, thinning hairline, handkerchief hanging halfway out of his rear pocket, and barely tied shoes. But he knew his stuff and loved the students, often giving them a boost on tests if he thought one or two of them might need just a nudge in the direction of success. The Rican Ranger male students all worked to get into Ray's classes and never skipped, back talked, chewed gum or anything that would bring them into disrepute with Ray.

As Rod Sr. thought about his son's report on the Ranger students' diligence and put that piece of news with their always having cash on hand, it was but a short leap to the news flash he got from Trixie McLoughlin, a local bar maid that cinched it. She had tried to make her call an anonymous tip, but by a stroke of luck, Rod Sr. had stumbled on her bar and took a chance by entering during the start of the "liquid lunch" hour. Sure enough, he put two and two together. Trixie gave up the ruse and informed him that these Rangers had run a few of her customers, all truck drivers, off the job. Rod then knew for sure there was some kind of connection to the mechanic's program at the high school.

"I don't know what exactly they're up to," Trixie had said, "but one trucker who got his *mob* walking papers said he noticed that one of his trailer rigs had two false gas tanks and a four foot false front right behind the nose of the trailer. It was some sort of storage compartment with a neat-as-you please welding job on all sides. He was lookin' on how to saw it open—was trying to figure out how to get into it, when a couple of those young honchos caught him in the act. They beat him senseless and ferried him home in his car, ringing the doorbell after plopping him on the front stoop. The guy *and his wife who answered the door* got the message—we know where you live Dude, so watch your step. I think he skipped town with his wife and kids, got some long haul trucking job with an Arizona outfit. Drives the I-10 corridor exclusively, Florida to California. Got as far away from Fitchburg as he could get…"

With that statement, Trixie had begged Rod to leave her alone. Rod had figured out who she was, partly because she gave her first name when she called in the tip, and she wore a name badge in the bar. So much for anonymity. Waitresses everywhere knew a name badge helped encourage tips.

Rod also had called his twin sons' shop teacher, Ray Peterson, ostensibly to thank him for training his boys so well. Rod used that pretext to ask Ray if he might stop by for a tour of the mechanics shop area at Fitchburg High School. At first, Ray was confused about why a police detective would be calling his home on a Saturday. Rod calmed him down and assured him it was completely innocent. Rod talked Ray into introducing Rod to the shop students as some sort of school board representative from Chelmsford, Massachusetts, seeking information on FHS's model mechanics program. Rod suggested that a cop showing up might scare some of the students. He persuaded Ray that the school board idea would work well. Rod brought lunch and Ray had two of his students, Cordero and Julio, do the meet and greet and provide a tour. During the subsequent "interview," which was more of a subtle interrogation, Cordero and Julio, themselves Rican Rangers, confirmed both that trucking companies loved Ray's graduates *and that they learned the art of welding.* That piece of the puzzle enabled Rod to tie off that line of inquiry. After all, what truck driver recruiter cares whether a new hire can weld? The hireling need only set his ass in the seat and be adept at backing a trailer down a narrow alley to offload inventory to a waiting vendor.

After the kidnapping, Jeremy had read the mind of José and now knew he kept careful watch over all of his recruited minions, paid them a weekly allowance—*for studying hard no less*, and for doing odd jobs that did not yet border on the criminal. Conor and Rod Jr. were classmates with some of the older gang members at FHS, and they interacted most often in shop class working on V-8 engines. Jeremy thought it'd be fun to get to know Conor and Rod Jr., and maybe they could take him under their wings and show him something about tuning cars and the like. He loved motors, especially the little one that powered his Erector Set inventions. All it needed was a D size Eveready battery.

Jeremy felt Ed's mind and understood how much he babied this car, always changing the oil religiously, tuning it up himself, anything he could do to make it last. He didn't quite understand why it was a *Wednesday* car, so he asked Ed.

"Col. McPherson?"

"Yes sir, Mr. Jeremy! What can I do you for?"

"Why'd you want to make sure this car was built on a Wednesday?"

"Ha!" Ed roared, not needing to ask why or how Jeremy knew that little piece of information. *Kid's a damned mind reader!* "Well let me tell you. Those assembly line workers, well some of them like to imbibe— make love to their vodka or gin, don't you know. They get pretty drunk on the weekends, and some of them start their drinking on Thursday nights. I figure that they pretty much have sobered up by the time Wednesday rolls around. That means that's when they are at their sharpest, not missing a beat on the assembly line. You know about assembly lines, Jeremy?'

"Not really, no sir."

"OK, well you've heard of Ford cars, right?"

"Yes. My grandpa Phillip says Ford stands for "Fix Or Repair Daily!"

"Oh yeah. Have heard that myself. Not sure it's true, though. Hell, this car's a Ford, but they gussy it up real fancy like and call it a Lincoln. Like the President. The guy who won the Civil War. Well he didn't actually win the War, but he sure as hell fought it. Some damned chicken mother assassinated him while he and his missus were watching a play in a theater. Hell, I just remembered the guy, name a John Wilkes Booth, killed Lincoln in Ford's Theater. How's that for a coincidence? Doubt Henry was a relation. I think Booth was some sort of Confederate sympathizer. An actor, too. Guess that's why no one paid him any mind when he was stalking around behind Lincoln's balcony seat. Came up right behind him and shot him dead. Coward. Ah, sorry, getting off track there young man. Anywho, assembly lines were the invention of none other than Henry Ford, the guy that pretty much invented the car, or at least the *mass produced* car."

"I've heard of him."

"I'll bet you have. You know what he used to tell his customers?"

"No sir."

"You can have a Ford Model T in any color you want as long as it's black! Hoo wee! May not a been much of a sense of humor, but it sure got his point across. He paid his workers five dollars a day! Pretty groundbreaking at the time. I think he figured he needed to pay them well enough so they could buy the cars they were making."

"My Grandpa Phillip used to pay my dad five dollars a week allowance! I only get a quarter."

"Ouch. Hard to make a living on two bits a week!"

"Two bits?"

"Ah, that's old timey speak for 25 cents. So, Henry had to figure out how to get a lot of cars built fast. He finally realized what he needed to do was line up all of the parts that have to go into the car. You make this long hallway like path inside a big plant building. Line up your workers on either side. Then start with the first part—hand it to that first guy, he then fastens it to the second part which the next guy is holding. They then pass it to a third guy who has the next part. I'm guessing they start with the chassis. You know, the car frame—sort of like God did with your skeleton. Your bones. Next, God built on your muscles, veins, nerves, and somewhere along the line installed your organs. You know, your heart, kidneys, liver and such. Same thing with these cars. After putting all the pieces/parts together, some guy at the end of the line starts her up and drives her off the line into a big parking lot all ready for the trucks or ships to move them out to the car dealers."

Mesmerized, Jeremy then asked, "So is that how the Germans made our car, the Volkswagen?"

"Yeah, I'd guess that was true. Those Germans are pretty efficient. You know that's where we learned to build our highways. Old General Eisenhower in World War II, once he got into Germany, he just couldn't believe their highways. They call one the Autobahn. No speed limit on that road. Scary I suppose. He came back from the war, ran for President and, after he got elected, he started us building highways, every direction imaginable. Odd numbered interstates go north, like I-93 or I-75, the even numbered ones go west like I-90 across New York, or I-40 down south. I think the interstates spelled the end of passenger trains, pretty much. Miss those I do."

As they traversed north, Jeremy marveled at what seemed like endless woods. He saw songbirds, hawks and even spotted a raccoon hiding behind a tree watching the cars pass by. He looked through the back window, easy to do since the seats didn't have headrests. Saw his parents talking animatedly. He realized they were thinking about the family's future—should they stay in Massachusetts, or should his dad start applying for minister's jobs in other states? Except for the kidnapping trauma, his parents' discussion might just have been routine-minister couple stuff.

The two cars made it to the McPherson compound and pulled into the drive. Ed punched in the code to the servo gate. Jeremy admired how it opened with the touch of some buttons. On came Pinky the Doberman wagging his tail, elated that his Master was home. Pinky chased the Lincoln back towards the house as David and Alex followed behind. Lily was waving from the back door, an oven mitt in her hand. As Alex got out of the VW Bug, she realized that, not only did they not have a change of underwear, they didn't have their toothbrushes or other daily necessaries.

"You folks come on in," Lily implored. "Pinky—you stay outside for now, you already *had* your dinner. Welcome Mr. Jeremy, and you, too, Rev. David and Alex.

I've got salad, hot rolls and baked lasagna all ready for everyone to enjoy. Get washed up. Bathroom's down the hall. Now Mr. Ed, you've got to give Momma a kiss here. I've been worried sick, I have. Figured you were OK after all the hullabaloo, but that detective seemed pretty upset at you, Ed, when he called. I think he said something about you disobeying a direct order. All I could think was not my Colonel Ed. He didn't rise up in the military by disobeying any *superior* officer. That feller just didn't understand where he fell in the chain of command!" Earlier that day, Det. McNamara had deputized Ed, with orders to stay put and keep David Hergenroeder safe. Ed hadn't obeyed.

Everyone ambled into the single story, 3,000 square foot compound, leaving Pinky wagging his tail with envy. Ed had insisted that Pinky's breeder not cut off Pinky's tail, figuring if God intended for Doberman's to have stub tails, then God surely would have made Pinky that way from the start. Who was Ed to argue with God, since it didn't work for that feller Job in the Old Testament? And by gum, that Mr. Job had a lot to complain about.

The two families enjoyed each other's company, even as they all anticipated trouble ahead. And it was about to come their way.

CHAPTER 4

Truman McPherson's Toy Box

After Lily's delectable dinner, Jeremy had a bath and Alex tucked him in. "I'm proud of you Jeremy. You were so brave today. Get some sleep. You don't have to say any prayers tonight since Col. McPherson did such a good job thanking God right before dinner. Rest up. We'll need our strength for what the next few days have in store."

Jeremy kissed his mom and watched her pull the door to, not quite closing it. Across the room he saw an imposing trunk. Big leather straps held it shut tight. Each strap had a shiny buckle. *That's gotta be what I think it is! A toy box for sure—must have been Truman McPherson's when he was little!* Truman was the McPherson's only son. He had died in Vietnam while on point with his Marine patrol. He'd signed up for the Marines the day after he graduated from Fitchburg High School in 1964.

Jeremy slid out of bed and tiptoed across the room. When a floor board creaked unexpectedly, Jeremy froze in place. He listened carefully in case any of the adults visiting downstairs came running. Finally satisfied that they'd missed the noise, he popped the big brass buckles and felt a whoosh of air as the top sprung open. It was spring loaded, sort of like the engine hood on Ed's fancy Lincoln.

Jeremy's jaw dropped as he took in the bounty of toys. Truman's collection included Tonka trucks and heavy equipment of every description, older model Matchbox cars, ones Jeremy had never seen before in the store, and off to the side leaning against the far corner of the trunk sat a cookie container with a loose lid. He popped open the lid and found a treasure trove of money, more than he'd ever seen in his life. He reached down and found the most curious coins—1943 U.S. pennies—steel, not copper. Jeremy remembered his Grandfather Phillip explaining that, during World War II, the U.S. Mint had substituted steel for copper, which had become increasingly scarce given the war demand. Searching deeper in the trunk he found a real Teddy Bear, so named for the former President, Theodore Roosevelt. It didn't smell like a bear and he wondered if it smelled like Truman. As Jeremy held the bear he found himself looking into Truman's eyes as a child on Christmas morning, the very day Truman's parents had given him the bear, or rather as Truman had thought, Santa had given it to him. *Truman loved this bear and it kept him safe from all the goblins under the bed!*

Next, Jeremy pulled out a Tonka truck that had a shovel that moved from the back of the vehicle to the front, sort of like a reverse snowplow. He pulled the shovel along its rail and found it had a hinge that enabled the operator to reverse the truck and pull snow or sand backwards, towards the truck. *I've never seen one of these before!* He felt Truman's head and realized he could actually feel his presence, as if Truman were sitting there with him all set to play. He saw Truman as a 17 year old, again on Christmas day, holding a little black puppy with a tail and flappy ears. *It's Pinky! When he was a puppy! What a doll baby he was.*

Jeremy yawned and realized how tired he was. He grabbed the Teddy Bear and remembered Truman called it...*Frankie*. Apparently, Truman had heard his dad bragging one day about how great a singer Frank Sinatra was. Truman figured if his dad liked that guy so much, then that's just gotta be a great name for my bear. So christened, Frankie became part of the McPherson family on a permanent basis. Even Col. McPherson and Lily knew to call the bear Frankie. The bear traveled everywhere Truman did up until another boy saw the bear and teased Truman mercilessly. The bully knew right away the bear belonged to Truman, especially since Truman was an only child. Truman then put Frankie away in the trunk for good. Jeremy felt Truman's shame, mixed with love for all the great and warm memories Frankie had provided Truman on lots of dark nights.

"C'mon Frankie. Let's you and I go to bed. I'll keep *you* company tonight. I might need your help tomorrow night, but tonight I'll be brave enough for both of us."

Jeremy dozed off and dreamed about owning a Lincoln Continental all his own. He drove it to his senior prom and picked up...Lori Kendall right next door from the parsonage. They had a marvelous time and he got her home by 11:59 p.m., right before he figured she'd turn into a pumpkin, or he'd turn into a frog. The rest of the night passed peacefully for Jeremy and Frankie. Just beyond the horizon, though, storm clouds full of trouble started brewing.

CHAPTER 5

Wednesday June 12, 1968—7:00 a.m.
Offices of Child Psychiatrist Dr. Azriel Rebovitz

D r. Rebovitz sat back in his chair and mused about all that had happened in the last week, and especially in the last 18 hours. A most remarkable patient had fallen in his lap, Jeremy Hergenroeder. Here was a five-year-old boy with a dangerous gift: mind reading. A gift that apparently was not limited by geographical boundaries, for how else could Jeremy have seen Sirhan Sirhan planning to assassinate Sen. Robert Kennedy in California? Dr. R's treatment goal, agreed upon with the Hergenroeder family, had been to help Jeremy develop a filter for his mind reading pronouncements.

After assuring the Hergenroeders that Jeremy was not schizophrenic, Dr. R realized they had a real problem. Nobody wants to have their mind read. So, how could they protect Jeremy and his gift? He cogitated for a few moments: *Our minds are the last vestige of real privacy, aren't they? Of course. But this child also reached into the mind of my own mother! And she had a childhood friend with the same gift. More amazing still, Mom could feel her friend and Jeremy reading her mind. This is just inconceivable! I'd never have believed it if I hadn't seen it all in action. Imagine if Jeremy had come to me last March, perhaps we could have warned Martin Luther King of the threat of assassination in April! Would anyone have believed the prediction anyway? Ah, water under the bridge.*

In an effort to protect Jeremy further, Dr. R and the Hergenroeders had decided that Jeremy would come to Dr. R's house on Sunday mornings for some private sessions. They had suspected, but couldn't be sure, that Dr. R's secretary, Velma Brodie, had sold out Jeremy to that Puerto Rican mob operation. Everything seemed so innocent at the time—just a discussion of the power of Jeremy's gift, why other people would find it disturbing, especially when they themselves were unaware of their own thoughts and feelings, many repressed—and often such repression was a healthy adaptation to slow the uptake of painful insights. *Dangit, those kidnappers got Jeremy on their radar when Velma told them his secret! In her halfwit mind, she thought that she could trade that information to get her husband Dan out from under a loan shark. Then, they kidnap Jeremy and somehow as the kidnappers, Pilar and Ricardo Gutiérrez, are racing around Worcester County having crammed Jeremy into the floorboard, Jeremy flies his little mind reading beam to Mom at the nursing home and she figures out he's in trouble. Then she calls me and...*

Dr. R sat up with a start when he heard the front office door open. *I thought I left the front door locked...too early for my first client.* As he arose from his chair, he then heard a faint knock on his door. He opened the door to find none other than Velma Brodie standing there, a curious look on her face. Before she could speak, Dr. R said, "Velma, I'm not sure I can take you back. You breached my trust *and* disclosed a patient secret. Those are the most severe derelictions of duty that I can think of. Why are you here?"

Velma started quietly weeping, realizing, once again, that she had thrown her whole life to the wolves. "I just need some forgiveness, I guess, Dr. Rebovitz. Dan and I are trying to patch things up and, believe it or not, I think he feels worse about this whole episode than I do."

"Alright, c'mon in for a minute, just a minute, and have a seat. I don't think I can employ you here, you do understand that don't you?"

"My brain tells me you're right, of course, but my heart doesn't understand yet. I'm too grief stricken thinking I almost, *almost* got a little boy killed, all to satisfy a gambling debt. I just don't know where to turn. Thank God Dan still has his welding job at General Dynamics. He took my car to Quincy early this morning. You know José and company took his truck. I suppose I ought to call the state police to see if they somehow confiscated it when they arrested José."

"I hate to sound heartless, but I don't really care about your truck or Dan's job. I'm sure that José can run his operations from his jail cell. He'll surely figure out a way to come after Jeremy again, don't you think? It all started with you, didn't it?" Dr. R pressed.

"Guilty as charged. I still want to help the Hergenroeders. I got the impression last night that Det. McNamara wasn't gonna arrest me or Dan for any crimes. Unbelievable as that may seem. I figure he must be giving us credit for helping to stop the kidnapping. Of course, he didn't come right out and say that, but I reckon he would have arrested us by now."

"Again, not my concern. Beyond Jeremy's needs and interests, and those of his parents, how would I explain to future patients who grace my door that, yes, my secretary breached patient confidentiality, but she's learned her lesson? Word gets out that you are still here and my patients, who have to muster up enough courage just to seek psychiatric counseling, then have to have the additional courage to trust you?"

"I, I…just don't know what to say. I *am* sorry."

"Suppose Dan relapses into gambling again? What steps would you be taking to enable his addiction? I'm thinking it hasn't even occurred to you that you need to start attending Gam-Anon. Do you know about the group?"

Velma shook her head.

"It's a 12-step recovery program for spouses, family members and close friends of gamblers. I'm willing to give you the benefit of the doubt and chalk up *part of this whole series of behaviors* to your own gambling disease."

"But *I* don't gamble!"

"No, but you empower Dan's gambling and, thus, his addiction. What you permit you promote. That's part of his disease process and you caught it like a virus. You are going to have to get into recovery yourself. Until you get some recovery under your belt, I can't even think of taking you back to work here. That is my immediate advice to you. Recovery is salvation on earth and you need it in my professional opinion. That's what Gam-Anon is—a mutual support group for the family members and spouses of gamblers. The group meets, ironically enough, at Rollstone Congregational Church, where David pastors. You can't help anyone, especially the Hergenroeders, until you help yourself. You can't even help Dan. Your whole thinking process is diseased and you don't even realize it," Dr. R offered, sitting back in his office chair. Velma started sobbing.

"Tell you what I'm going to do," Dr. R continued. "I'm cutting you a $1,000 severance check to help buy you some time to get with the program. I'll keep you on the health insurance for another three months. But before I give you that check, you must agree to two conditions. First, do not, under any circumstances, contact the Hergenroeders. Second, attend 90 Gam-Anon meetings in the next 90 days. After the 90th meeting, send me a signed note from your sponsor. You'll have to get a sponsor by the way, who'll confirm that you've been to all those meetings. No excuses."

"90 meetings in 90 days! How can I possibly do that?"

"Once again, not my problem. It *was* my problem, but only because you put Jeremy's life in harrowing danger by throwing him *and* his family to those mobsters. And, because I made a bad hiring decision. Lord knows we all have our own addictive tendencies. Mine used to be trying to fix and save every Korean War veteran I ran into. But I've moved on and gotten recovery from that set of demons. Now it's your turn," Dr. R finished as he pulled out his large check register. He cut Velma a $1,000 check and handed it to her as she started weeping again.

"Thank you. I know I don't deserve this chance and especially a severance after the way I've treated you and the Hergenroeders."

"Go get help Velma. It's out there waiting for you. Go, even and especially if Dan starts gambling again. It's your only way out of the hell hole that you've dug for yourself."

As she departed, Dr. R telephoned a local temp agency to get a replacement. The agency rep promised to have a candidate to him by 10:30 a.m. For the next two hours, Dr. R studied up on a couple of his patient charts in preparation for the day's appointments. His patient load, all children ranging in ages from 5 to 17, was substantial enough that he always felt better reviewing his prior findings to be ready for the surprises that his patients would throw at him *and themselves* during their psychotherapy. He found that mutual journey most compelling—plumbing the depths of patients' rich psyches and personalities.

At 10:00 a.m. sharp, he placed a call to the McPherson residence.

"Hello," Lily McPherson answered.

"Ah, yes, my name is Dr. Rebovitz…"

"Oh sure, hi Dr. R, that's what Jeremy calls you right?"

"Yes, Ma'am, but please call me Azriel."

"OK, Azriel, what can I do you for?"

"Um, is David or Alex where I could speak to them?"

"Alex is here, but David and Ed are out at our gun range. Jeremy is upstairs playing with Truman's toy collection, something we just have not gotten rid of since Truman died in Vietnam."

"Oh my, I'm sorry to hear of your son's death. I didn't realize he served in the War."

"Yes, he signed up as soon as he turned 18, didn't even wait to get his draft card or see where he might have fallen out in the draft lottery. Went right into the Marines. Did his basic training at Parris Island. You know, he didn't fall far from his father's tree. I'm guessing you are wondering about Jeremy, too. We all decided at breakfast this morning that he should try to go back to school tomorrow. Ed checked with the school district and they informed us that Edgerly is closed today. They are doing a security check of some sort. Makes sense I suppose."

"Indeed it does, Ma'am. Indeed it does."

"I think the plan, assuming the school opens back up tomorrow morning, is for Ed and David to take Jeremy to Edgerly School first thing. They'd have to leave at 7:00 a.m. to make it before the 8:15 a.m. bell. Like I said, everyone agreed, including Jeremy, that it was best to get back on the horse after we all got thrown off. Plus, Det. McNamara, I understand, will be putting a couple of officers at the school to stand vigil and guard the kids."

"Oh, that's great. I'm so glad Jeremy's going to be able to stick with that accelerated program. Hate to see his intellect wither on the vine."

"Let me get Alex for you. Just a minute," Lily said as she put the phone down.

Dr. R could hear Lily calling for Alex. "Hello? Dr. R?"

"Yes, Alex. Good to hear your voice. How are you all doing?"

"Well, as you can imagine we're still taking stock. We have mulled it over and do want to get Jeremy back to school. Seems like the best move for the moment. Keeps a semblance of normalcy going. Do you think that is wise?"

"Absolutely. I'm also glad that Detective McNamara is thinking ahead to get a police presence at the school. I understand the school is closed today."

"Yes, yes it is. I think even the School Superintendent got involved. It was his idea. Everyone sort of rallied around making sure Jeremy and the other students would be safe going forward. Most of them will be on summer break in the next few days, but Jeremy's class will continue."

"I think that is ideal," Dr. R agreed. "Routine is a great salve for trauma—this has been a shock to all of our systems, especially yours. I've got to visit my mother to thank her for saving us all. Still unbelievable what you learn about your parents that they never tell you when you're growing up!"

"So true. Your mother saved the day. Jeremy told David and me last night after dinner how he did it. Went back into her mind after she forbade him from ever doing it again. I still don't know how she put two and two together—it's not like she could read *his* mind, for heaven's sakes."

"Well, that's for sure. I'll let you know what I find out, assuming she'll tell me. I'm still her baby boy don't you know. She's still in charge of taking care of me, right—sort of like you with Jeremy!" Dr. R roared with laughter and Alex joined in.

"Please let Jeremy and David know that I called. I should tell you that I let Velma go today. Gave her a severance check on the condition that she *not* contact you all and that she attend 90 Gam-Anon meetings in the next 90 days. She didn't really understand, but did agree not to call you. If she does, please let me know immediately."

"I will. Or we will. Did you know that Rollstone has regular Gam-Anon meetings in the fellowship hall most weekdays at 7:00 a.m.?"

"Yes, I told her about Rollstone. I'm quite sure the irony eluded her—you know that the very minister whose family she threw under the bus would as yet help her find some salvation on earth."

"Wow."

"Yes, well said. I'm still happy to meet with Jeremy this coming Sunday if you all are up for it. No pressure of course. I do think he's figured out his filter. Perhaps I could help him address some of the trauma he's been through. He's so sharp, though, and I'm thinking he may already be working through the emotions."

"Oh my, no, I doubt that. Let's plan on it and thank you so much. We still have to figure out something about our living arrangements. I'm going to call Det. McNamara to see if he thinks it's yet safe for us to return to Pearl Hill Road. There's a roast I left out on the kitchen counter to thaw, must be getting plenty ripe by now. My, how life can throw you a curveball!"

"That's one decision I can't help you with Alex. Way beyond my level of expertise. Do be careful though and call me any time of the day or night. All you have to do is call my office number and my answering service will track me down. We doctors learn to sneak by without much sleep on some nights. Doesn't work all that well, but we put up a brave front."

"Thanks again, Dr. R. I'll be in touch if we can't make it on Sunday," Alex offered as she rang off.

CHAPTER 6

Wednesday June 12, 1968—Morning
Waking Up In The Intensive Care Unit (ICU)—Burbank Hospital

Ricardo Gutierrez slept in fits and starts, odd dreams invading his psyche. One dream found him flapping his arms in a vain attempt at staying aloft in the clouds, and then falling to earth at light speed, crushed to death. Nurses had woken him every two hours during the night to check his vitals, but he only groggily sensed their presence. As his narcotics started wearing off, he awoke and tried sitting up in bed. To no avail.

"Goddamnit!" he shouted, finding once again that the nightmare was true. That bastard *had* shot off his left hand. How was he supposed to do anything now? *That's my writing and shooting hand. Was my writing and shooting hand.* Almost as bad, part of his left knee had a chunk missing. Ricardo tried to rise up so he could get a better view of his leg, which seemed to be in a long cast. As he did so, vertigo rushed in and he collapsed back onto his pillow. He tried to reach the cast with his right hand and finally succeeded, feeling the structure of the thing. *What a frickin' horror show!* He looked at the tube going into his right arm from the IV pole. He read aloud the name on the bag of liquid: g, l, u, c, o, s, e…*glucose*. He thought for a minute. *OK, that's just sugar water or something. At least I'm alive. Wonder how Pilar is doing down the hall?*

Ricardo and Pilar, cousins in the wider Gutiérrez family, were fortunate that, unlike most small town hospitals, Burbank had state-of-the-art facilities. It benefitted from both a generous donor base and the presence of whip smart medical residents who haled from Boston's best medical schools. The hospital sat atop a big hill, which doubled as a free ski slope during the winter. The city had installed a free rope tow that enabled many a Fitchburg youngster, who could only afford a used pair of skis, to learn the sport.

Ricardo heard a knock on the door and said, "Come in."

Two heads appeared, the shorter of whom was an attractive nurse and the taller man, a member of Fitchburg's finest. They both entered, the nurse leading the way.

"How is *my* patient doing this morning?" asked Nurse Benita Cruz, as she whisked to his bedside, her brown eyes beaming. She stood just north of five feet tall, but filled the room nonetheless. Ricardo took an immediate liking to her, breathed in her pleasant yet subtle perfume and felt enthralled by her bewitching smile. He'd anticipated facing a mean old witch for a nurse, a battle-ax who would scowl at him for kidnapping a five-year-old kid. *No dismissing frown here!*

"I'm in a lot of pain Ma'am," Ricardo said. As he spoke, he got a start. Momentarily stunned, he quickly recovered. *Oh my God. I know her. She's the sister of one of our younger Rangers. Cedro...that's his name. I hope this is a lucky break. She's Puerto Rican!*

"Mr. Gutiérrez, my name is Officer William Testarossa. I'm guarding your room."

Testarossa towered over Nurse Cruz and Ricardo, easily six foot three or four inches tall. He seemed to have black eyes that matched his black hair, with the countenance of an executioner. *The guy must weigh 250 pounds easy—I ain't afraid of him!* Ricardo tried to convince himself.

"You've been placed under arrest and our detectives need to speak..."

Before Testarossa could finish, Nurse Cruz interrupted, "Officer, all in good time. This is the first moment Mr. Ricardo, err, Mr. Gutiérrez has awoken since his *emergency* surgery last night." She emphasized emergency, stretching the word out for effect. "We heard you cursing from the pain, Mr. Gutiérrez. Please let's wait a bit, Officer, before you all start interrogating him. He's not going anywhere. It'll be several days before he can even walk, and that will require intense physical therapy. He'll need an occupational therapist to figure out how he's going to adjust to switching from being left handed to right."

"Of course, Ma'am. I didn't mean to rush things, but I'm under strict orders from my command to alert them the minute he wakes up."

"I ain't talkin' to no cops, Officer Testarossa. I want a lawyer, now!"

"Certainly that is your right..."

"Officer, I hate to interrupt *again*, but I need you to let me do my job, check his vitals, make sure he goes potty if he needs to and advise the surgeon that he's now awake. Why don't you go out and call your Sergeant or whomever you need to call?"

Testarossa left the room in a huff, but not before warning Nurse Cruz that Ricardo was a known and dangerous criminal. "You just give a shout and I'll come running if this Bozo tries any funny business."

Ricardo did his best to lean toward Nurse Cruz conspiratorially and said, "I know your brother Cedro, Ma'am."

"Yes, I know you do."

Benita angled in close to Ricardo. "We should whisper. The walls may have ears. You and José have done a lot for our family and we're, no, *I'm* grateful. You guys helped pay my nursing school tuition. But I doubt I can help you much here. Even the DA, some guy named Chris Johnson, keeps calling to see if you and Pilar are up and at 'em. I've only heard rumors, but what in blazes were you doing yesterday to bring down all these John Q. Law types to our hospital?"

"I better not say nothin', else you'll get cornered or charged as an accessory, *Senorita*!"

Just then the chief nursing officer, Parma Ventura, whisked into the room, without knocking, and with Testarossa tailing her. Her parents had named her after the town their car broke down in during their honeymoon on the way to Put-in-Bay, Ohio, off Lake Erie: Parma. They'd given up trying to agree on using any of either spouse's family names. Ventura stood just five feet tall but ruled the ICU like Patton commanded the Seventh Army. Not a fat cell on her body, she regularly practiced yoga, long before it came into vogue. Her ice blue eyes peered into the room, locking on Benita whom she found leaning in way too close to Ricardo. Benita got a start and tried backing away subtly as if she had been examining Ricardo's head. The trick failed.

"Nurse Cruz! What are you doing in here unattended by the guard? And what's this I hear about your denying the detectives' access to this *prisoner*? I gave you strict instructions to inform the police guard the minute the *prisoner* awoke. Why did you disobey my direct order?"

Stunned and shaken, Benita Cruz's throat constricted. Classic fear response and nowhere to run. Exercising her supervisory authority as CNO, Ventura had only just promoted Benita to the ICU in the last 30 days and she'd barely finished half of her probationary period. Benita had long dreamed of working in an intensive care unit with its all-hands-on-deck atmosphere, and here she was about to throw it all away by trying to help. A friend.

"Ah, well, you see, Ma'am, it was my *professional* opinion that the *prisoner* was not yet fit for a full interrogation. He even asked for an attorney..."

"Now that statement right there should have informed your *professional* judgment, should it have not? He's sharp enough to lawyer up and you think he's impaired mentally? What were you doing leaning in so close to him? Do you *know* him?"

Supervisor Ventura had the look of an evil apparition. She'd been practicing nursing for 25 years, starting out as a licensed practical nurse, an LPN, at a nearby nursing home, slogging through all the scut work, clawing her way through RN school at night, finally getting her Bachelor's degree and a full nursing license. She didn't stop there— going to evening classes for an MBA and even a Master's in Public Health to round out her health industry acumen. She'd never married—too busy with her career and schooling, never dated in fact and feared she might be lesbian. Something her long dead mother would have disowned her for if Parma ever came out of that closet. Her graying hair told the tale of long hours, medicating her feelings with work, like some drug addicts did with opiates.

"We will discuss this later in rounds with the ICU Medical Director," Ventura continued. "What do *you* think I should tell him? That a brand new ICU nurse, not even here one month, decided on her own to stop a police investigation in its tracks—without first consulting me or the physician in charge? He'll question *my* judgment now. Was I a fool for promoting you to the ICU from the med-surg unit?"

As Benita cowered back a few steps, Ricardo chimed in, "Ma'am, I'm sorry, this is my fault." Pointing at Testarossa, Ricardo continued, "I asked that policeman to leave until I could get my strength back and wind down from the effects of the pain medication."

"Don't you start with me, Mister! This matter is between Nurse Cruz and me as her supervisor. Nurse Cruz—and I expect an honest answer, is that *precisely* what this *prisoner* told Officer Testarossa? Be careful how you answer since your job is now most definitely on the line."

"So, yeah, I guess so. It all happened so fast, I'm having trouble remembering word for word. I was worried about the patient's condition and the officer seemed aggressive. But no, we did not discuss his pain medications."

"Follow me to the nurse's station right *now* and we'll finish this *line of inquiry* in the presence of the ICU Chief, Dr. Baker *and* Officer Testarossa. I believe lying to a police officer is against the law. Isn't that correct, Officer?"

Without giving Testarossa a chance to speak, Ventura pressed on, "So, it sounds to my ears like you're prevaricating, Nurse Cruz, telling me only half truths. I hope I'm wrong. We'll let Dr. Baker and Officer Testarossa make that call. I think the DA might chime in as well. Mr. Gutiérrez, I sense that you are taking advantage of my new ICU nurse, or perhaps you two know each other outside of work. She is now off your case. You may think you have constitutional rights that trump what goes on in *my* ICU, but you're dead wrong. Take that up with the judge who'll try your case. In the meantime, I'll see that you have an *experienced male* nurse attending to your *ICU* care needs. Don't try your con game on him or me."

Cruz and Ventura exited with a whoosh of cold air. Ms. Ventura, much to her dismay, could not find Dr. Baker on the floor and turned to Nurse Cruz advising her, "We'll take this up later. Report to the 5th floor med-surg unit. For now you're back on evening shift on that unit. Until proven otherwise, I consider your actions a severe breach of trust. You literally have not a clue the position you've just put me in or this hospital. I thought you had better judgment."

In tears, Benita ran to the elevator, not sure whether to head to HR and submit her resignation or just report to the med-surg unit. *How will I explain this demotion to my old supervisor—after she went to bat for me? This is a career disaster! What Ricardo and José did for our family isn't worth this sacrifice!*

Meanwhile, Ricardo stewed in his own conspiratorial juices. He'd fended off the cop. For now. But he had put a potential ally at risk not just for her job but, worse, he may have put Benita in the position of having to turn state's evidence against him. *It wouldn't take two minutes for any district attorney worth his salt to get her to cave!*

Next door, under the watchful eye of a separate guard, Pilar stirred in delirium. The guard covered his ears as Pilar's monitor gave off a shrill alarm. Ricardo heard the noise and wondered what it meant. The ICU code team rushed into Pilar's room to find him coughing up blood and gasping for breath. The lead nurse noted again that Pilar's face was a noxious mess from his fall after the cops(?) shot him in the leg. He'd obviously landed on some sort of gravel-like surface and *kept sliding*. Just back on the unit, Dr. Baker pulled off Pilar's smock to note an entry wound the team had somehow missed.

"Nurse, call a stat now, and get a crash cart in here ASAP!" Baker shouted. A crash cart was hospital jargon for a cabinet on wheels that has emergency equipment and supplies that a physician/nurse team would deploy to save a dying patient's life. A well-stocked cart in 1968 likely would have had suction devices, sponges, swabs, forceps, pain medicine, IV supplies and an oxygen tank.

As the stat team gathered around Dr. Baker, he asked, "How did we not see this knife wound everyone? Quick, let's get him to surgery now. We can clean up this wound while we wait for a gurney. Move that crash cart over here and give me the laryngoscope! He's obviously bleeding internally."

Pilar, semi-comatose, was barely breathing, but some breath trumped no breath any day of the ICU week. As one nurse cleaned around his mouth and neck where the blood and vomit had spilled, Dr. Baker pulled open Pilar's eyelids, shining his flashlight into Pilar's eyes looking for a pupillary reaction. Thankfully, the pupils reacted just as Pilar coughed again.

"Pilar!" Dr. Baker shouted. "Wake up—stay with us!" Pilar awoke for a brief period and eked out, "My chest doc, it hurts to breathe. I'm having trouble..." Pilar passed out before he could finish the thought.

"I thought this guy just had a gunshot wound to the leg. He must have had a knife jammed into his belt during the scuffle!" Dr. Baker said to the code team. "Looks like he stabbed himself with his own knife as he fell to the pavement. The wound is in the suprapubic area and I can't tell how deep it is or if the knife hit upwards towards the kidneys, the aorta or the vena cava. He certainly is in shock. The wound already looks severely infected. Must have been one hell of a dirty knife to get infected that fast. Look at that wound—how did the team miss it during surgery last night?"

Ricardo heard all the commotion next door realizing Pilar was in far worse shape than him. *The moron had a knife under his belt! Jesus. What if he talks—people spout all sorts of things on their way into surgery. Everyone knows the jokes the docs like to play as folks fall asleep under anesthesia. Now count backwards from 100 and tell us who you are stealing from, Mr. Patient. Pilar could give up the whole gang and shootin' match. That lawyer José has on retainer, Pablo Gomez, better be ready with some kinda answer. Gotta find some way to get a message to José.*

CHAPTER 7

Wednesday June 12, 1968—Morning
Ed Counsels Jeremy; Rican Ranger Trainees Find
Themselves in Sudden Disarray

Jeremy awoke at 4:30 a.m. and headed to Lily's kitchen for a glass of water. He found Col. Ed sitting at the kitchen table enjoying his first cup of coffee.

"Good morning, young soldier—how'd you sleep in that big bed?"

"I did great, sir. I found Truman's Teddy Bear, Frankie, and he helped me. But I'm worried about putting my mom and dad in danger."

"Oh, my. Howse about settin' down and tellin' me about it?"

Jeremy paused a moment, and then said, "It all started with Mr. Kennedy. My Dad called him RFK."

"Yup, that's what I called him, too. Before he died. I guess I'll still call him by his initials."

"I tried to warn my parents that a guy I thought was named Sir Hand hated Mr. Kennedy. I knew he was up to no good."

"Yes. Your Dad told me about your, ahh, your vision."

"My parents didn't think I could possibly feel that guy's head from 3,000 miles away. Even if they had listened, what could they have done anyway? Nothing. What good is my gift if all it does is bring us trouble? Look what's happened now! We can't even go home—Ricardo and Pilar have friends who will come after me, I bet. Maybe hurt Mom and Dad!"

"So you think maybe it would have been better if you never said anything?"

"Well, sir, I am afraid I'm causing my parents to be in danger because I couldn't keep my mouth shut. Dr. R wanted to help me *filter* my gift, but it's too late for that. My secret's out! All thanks to that Velma woman. I hate her!"

"That makes perfect sense to me, young man."

"It does? I figured you'd say I was just being silly."

"What, you couldn't read my mind just then?"

"No, Dr. R and my folks say I can't do it when someone is thinking about me with love. You must have been feeling love for me. I can't read that."

"Well I'll be a monkey's uncle. No, I don't think you are being silly. I'd have a *distaste* for Ms. Velma too, if I were in your shoes. But you know what, even though she sold you down the pike to those hoodlums, she did step up and help Det. McNamara figure this whole thing out. That took some guts on her part. I think Dr. R is about to fire her for not keeping your secret. You know, like your dad does when he counsels parishioners, doctors have to keep their patients' secrets too. That means folks who work in doctors' offices have to do the same thing. Did Dr. R mention that to you?"

"No, all we did at his house last Sunday was have our secret counseling session. He told me that some folks whose minds I read might not want me to do that. They wouldn't want me knowing what they were thinking. He also said they might not even know themselves what they are really feeling. So I have to be careful speaking about their thoughts."

"That's great advice. Back to the point. Even though I say I *understand* that you hate Velma and that you *think* you are the cause of everyone's problems including and especially your folks', that's just not true. I want you to understand something. It took me a long time to figure this out for myself. The only person I can control is me. That means Ricardo and that Pilar—you're not responsible for them putting Dr. R in harm's way, or your parents. Those guys, they made their own *choices*. Do you understand what I'm saying?"

"No! If I'd never opened my mouth, they'd have never come after me and my parents."

"OK, you've got a point. Gosh, you are smart. Look, what I'm trying to say is that you should always feel your feelings. Don't pretend they don't exist. They'll eat you alive otherwise. But give yourself a break. You're only five years old for Chrissakes! That's two years short of a dog's year. You've got your whole life ahead of you. You're taking on way too much responsibility. I want you to let go of that guilt. That's what it is. I've not heard your parents blame you for anything. In fact, they've done everything they can to help you. Didn't they get you into some sort of judo class? *And, get you to visit with Dr. R, too?*"

"Yeah, I guess."

"Good. Give them a break too. We're all trying to figure this out *together*. When I was in the military I had lots of guys under me—smart ones, dumb ones, wise guys, jokers, you name it. But when the going got tough, they all came together as a unit to defend our country and each other. Think about all of your family and friends the same way. We're all coming together. We're taking it one day at a time. When that gets too tough, why we'll take it one hour at a time. You know who we need to thank, don't you?"

"Who?"

"None other than Dr. R's mother. She's the one who called him didn't she—to say the bad guys were on their way? How'd she know to do that, by the way?"

"Ah, well, I broke her rule."

"What rule? What are you talking about?" Ed demanded, perhaps a bit too militaristically.

"Um, well, Mrs. Eva, ahh, when we visited her, we talked about stuff. I felt her head and she had a bad memory from Germany, where our Volkswagen got built."

"You mean she was in Germany when Hitler came to power?" Ed asked.

"Yeah, I think. I saw her, her husband and Dr. R when he was a 12-year-old boy, looking out their hat shop window. There was a bunch of people coming down the street, throwing rocks and stuff. They were setting buildings on fire, too."

"Oh shit, you saw Kristallnacht happening didn't you? In her head I mean. The night of the broken glass." It never would have occurred to Ed not to swear. It was second nature and got his point across every time, except he never swore in church. Jeremy didn't care, since his Grandpa Phillip liked to swear, too, and he found it kind of funny when his mother would get all red faced when she heard Grandpa going off. He understood that Grandpa swore to blow off steam, especially when he was working in his garage wood shop on all manner of creations. Phillip routinely got distracted when he was hammering away and always had a black nail on one of his fingers where he'd missed the target. That called for Phillip to shout lots of swear words while he flailed about in a vain attempt at stanching the pain.

"Yes," Jeremy continued. "She didn't want me to see it, but I couldn't help it. She got upset and my dad got mad at me for being rude."

"OK, I get that. What happened then?"

"She asked me not to do that again. She said she had a friend when she was a little girl who had my gift for reading minds. But Ms. Eva had a gift too!"

"Really? Do tell."

"She could feel her friend looking around in her head, reading her thoughts. Her name was Helga something. Shi...vish, I can't remember exactly because I couldn't spell it."

"Shivitz? Was that it?"

"Yes! Shivitz. With a z on the end. They played this game back and forth every chance they got. Then Helga moved to America and Eva, Mrs. Eva, never saw her again. She never knew if Helga got into trouble like me with her gift."

"Alright, so how did Mrs. Eva know to call Dr. R?"

"When I was in Ricardo's stolen car, I looked into his head and Pilar's and saw that they planned to hurt Dr. R. They'd hurt him if he didn't help them. So I disobeyed Eva. I went back into her head and looked at her memories of the broken glass night. I could tell I upset her. But she figured out something was wrong. I guess she knew I'd never do it unless I had to. That's when she called Dr. R. It was sort of funny. She had to get down the hallway of the nursing home. Some guy was talking on the hall phone and she asked him if she could use it. He said no. He got real angry. But she got angrier and pushed his wheelchair out of the way. Called Dr. R's office. Told Velma to shut up and get her son on the phone. Mrs. Eva was forthright—that's the word Dad used with Nurse Missy. That's a good word."

"Yes it is Jeremy. So, I'm guessing she told her son to call the cops. That's when they called Mom, I mean my wife, and she got me on the CB. That explains everything. I'd not had a chance to think it all through—happened so fast. Your Dad and I got on top of that building just in the nick of time. I had my rifle at the ready and your dad kept watch with my military binoculars. We saw that Ricardo had a gun—not a good sign. You did the right thing and I think the next time you see Mrs. Eva she'll agree that it was OK to break her rule, just this one time. You know the cops never would have gotten there in time. You had to break that rule, Jeremy. No tellin' what would have happened. You all might have been on the way to Quincy—and they might have killed Dr. R if he got sideways with them. I hated shootin' them two fellers, but they really left me no choice. There's that word again, *choice*."

"Yeah, choice. I guess you're right. We're all OK for now. We just have to help each other, but you didn't have to help us. I bet my parents will thank you. I want to thank you. You saved my life, too!" Jeremy said, as he slid off his chair and came around the table to hug Col. McPherson around the neck.

"You're a good man, Jeremy. Yessiree. We can spend the day here at the compound, play with Pinky—and see what we need to do in the next couple of days. That make sense to you?"

"Yes sir."

"Good. You can lend a hand with the chores. I'm pretty sure school is optional for you today. Hell, I can't imagine the principal and the school board letting Edgerly School get back in session today, what with all of the hullabaloo yesterday."

The pair left the kitchen to go find Pinky, unaware that other people had plans for the day, too.

CHAPTER 8

Wednesday June 12, 1968—6:30 p.m.
Judge Chuck Melanson's Chambers—Boston Superior Court

After getting word from Gordon Wilde, the criminal court clerk, that Judge Charles "Chuck" Melanson would hear José's case, Pablo Gomez phoned Penny Montgomery. José's instructions and her contact information stood out prominently in the firm's Rican Ranger client file. José and company had, months ago, found a weakness with this particular judge, and had bribed the court clerk who was in charge of case assignments. Wilde made sure that the randomized system for case assignments to the various criminal court judges wasn't so random. He conveniently arranged case assignments so that any and all Rican Ranger defendants always ended up on Melanson's docket. The judge had not a clue about the Wilde influence.

Penny Montgomery, José's madam, called Judge Melanson in the late afternoon, and used his direct line. "Judge-y baby, it's your love-struck girl Penny. How's my pookey bear doin'? I'm just itching to get under that big robe of yours."

"Ah, Penny, yes, busy day today. I'm a bit whipped already and may call it an early night. What's up?"

"Oh, sugar, please don't put me off tonight. I can't stand the tension and I need you so bad! Plus, I got a friend who's in a bit of trouble. Name's José. He's got some kind of arrangement before you tomorrow."

"You mean an arraignment?"

"Yeah, what you said. I don't know the law stuff," Penny cooed, feigning ignorance.

"I can't help you with that case. Too high profile! The press'll be all over it."

"Well hows-about I just *cum* by your office after hours and I'll help you understand."

"OK, but just for a quickie."

"You got it. Let's just see how much time you'll give me when we hop on that desk of yours."

"OK, you win. Meet me at the back door at 7:00 p.m. sharp."

"Will do, lover boy!"

Unbeknownst to the hapless judge, the Rangers several months ago had stepped in to service the judicial libido by satisfying his aberrant sexual proclivities. They'd hired Penny, a special services prostitute, to do their bidding. A voluptuous blonde, she "understood" the Judge's needs, wants and desires, and had approached him for legal assistance in a swanky hotel bar one night after he'd adjourned court. Demurring, Melanson had tried to advise Penny that she should seek competent counsel from any of a number of firms locally. He was in no "position," he'd urged, to represent her. Feigning the most profound disappointment, she'd harped on his mentioning of "position" noting that, yes, she did need an attorney, but her boyfriend had just dumped her for another *lover* and her grief had paralyzed her. He offered to buy her a drink as solace, and from there it was just a matter of a credit card and a nice clean room on the fifth floor for him to realize he'd finally found his sexual soul mate.

As their "relationship" blossomed (the Rangers paid her fees), Penny gained all manner of intelligence about the Judge's personal problems including his exorbitant alimony—punishment in another jurisdiction, apparently, for his having had an extra-marital affair. She also learned of the extensive bribes he'd had to make to judicial council colleagues to persuade them to look the other way so that his appointment to the bench could move on through. He also complained that judges just didn't make the kind of money private firm attorneys did. For him, paying for the finer things in life had proved impossible.

Melanson lived a coupon cutting existence and was thrilled to learn that Penny herself had been the beneficiary of an enormous inheritance from a long dead uncle, and didn't want for anything. Yes, she could help him a bit if he'd help her in return. He lost himself in her aura every time she'd gently remove her garments to reveal a bounty worthy of the Song of Solomon. He found her biblical garden irresistible and she satisfied his peculiar appetites. Even though the voice inside his inner child warned him that this was all way too easy, he gave in knowing there might be a heavy price to pay down the road. The flesh was indeed weak. Today the tax had finally come due.

Penny had amassed lots of photos of their dalliances to share should Judge Melanson's conscience ever get the best of him. The waiting press would take only minutes to connect the dots. She herself had compiled an impressive rap sheet, having been convicted of prostitution in several locales the prior 24 months. Melanson, of course, was unaware. On her last charge, the Ranger team had intervened with another store-bought judge and she'd gotten off scot free. They'd approached her following her case's dismissal, asking if she might consider returning the favor down the road, almost like the Godfather did when he asked the mortician to fix up his bullet-ridden child, Sonny, for his open casket funeral. She agreed, if they'd remove her abusive pimp from the Bay State. They dispatched him within 24 hours with a one-way bus ticket to Little Rock and strict instructions never to return. He agreed, not that he could speak, since several of his teeth came up missing and his tongue had swollen to three times its normal size.

Now if her sexual favors couldn't win the day with Melanson on the matter of bail, the Rangers would drop ship to the Judge a sample of the numerous photos they had captured from adjoining hotel rooms. Nothing persuades like the fear of a public humiliation. Melanson surely would then reconvene court and get the matter addressed properly. The Rangers need not have worried. Melanson wasn't that stupid. He realized that, to keep Penny happy, he would be assisting Mr. José by finding in favor of the defense team's evidentiary motions that Gomez soon would be filing. The Rangers had several bites at the apple at the ready. After all, the arraignment was just round one—all José really needed was a decent bail amount to get back in business. Melanson knew his job was to make it look difficult for the defense.

At the age of 49, Melanson should have been at the apex of his legal career. Instead, he was sinking fast. Penny appeared at their prearranged time, whisking through the same back door that the judge used in other high profile cases to escape the TV news cameras and bolt out to his car. Ever the psychologist, Penny had worn his favorite mini-skirt. Her halter-top was extra loose and she bounced and jiggled all the way up the elevator, rubbing against the judicial robe for enticement. Melanson couldn't resist her charms and his desk provided his only support. He wondered if he'd fallen in love and pined for a long-term relationship with Penny. His law clerks and court officer were none the wiser and Penny had conspired with him to be discrete. In minutes she had gotten him into a forgiving mood. But not before she had stopped right in the middle of his sexual crescendo to press her case. Melanson had begged her to continue.

Through alligator tears, Penny had moaned, "Please! José's like kin to me! Don't worry Judge. I wouldn't want pookey bear to get in trouble. Now you just let Momma take care of everything."

Unbeknownst to everyone on José's legal team, the Boston District Attorney's office had started a file on Melanson. But so far the evidence of corruption had proved too scant to build any kind of case. Not yet anyway. For starters, Melanson appeared to be living above his means. More obvious, he had switched from having a reputation as a hanging judge who never disagreed with any prosecution motion, to one who suddenly had taken a distinct liking to the criminal defense bar. Judges just don't switch that quickly. And the problem for Melanson was that the Boston DAs had grown accustomed to preferential treatment. The easy cheesy protocols Melanson had launched in the prosecutions' favor all started just minutes after his swearing in. Upon their election to the bench, most judges, as practicing lawyers would tell anyone who would listen, contract a particularly distressing disease called robe-itis. They quickly forget the vicissitudes of law practice. Hang 'em high judges like Melanson should get *more* curmudgeonly, not less. It's the natural evolution of things. So, Penny and José had already cooked Melanson's goose. He just hadn't yet smelled the campfire that was razing his reputation for integrity.

CHAPTER 9

Thursday June 13, 1968—9:15 a.m.
Boston Superior Court—José's Arraignment

F estooned in the standard issue orange jump suit, José shuffled with his guards into Judge Melanson's courtroom. As his leg irons and wrist restraints rattled, José struggled to stay upright. Pablo Gomez, JD, Esq., with a subtle smirk on his face, waited at the defense table, which was set perpendicular to the jury box. Only the DA's table faced the jury, homage to the prosecutor's burden of proof.

Gomez had not made it to the jail to speak to his client before the arraignment, but they both knew the drill, even though it was José's first venture *personally* into the criminal justice system. Many of his Rangers had been in trouble before. Nevertheless, the firm of Pellatino, Degrazio and Gomez always managed to get them off outright on a motion to dismiss for lack of evidence (*despite our subpoena, your Honor, our witness in chief seems to have absconded from the district*) or some simple misdemeanor plea that kept the prying eyes of the police away from Rican Ranger operations. José never ventured into court to witness any of those proceedings. He knew he needed to stay well off the justice system's radar. Unlike most firebugs who couldn't resist watching with the rest of the crowd their torched buildings collapse, José had no such psychological predilection to view any Rican Ranger crime scenes. What was there to view anyway? In 99% of their hauls, as soon as his teams loaded the ill-gotten gains onto a semi-trailer, they'd weld the goods into the ready-made compartment right behind the front nose of the trailer. Off-loading always happened in a secure warehouse off the beaten path. Even if the cops caught the Rangers during the loading phase, they'd just assume that the welding equipment the Rangers had with them was a tool of the trade, not part of some illegal haul.

"All rise!" court officer Mack Bistowish intoned. Mack looked the part, complete with a 45 automatic belted to his hip, a nightstick swaying from the other hip and a swagger to finish off his countenance. Mack had served one tour in Vietnam as an infantryman, rising to corporal before his duty period ended. Melanson chuckled to himself at the *all rise* pun, reflecting on the ascending passion of the night before, his desk just a few feet away on the other side of the court wall. As he alighted to the bench, he scanned the courtroom and, much to his dismay, saw Penny smiling at him from the rear of the courtroom. He looked away realizing how much trouble he was about to affix to his career, if he got caught anyway.

José felt good because Melanson was his patsy. Penny had made her presence known to Gomez and José, with a quick and discrete wink as she entered the courtroom. Gomez had taken her confirmatory call at home just around midnight. He left nothing to chance.

"Call the first case," Melanson bellowed to Mack.

"State v. José Gutiérrez!" Mack hollered much louder than necessary. He handed Melanson the case file and stepped back into his corner, eyeballing the packed courtroom.

"General Fiandaca, *ma'am*, are you ready, ahh, to ahh, um, proceed?" Melanson squeaked out, his baritone losing its base tone as if he'd become a 13-year-old boy again. Melanson ogled the Assistant District Attorney General, undressing her in his mind's eye. Tammy Fiandaca, JD, aged 32, stood five foot five, sported a chin-length contour cut, pageboy hairdo, blond of course, and was whip smart, having finished second in her law class at Boston College in 1963. She saw right through Melanson's sex crazed emotional state, and used it to her advantage. Penny, too, noticed the Judge having trouble getting his words out. Even José drank in Melanson's star-crossed demeanor and leaned over to Gomez whispering, "No wonder Penny got him into bed minutes after meeting him that first time!"

"Thank you, your honor. Yes, we are ready."

Gomez rose quickly, "Waive reading of the charges, your honor. My client pleads not guilty."

Melanson eyed José. "Mr. Gutiérrez, you stand in my court when spoken to. Now get up out of that chair and show some respect."

José stood with a gleam in his eye realizing that Melanson was just putting on a false show of force.

"How do *you* plead Mr. Gutiérrez? I'm not interested in hearing how your attorney thinks you are pleading, and do *you* waive the reading of the list of charges? Have you even *read* the charges?"

For a millisecond, Melanson's extra dose of sarcasm caught José off guard. Recovering, José responded, "Yes, your honor. I plead not guilty. These charges are completely false and, of course, I've read them. The DA even got my middle name wrong. It's Gustav not Jorge, so what I'm asking is, do they really have the right Defendant?"

Fiandaca, still standing, glared at José. "Your honor that's just a typo, we've got the right Defendant. Since Mr. Gutiérrez is so adept at the law, perhaps we could move right now to conduct the preliminary hearing. I have our arresting officers here and we are ready to proceed in the name of judicial economy."

"I object your honor. This is completely out of line!" Gomez broadcast for all the courtroom to hear, including the press. It was cases like this one, so soon to be high profile, that would assure his firm had clients waiting in the wings for months to come. Paying clients. Drug dealers—they were the ones who could fork over the cash up front to carry the day and pay the overhead. Gomez had a motto—the next client might be the last, so treat them *all* well. Always return your calls before the end of the day and, no, this is not plumbing where at least at day's end you can clean the shit off your hands!

"Objection sustained. *Ms.* Fiandaca!" Melanson said, emphasizing his awareness of the budding women's lib movement, which removed the "r" from Mrs. since women were no longer chattel or bound to their "M*r*." husbands. Back in 1968, the women's lib movement paralleled what the Nation of Islam followers had done when they adopted Muslim last names in place of their former slave owners' last names. Malcolm X had made that point loud and clear, scaring White America to no end with his prophetic laser beam.

"I'm not sure what you are trying to pull here," Melanson continued. "Mr. Gutiérrez, sit down and shut up.

This is not the time for defense speeches. You are not before a jury yet, so save it or I will put you on the stand and serve you up for cross-examination by Ms. Fiandaca. Now, am I setting a date for a preliminary hearing or...?"

Gomez didn't wait for José to speak and quickly said, "Waive preliminary hearing, your Honor. And I apologize for my client's outburst. This is his first day in court *ever*. He's never been in trouble before and is quite traumatized by his mistreatment at the hands of the state police. A matter I may have to take up with a preliminary motion before this case proceeds any further. I have reason to believe that, during my client's phone call to my offices, the police guards were trying to listen in on our attorney-client confidential *and privileged* discourse!"

Melanson realized things were getting out of hand and fast, a situation he hadn't envisioned and now hoped to nip in the bud with what should have been a quick arraignment and bail hearing. But the circus had come to town and set up its big top right in front of his bench. José now serving as the ringmaster, calling the elephants and tigers to enter stage left. Melanson scanned over the press corps (no TV cameras yet allowed in courts), all of whom were madly taking notes in their reporters' pads. *Oh shit, this really is going to be on the front page and above the fold in tomorrow's Globe. Gotta rein in these clowns.*

"...move to call the guard, Officer Vic Langston, to the stand to respond to these spurious charges." Fiandaca stopped speaking, and then said, "Your Honor, I seem to have lost the court. Do I need to restate my request?"

By this time, Penny and José were rolling their eyes. They got the circus feeling too, and admission was free today. "No, Ms. Fiandaca. We are not going to give any weight today to Mr. Gomez's assertions. I don't need to hear from, what was the officer's name again?" Melanson asked sheepishly.

"Langston, your Honor. He's right behind counsel's table," Fiandaca pointed to Vic who stood up ramrod straight, ready for duty. Langston looked at Melanson with only partially concealed contempt, having figured out months ago that this guy was corrupt. To the bone.

"Again, need I remind both counsel for the State and the Defendant that this is only an arraignment? Since Mr. Gutiérrez has pleaded not guilty, are both sides ready to take up the question of bail?"

"Defendant is ready, your Honor!" Gomez eagerly announced.

"State is ready."

"Well, let's proceed. I'm concerned with the State's aggressiveness here, Ms. Fiandaca. It's true, is it not, that Mr. Gutiérrez has never served a day in jail or been convicted of a crime?"

José sat gleefully next to Gomez, complete with a false look of concern, playing to the hilt his bit part.

"No, your Honor," Fiandaca exclaimed, as Gomez sat down to watch his client's bribe payments purchasing the judge's favor. "Mr. Gutiérrez has, indeed, never been *convicted* of any charges and..."

"Your Honor, I must object to Ms. Fiandaca's efforts to bring in my client's prior arrest record. Did I leave the United States of America and land in some banana republic? Does the presumption of innocence not still weigh heavily as it should in this courtroom? No bail is needed or justified in this instance, and I urge this court to release Mr. Gutiérrez on his own recognizance or, if that is not sufficient, into the custody of his grandmother back in Fitchburg. He will be here for trial and we have already begun preparations for a vigorous defense against these spurious, ridiculous and overblown charges. Indeed, they amount to a piling on as if *Miss* Fiandaca got out her DA's manual and cut and pasted from every felony charge she could find," Gomez asserted as he took his seat.

Melanson sat back in his judicial throne, staring at the ceiling as if looking to God for salvation. He took a deep breath that resonated through the courtroom. "Ms. Fiandaca, I'm not going to hear evidence of an arrest record particularly, as here, where the Defendant has no, *zero*, convictions on his record. Mr. Gomez, please refrain from starting the trial too early. This is a bail hearing. Ms. Fiandaca, let's stick to your standard bail script, which this court has heard *ad nauseam* in more cases than I care to count. If this Defendant is a flight risk, then I need to hear why."

Nodding, Fiandaca responded, "If you will allow me to proceed your Honor, I have other indicators that this Defendant will abscond from the district, especially since he has pending charges to the west, in Fitchburg. Worcester County. Mr. Gutiérrez has no gainful employment whatsoever, which causes me and the District Attorney's office grave concern. He has no ties to Boston, no family or relatives in any of the surrounding bedroom communities either on the North or South Shore, and appears to hide out in Fitchburg living off of, what, the generosity of friends and neighbors?" Fiandaca paused for effect, hoping, again, that she might sway Melanson with the substance of her arguments.

"The charges here are far from some of the cases we see with small fry defendants, those who have committed nonviolent, petty misdemeanors. Every charge here is a felony that carries a substantial prison term. Worse, I have been unable to confirm that Mr. Gutiérrez is even a U.S. citizen, which makes the likelihood of a flight to Mexico or Canada a concern for the People. No bail amount that the State can think of would be high enough to ensure this Defendant's attendance at trial. I should not have to reiterate that the charges here are quite serious: loan sharking, extortion, conspiracy to transport stolen goods across state lines, assault, *and* we are investigating Defendant's possible connection to other crimes. Your Honor, we only just arrested this Defendant two days ago, but it appears from our preliminary investigation that his criminal influence reaches far and wide. We also know that, on the day of his arrest, two of his cousins, also from Fitchburg, kidnapped a five-year-old minister's son. That is the basis for Defendant's pending arrest warrant out of Fitchburg for conspiracy to commit kidnapping.

"Need I remind the court that the charges of conspiracy amount to the very criminal act that a defendant has *conspired* with others to commit—just as if he did the act himself? A five-year-old child, your Honor. The State is gravely concerned for the safety of that child and his parents! This is precisely why no bail is appropriate in this case. Do not let this Defendant go free. If ever there was a case for no bail, this is it, Judge."

With that statement and some oohs and ahhs from the gathered press corps, Ms. Fiandaca sat down to await Mr. Gomez's best.

"Mr. Gomez, how do you respond? Should the Court be concerned with the safety of a minister's family and child? I'm not sure I yet understand the connection. It sounds to me like the State has a good point. What am I missing?" Melanson sat back and his antique chair creaked in protest. *I hope Gomez has a decent argument ready.* Melanson would not be disappointed.

"If your Honor, please, let's take a look at what the police and the DA have so far. No stolen goods. No evidence of any connection to any kidnapping. He's not charged with that crime in this jurisdiction. Mr. Gutiérrez is a citizen and we will be happy to provide his birth certificate as an exhibit at trial if need be," Gomez offered, hoping to God that José indeed had not entered the country illegally. After all, it was not like he was from Cuba. *Puerto Rico was a territory...wasn't it?* "I'm appalled that the DA would impugn my client's heritage. He is from Puerto Rico, which, we all should know from our sixth grade civics class, is a U.S. territory, making all such inhabitants of that island presumptive citizens of this country. They even vote in our presidential elections, so I don't know where Ms. Fiandaca was headed with that unfair and scurrilous accusation. Again, as to extortion, we have no witnesses coming forward or mentioned in the charges, so I am unable to respond to those baseless claims.

"The State Police arrested Mr. Gutiérrez while he was driving the speed limit from Fitchburg to Quincy to see a family member named Dominic Sangria, who works at the

General Dynamics facility. My client tells me he was interested in applying for a job at the shipyard. Mr. Sangria planned to introduce him to the foreman, who had put out the word he needed a couple of experienced welders. You know, with all the war time build up, the shipyard is running two shifts just to keep up with the demand from the Defense Department. Yes, my client has been unemployed for some time your Honor, but he was making a sincere effort to get off the bench and get hired in a decent job. Why punish those efforts now? And, with the press here, I can only hope he'll still be able to get that shipyard job.

"Worse yet, throwing him in jail will surely prevent that employment from ever coming to fruition. In fact, it would be a second form of punishment, all without a trial. The DA can't on the one hand bad mouth my client for not having a job and then on the other keep him in jail to prevent him from finding gainful employment. And, he surely was going to get a job since Mr. Sangria is a member of the IUMSWA, the Industrial Union of Marine and Shipbuilding Workers of *America!*" Gomez adding the America for effect.

Meanwhile, José thought to himself, *Damn, this has been money well spent. Where the hell did Gomez come up with that line for Chrissakes?*

"I gather you are finished, Mr. Gomez, since you have retaken your seat?"

Half rising out of his chair, Gomez nodded, "My apologies, your Honor. Yes, I'm finished, unless the Court has any questions."

"No. Ms. Fiandaca, any rebuttal?"

"Of course, your Honor. Without fully revealing all of the facts and evidence we have been gathering including what the Massachusetts State Police have *amassed*..." Fiandaca loved that word and hoped it would have the intended effect, namely, that José would soon be off to prison permanently merely from the weight of the evidence that would surely crush him at trial. "I am not at liberty to divulge some of this evidence at this time because law enforcement has justifiable fears for the lives and safety of several, and I do mean *several*, confidential informants. We are concerned that the Defendant is in league with several underbosses in the Puerto Rican mobs.

"As I understand it, he himself runs a syndicate of some notoriety, although the press has not discovered their reach, so the average juror candidate walking the street wouldn't have become biased against Mr. Gutiérrez. This undercurrent of mob activity is, in part, the basis for the charges related to the interstate movement of stolen goods. We have one witness whom Defendant's henchmen beat up within an inch of his life. He now is in the witness protection program ready to testify at trial. We will, of course, disclose his former name to defense counsel as part of the normal discovery process. We have bills of lading, all falsified, showing how Defendant's own henchmen diverted long haul trucks to destinations separate and apart from their offload sites where the unwitting trucking companies' clients had expected *and received* delivery. You see, the brilliance of Defendant's scheme involved dual purpose trucking runs. Regular clients got their goods delivered in a timely fashion and Defendant's illicit operations delivered the illegal goods right on deadline.

"It is our understanding that Defendant's gang, if you will, chose Fitchburg on purpose both for its proximity to Route 2 and for its semi-anonymous, off the map location. Most folks know Fitchburg for its dye industry and chair manufacturing. I believe it is considered the chair capital of America. It's a small town, with but 40,000 residents, so I'm quite sure local law enforcement only became aware of Defendant's exploits in the last 72 hours with the kidnapping of the five-year-old child. The state police are now working closely with Assistant DA Chris Johnson of Fitchburg to close off this venomous criminal enterprise once and for all."

At the mention of the five-year-old kidnapping victim, Joe Garibaldi, a Boston Globe reporter, shot out of the courtroom, racing to the pay phones to warn his editor that there was indeed more to this story than some sort of illegal shipping conspiracy. Balding and a bit of a barfly, Garibaldi had a bloodhound's nose for a good story. He had connections across the state with other reporters, feeding them tips and in return getting great lines on intrastate conspiracies. This little puppy was shaping up to be an *interstate* conspiracy, and the child's kidnapping only added napalm to the bonfire. *Gotta beat Channel 4 News to this one!*

Incensed at the disruption, Melanson raised his voice, "Ms. Fiandaca, I see you have now warned the press about this five year old. I'm betting that, even as we speak, the Globe reporter who just bolted from the courtroom is getting on the phone to his colleagues to chase down this child's name and particulars. Was that your intent?"

"Of course not, your Honor. It's why I didn't mention any names, of the child or the family in question." Ignoring the diversion, Fiandaca pressed on. "More to the point, however, releasing Mr. Gutiérrez..." Fiandaca hated using José's name because it humanized him in the eyes of the court, but she was keenly aware that Melanson might once again be siding with the defense. She hoped that she still might curry favor with the court and get a high bail set, even if she couldn't keep this SOB in jail, "...would enable him to claw back control of the situation with his mob members and guide them away from the long arm of our laws. The community faces a substantial risk of Defendant orchestrating many more crimes between now and trial. I urge you on behalf of the State to keep this man in jail until that trial. If only for the safety of the five-year-old kidnap victim!" With that, Fiandaca sat down. Vic reached over the bar and patted her on the shoulder, signaling that he knew she had done everything she could to bring about a just result.

"Mr. Gomez, I assume that you would argue that everything Ms. Fiandaca said was mere conjecture and baseless, and further that you and your client are unable to respond to evidence that remains well hidden behind law enforcement's investigatory veil? Am I correct?"

Incredulous, Fiandaca stared down Melanson, but chose not to object.

Gomez shot to his feet. "Of course, your Honor. I could not have said it better myself. Thank you."

"Well, the Court is indeed impressed with defense counsel's assertions that Mr. Gutiérrez was most likely on his way to apply for a job with General Dynamics. I have seen the ads in the *Globe* for all manner of workers at those facilities. I am not unimpressed, however, with the allegations of a kidnapping conspiracy involving a five-year-old boy, one of such tender years. A kidnapping, Mr. Gomez and Mr. Gutiérrez, that occurred not quite two days ago. But I must remind the State that the Defendant was nowhere near Fitchburg where this kidnapping allegedly occurred..."

Fiandaca saw where this was headed and bolted to her feet, "But your Honor, that is the essence of a conspiracy, is it not? Conspirators by design are not all at the scene of the crime or crimes they collaborate in committing! Each individual has a singular role..."

Melanson cut her off. "I understand the law on conspiracy, Ms. Fiandaca, and I appreciate the State's position. Lack of proximity does not a conspiracy defeat. But the Boston D.A.'s office has not charged Mr. Gutiérrez with kidnapping here. Further, your weak and unfounded accusation that Mr. Gutiérrez lacks citizenship, however, seems a callous attempt at painting this Defendant in the worst possible light. You implied that his entrance into *our* United States was his first crime on our soil. A beginning to a long crime spree, yes? Regardless, unless you have additional arguments and *evidence* that you are able to disclose, I am inclined to release this Defendant with a modest bail, especially since he remains unemployed. I will set a bail amount that would, in the eyes of this Court at least, persuade him to return for trial. I also remain convinced that, based on your argument, Fitchburg's finest will re-arrest Defendant as soon as he walks out of this courtroom."

"But your honor, that police department has no jurisdiction in Boston…"

Melanson interrupted Fiandaca again, "Of course, but that DA's office has procedures for issuing warrants through this Court and I remain ready to facilitate appropriate process the moment I am so requested. I am ordering this Defendant be released on $10,000 bail. Mr. Gomez, I assume that amount will not unduly burden your client and that I have your word that he will return for trial?"

"Yes, your Honor, my client advises me that his family will step in to assist him with *amassing* that bail amount. I do want to reiterate that he is unemployed and such an amount is most certainly a burden," Gomez finished, chuckling to himself at getting to use Fiandaca's *amassing* phrase in rebuttal. *What's good for the goose.*

"Very good. Please get out your calendars Mr. Gomez and Ms. Fiandaca. Do you two agree that we should set both a trial date and the time for a scheduling conference to address any motions and other preliminary matters after we actually receive a grand jury indictment?"

Both attorneys nodded their agreement, with Fiandaca feigning respect, and Gomez barely suppressing his glee.

"José," Gomez said, as Bistowish started ushering José back to the holding cell, "I'll meet you in a few minutes and we'll get bail taken care of. You be a good boy with Officer Mack now."

Ignoring Gomez, Fiandaca jammed José's file back in her brief case, and prepared to exit. Her boss, Solomon Purdy, the popularly elected District Attorney General for Boston, had warned her to expect Melanson to allow bail, but she refused to believe it with such drastic charges and a five-year-old boy's safety at stake. "Wait till Purdy hears this crapola," Fiandaca whispered to no one. Just in the last few weeks, Purdy had learned of plans for a sting operation on Melanson, but hadn't let on with Fiandaca, since he needed her at her advocating and zealous best to keep up the appearance that no one in law enforcement was the wiser. As Fiandaca finished packing, she turned and saw Garibaldi skulking back into court with a look on his face that said he'd had no luck with his Fitchburg contacts.

Not believing the fluke that Fiandaca hadn't exited yet, Garibaldi scurried over to her. As she caught sight of him, she rolled her eyes in muted contempt.

"You gotta give me something, Ms. Fiandaca!"

"No comment, Mr. Garibaldi. I'd have thought you'd have heard enough to fill two newspapers with today's proceedings."

"But I missed much of the show."

"Then I suggest you follow the money trail!"

"What money trail?"

Fiandaca just smirked and left Garibaldi standing by counsel's table. *Maybe we can get this reporter to do some of our work for us!* Fiandaca mused to herself.

CHAPTER 10

Thursday June 13, 1968—7:00 a.m.
Back to Edgerly School

"Jeremy! It's time to brush your teeth. Lily made you a lunch for school. Here's your milk money," Alex instructed, as the two families finished a farmhouse style breakfast of scrambled eggs, a huge platter of bacon, buttered toast (Wonder Bread no less) and steel cut oatmeal. A Lily McPherson specialty. She even folded Vermont cheddar cheese into the eggs and real maple syrup on the oatmeal.

"OK, Mom. Thanks Col. McPherson and Mrs. McPherson for letting us stay here the last two nights," Jeremy exclaimed.

"Think nothing of it young man. You'd have done the same for me had we switched places, now wouldn't you?"

"Oh, yes, of course. Right Mom?"

"Yes, honey, we all stick together like eggs and bacon," Alex agreed.

David stood up and asked, "Ed, do you mind if I ride with you and you can take me on over to the church after you drop off Jeremy? I'm thinking I don't need to have my VW Bug sitting out pretty as you like at the church. Wouldn't want any of those Rican Rangers to think I'm just waiting on them to kidnap me."

"Of course, David. Probably be best if I hung out a spell there. Are you thinking you'll grab some work and leave directly?"

"Yes, I hadn't thought it through like that, but your notion makes all kinds of sense. It's a big church and I don't need to sit in my office fearing every creak and odd noise. They'd throw me off my game. I'll need to visit briefly with my staff, Linda, Bill and Roger, and get their input."

Linda Dunn was David's secretary, Bill Fontaine served as the church organist and Roger Tomlinson was the church sexton (ecclesial jargon for property manager and all around fix-it guy). The foursome ran the church, often with the advice and counsel of Kurt Crider, who served capably as the church moderator, sort of the chairman of the board.

"Might have to give Kurt a call, too, but I'm guessing he's already been calling Linda wondering about all the what fors."

"Tell you what preacher, I'll just hop on down the street to Ronnie Bryant's barber shop where they're afraid of preachers like you! Get me a bit of a trim."

"How'd you know that?"

"Ah, hell, David, I've heard the talk. They're all afraid of looking sinful when you or those other ministers cross that threshold. Forget that you're a regular guy and all. Best to keep up appearances, nonetheless. I'll put in a good word for you if anyone asks."

Lily chimed in, "Now, Ed, don't let Ronnie cut too much off. Your hair is short enough. Let's let it grow out just a bit. It's the current style you know, just like those big ties all the men are wearing now. I saw one advertised the other day that was four inches wide. Like to never have seen such a thing when I was a little girl. Model looked like a clown!"

"Now Mah, you know I like this butch cut. Military has a point. Keep it short and it takes care of itself. No worries. Plus Pinky wouldn't recognize me with a Rolling Stones haircut. Say David, have you heard that new song by the Stones called *Jumpin' Jack Flash*? I think it's about a car or something cause they sing it's a 'gas, gas, gas!'"

"Wait just a doggone minute," Alex chimed in. "I like the Rolling Stones and Ed you are just too old fashioned to get their groove. I read somewhere that the Jack they're singing about was the gardener of their guitarist, Keith Richards."

"You nailed me, Alex. I did hear the song the other day and even at my age I found it kind of catchy. Couldn't help tapping my foot to the beat. Don't tell anyone at church though. It'd ruin my stoic image," Ed pleaded with a smirk. "And while I'm thinking about who you should be talking to David, you probably ought to call Mark Gallagher, since it was his judo lessons that helped Jeremy scream out about dying that caught the attention of that Anttonen couple. You probably ought to call them while you are at it, too, show them some gratitude. Tell you what, while you get gussied up, I'll look up their number."

"OK, I'd forgotten about them in all the chaos. I do need to thank them. They stuck their necks out a bit when most folks would have looked the other way."

Just then everyone heard Jeremy bounding down the stairs after brushing his teeth. He had a great set of incisors and oncoming molars, all thanks to Alex giving him fluoride drops every night before bed. Fluoridated water hadn't yet hit Fitchburg.

"I'm going to run out and say hello to Pinky. Is that OK Col. McPherson?" Jeremy asked.

Lily intervened. "Let's you and I take him out some dog food and check to make sure his water dish has some H_2O in it. How's that sound? He loves folks who feed him!"

"Awright! Neat-o-cool!"

After feeding Pinky, Jeremy hopped in Ed's Lincoln and marveled again at the push button windows. While Ed and David sat up front, Jeremy played with the window controls, up and down, up and down. As Ed steered past the security gate, he pressed the master control switch disabling the back seat window controls, and Jeremy's window button stopped working. "I'm sorry Col McPherson, but that button is just so cool. We have to crank the windows in our Bug. This is luxury!"

Ed didn't respond and David turned around to tell Jeremy not to mess with the car's accessories. The threesome daydreamed without a word for much of the trip down to Fitchburg. As they pulled up in front of Edgerly School, they saw a police officer standing by the front walk, keeping watch. The officer recognized Jeremy and casually strolled up to the Lincoln as David and Jeremy got out.

"Howdy do, gentlemen!" Officer Gerald "Jerry" Callahan announced. "Been awhile since I attended elementary school, don't you know. Glad to be back though. Good chance to catch up on some of my math skills!" Callahan guffawed.

"Officer, thank you so much for helping us and the school," David said, as he reached out to shake Callahan's big mitt of a hand. "This means a lot to me. I'm guessing you recognize Jeremy."

"Yes. I've been greeting all of the parents as they drive up here to drop their kids off. Folks are scared and then they see me and they seem to calm down. Nice to make your acquaintance young man," Callahan said, as he leaned down to Jeremy's eye level. "Put her there pardner!" Callahan said as he offered his hand, which Jeremy shook vigorously. "My, you've got some kind of vice grip there young man!"

Jeremy tried to look into Callahan's mind, but didn't see anything. He realized that the officer loved his job and the children he was duty bound to guard today.

David handed Jeremy his lunch box. "You keep your eyes peeled today Jeremy..."

Before David could finish, Jeremy's neighbor, Jimmy Kendall came running up. "Hey Jeremy, where have you been? I saw them kidnappers grab you. They pushed over Mrs. Murphy—she fell right on her butt. She's OK though. Are you OK or what? You haven't been home the last couple of nights."

David backed away so Jeremy could get back into the fold with his friends and classmates, and hopped back in Ed's car. The pair drove off toward Rollstone.

Jeremy looked at Jimmy and said, "Yeah, it's been pretty scary. They took me to the hospital after the cops arrested those men."

Overhearing the exchange, Officer Callahan stepped in and said, "Mr. Jeremy, you probably don't want to do too much talking about what happened Tuesday. We don't want word getting out that you're back at school now do we?"

"No sir, I guess not."

"Best be on your way then into the building. You come running or give a shout if you see any trouble brewing, you hear?"

"Sure thing officer," Jimmy countered. "We're on our way now!"

Eager to start their day, the pair ran up the steps into the school. Just before they reached the front door, a Fitchburg Teachers College student with a pair of binoculars spied Jeremy. Acosta Gutiérrez, Pilar and Ricardo's second cousin, and a long time Rican Ranger, had been on watch. He'd heard about all the fuss and had actually seen the kidnapping in progress from the adjacent junior high school building. A student teacher himself, he'd just let his eighth grade class out for lunch recess and was admiring the view on the quadrangle when, lo and behold, he spotted his cousin Pilar grabbing some kid and pushing over a teacher who tried to stop him. Acosta made a mental note of the kid's face and now recognized him coming back to school. Later, he'd read the piece in the *Sentinel* and, like the other Rangers, had put two and two together. He'd tried to visit Ricardo yesterday at Burbank Hospital, but thought the better of it when he saw a police guard standing watch next to Ricardo's room. *OK, I'm not sure what all this means. But I'll have to get word to José when he gets back home. Sure hope that Gomez firm gets him out and fast.*

The accelerated kindergarten class teacher, Mrs. Helen Murphy, greeted Jeremy and Jimmy as they entered her classroom. She pulled Jeremy aside to have a quiet word. "So, are you OK, Jeremy? I certainly didn't expect to see you back so quickly. We'd have excused you and if you want to call your folks you don't have to stay all day. I'll be happy to send some work home with you. The principal wants to speak with us today about the kidnapping and there'll be some social workers here today to talk to the students."

"I'm OK Ma'am," Jeremy offered. "Thanks for trying to save me. I'm sorry that Pilar pushed you over so hard. He's really mean. But that police officer said we shouldn't be talking about what happened."

"He did, did he? Well, I think what he means is that we shouldn't discuss the events outside of the school setting, like at the Piggly Wiggly or on the street corner. But in my humble opinion, we all got a big shock and you got the biggest of all. Talking through our feelings and emotions is a good thing. We don't need to theorize about the criminals' work—maybe that's what he meant. But thank you, nonetheless. I'll mention the Officer's concerns to Principal Chandler. He's in charge of our school. And, thank you for your concern. I'm a little bruised up. You'll want to thank Mrs. Lovejoy—she's the one who called the police after you got kidnapped. I tried to see the license plate of the kidnapper's car, but there was too much dust swirling around for me to make out the numbers."

"Yes, I…" Jeremy stopped just in time before letting Mrs. Murphy know that he had seen into her mind and realized she couldn't make out the plate. "I will thank her, ma'am."

"Now go find your seat and we'll get started in a few minutes."

Just then the Principal, Dr. Joseph Chandler, stepped into the classroom. He was the first Black teacher in the district to be named a principal by Superintendent Alfred

Gonyer. He stood six foot three inches tall, had a short afro haircut, and always wore spit shined shoes that had a distinctive squeak as he walked the halls. Gonyer had looked at all the applicants and chose Chandler, not even realizing from memory that he was black. At first. Later, when he made the call to Chandler, he congratulated him on that fact—"Didn't even realize we were being historic here, Joe, you being the first black principal and all in the district. I do want you to know, though, that with your Master's degree and prior business background, you had many qualities that I just found irresistible. It's a proud day for Fitchburg and I think we ought to hold a press conference, don't you?" Chandler had begged off, not wanting to make a big deal out of the promotion, but his wife Mrs. Hattie Chandler had scolded him when she heard the news at dinner. "You call that man right back tomorrow Joe and tell him that, of course, *we'll* help with a press conference, you hear me?"

Chandler had demurred in the name of marital harmony, but had yet to make the call. Shy by nature, he believed that one's actions defined the man. *Why should I seek publicity and look like a token? It'll make it look like he chose me just because I am black!*

"Well, greetings Mr. Chandler," Mrs. Murphy announced. "It's an honor to have you join us. Please say hello, children."

"Hello, Principal Chandler!" they all hoo-raad in unison.

"Mrs. Murphy, has your class had a chance to say the Pledge of Allegiance?"

"Why no we haven't sir. Class please stand and let's say the Pledge."

As the class did so, Jeremy felt Principal Chandler's head and found abject fear tempered with resolve to protect his school, his teachers and *his* students. Chandler was proud of his position and meant to do right by everyone. He'd fielded a number of calls from worried parents well into last night, with a final call coming at 11:30 p.m. His promise of a police presence seemed to carry the day with most parents.

As the students retook their seats, Chandler asked, "Mrs. Murphy, may I speak to your class for a few minutes?"

"Please sir!"

"Well children, I want you to know that you are all heroes. I'm proud of you. We had an awful crime get committed here just two days ago and you were all witness to it. I'm glad, as I know you are, that Jeremy here (Chandler pointed to Jeremy and walked over beside him, touching his shoulder), is safe and sound. We have two policemen here today and they'll be with us over the summer to protect us all. I'm calling you heroes because you followed your teachers' directions right after the kidnapping. You got right back into this building where you were safe. The police told me how proud they were of all of you too. I've brought in two social workers who will want to speak with you later today. This was scary was it not? How many of you were scared? Raise your hands."

Everyone including Mrs. Murphy raised their hands skyward. So did Mr. Chandler.

"Are you surprised I was scared, too?"

Several of Jeremy's classmates nodded their heads.

"That's right, just because I'm a big man doesn't mean I don't get scared too. It's a natural feeling. And it's OK to be scared. Do you know why?" Chandler hid the look of surprise on his face when he saw Jeremy raise his hand.

"Yes, Jeremy."

"Well, sir, I learned the other day that fear can be a good thing if I pay attention to its energy."

"Yes, indeed. That's just what I meant. The worse thing we can do is pretend we are not afraid. Because I was scared, I took action. I called the District office and asked for help. That's what you should do when you are afraid. *Ask for help!* And that's what I want each of us to do today and in the coming weeks. If you are afraid of anything, really anything at all, ask any teacher in this school or me for help. Ask the policemen, too. That is part of the reason we are all here—to help each other. Does that make sense to you?"

Some of the students nodded. Cathy Lundberg raised her hand. Mrs. Murphy saw her and said, "Principal Chandler, Miss Lundberg has a question for you."

Cathy had long auburn hair, fetching brown eyes and a smile that could beat the band. "My Mom told me our class might get cancelled for the summer. Is that true?"

"Great question Miss Lundberg. I did discuss that idea with School Superintendent Gonyer. We thought long and hard about it. But you know what? You all are so special and this is such a great learning opportunity, that we decided we shouldn't cancel this class. It's going to get easier for us in a couple of weeks. All the other grades will go home for the summer. We may move your class to a different building and we'll let you know, but for now we are going to go forward right here. That reminds me. If any of you or your parents have questions in the coming days just give me a call. I'm right in the phone book, too, so have your parents call me at home. Tell them not to be bashful. And you can tell them that's just what I said. Bashful!"

"Sir, what happened to the men who took Jeremy?" asked Duane Gurk. Duane had brownish almost black eyes and a fresh tan from a visit to the beach last weekend.

Mrs. Murphy chimed in. "Thank you, Mr. Gurk."

Taking his cue, Chandler said, "Yes, Mr. Gurk, your parents may have read in the paper that the two men were arrested just a couple of hours after they…kidnapped Jeremy."

Chandler had hesitated, but quickly realized that naming the event for what it was, a kidnapping, took away some of the power of the criminal act. It was a lesson he learned from his grandfather who was an AME, African Methodist Episcopal, preacher in Virginia. "Joey," his grandfather would say, for he alone called him Joey, "you have got to name injustices wherever you find them. Loosens the vice grip on you and the family. Don't hold back. It's what the prophets did and for good reason. Don't you ever forget that, son!"

"I heard one of the cops shot off the hand of one of the kidnappers, sir. Is that true?" Jimmy Kendall asked.

"Yes, I believe that's correct. The two kidnappers are under police custody at Burbank Hospital. They will go to jail right after the doctors release them. I doubt they'll be bothering anyone else for many years."

"Will we still get recess from now on?" Wendy Thomas asked from the back of the room. Wendy had green eyes and blond hair. The morning sun caught her eyes just so and to Chandler they looked like big emeralds.

Mrs. Murphy whispered to Chandler Wendy Thomas's name. "Yes, Miss Thomas, you all will get recess just like before. We'll make sure there's a policeman out on the schoolyard. This late spring weather is just too nice to stay holed up in this classroom till 2:00 p.m. I'll be out on the schoolyard, too, as will several more of our teachers.

"Are you going to be OK, Mrs. Murphy? You have that big bandage on your leg?" asked Josephine Collier, a precocious lover of buttercups and butterflies. Josephine had jet-black hair, a cherubic smile and a twinkle in her puppy dog eyes.

"Yes, I took quite a tumble. That man pushed me over and tried to hurt me. But you know what? I got right back up on my feet and I'll be OK. Do I look OK to all of you?"

The class giggled, as did Principal Chandler, who said, "Now, I've got a special treat for you all. This coming Saturday I want you all to come by my family's ice cream shoppe right up Main Street for a free ice cream cone. Does that sound OK? We'll celebrate being brave and asking questions when we get scared. You just tell the folks at the shoppe that you are from Edgerly and are here for your free cone. Is that a good idea?"

"Yea!!!!!" the class shouted in glee.

"OK, I'm going to run by some of the other classes and say hello. Thank you all for coming to school today. You are brave and I'm proud of you and your parents." With that, Chandler bowed to both the class and Mrs. Murphy, and made haste to exit the classroom.

"Alright class, I want to start today's lesson with a math problem. I want you to choose a partner and since there's fifteen of you we have a problem don't we? Can anyone tell me what that problem is?"

Josephine raised her hand.

"Yes, Josephine?"

"Ma'am, someone won't have a partner because there's one extra of us."

"Correct. May I ask that you work with Jimmy and Jeremy? Just pull your chair over in their direction. I'll hand out the problem, so get ready with your pencils..."

With that instruction the class got to work, just as the Rican Ranger CEO fixed a plan in his mind.

CHAPTER 11

Thursday June 13, 1968—12:30 p.m.
Falconi Bail Bonds

"Alright, José, you be a good boy, you hear?" Attorney Pablo Gomez said to his client using a falsetto voice. "This must have been the fastest title filing in the history of the Boston underworld. Good thing I had my clerk run on up to your grandmother's house in Fitchburg early this morning at the same time we were in court. Just sign here on the dotted line and you are free, my man."

José grabbed the pen while eyeing the bondsman through the iron grate window, protection he supposed against "clients" who might not appreciate handing over their hard-earned cash to someone who fed off their misfortune. *Cost of business. Deal with it, man.*

"Yeah, yeah, Pablo, you are so frickin' hilarious. Send me your bill, too, and I'll put it in line for payment. Lemme get this straight, not only do I gotta pay you, but *mi abuela*, my grandmother, has to put up her house *and* I'm still out 10% of the bail? That's another thousand bucks!"

"Correct. Let's move on out in the hall. We can discuss it outside," Gomez said, pointing the way. The pair moved out into the empty hallway. "Now, the retainer you've been paying me each month is to *reserve* my services, *comprende*? We've discussed this before. Melanson got you your bail, but I'm starting to get a feeling he's not well liked in the Boston law enforcement community. I don't know if he can hold it together. Did you see how he noticed Penny in the back of the courtroom? He kept eyeballing her, alternating between looks of lust and outright terror."

"Ah, that's our Penny. Working every angle."

"Yes indeed. She was puttin' on quite a show. No wonder Melanson couldn't think straight. She's some dish. Gives a whole new meaning to the word "retainer," doesn't it?"

"Yeah, yeah. What's this about your fee? I thought all of those retainers ought to have added up enough to get me through this trial and more."

"Not quite, *mi amigo*. I need $15,000 up front to continue in this case. That's a reduction from my standard felony trial fee which, as you might guess, is $25,000."

"The hell you need that kind of money for? You saw the act Melanson put on. This trial ain't never gonna happen. He'll throw out the evidence or we'll throw him to the press. He wants to stay on the bench, he better play by *Rican Ranger* rules. I own that S.O.B. and I expect just-us, ya know, justice!"

"Oh, you'll get justice alright. You misunderstand me. It's $15,000 each for *both* trials, the one here and the one in Fitchburg. I'm guessing you're about to be hit with an arrest warrant the minute you cross the Worcester County line."

"Thirty thousand? You're crazy. Let's be reasonable here. I got expenses. My crew needs to eat, pay rent, and pay off the Melansons of the world. How much business you get from me and my referrals each year, huh? I've helped make your firm rich. I've seen the walnut paneling, the fine art on the wall, the palace like furnishings."

"Hey, I'm grateful, believe me. So are my partners. But the $30 large is to ensure I get paid, *our firm gets paid*, in case you get convicted in one of these cases. Melanson can only get us so far. We gotta get past *two* juries, *hombre*. And I don't even want to know your plans for influence peddling in Fitchburg."

"I ain't goin' to prison. No way. There's too much business riding on my walking. I'll get you the cash by July 1st. This ain't walkin' around money you understan'. I don't have that kind of guacamole just hiding under my mattress at home. You gonna work with me on this?"

"Absolutely. July 1st will be fine. My advice to you is to steer clear of your grandmother's house for the next few days. I'm guessing Fitchburg's finest is on the lookout for you. Fiandaca sure as hell called DA Johnson to give him the sad news that you are a free bird once more. I can feel Johnson salivating 90 miles away. Falconi here's a good man, best bail bondsman in the city. It's why I use him exclusively, but he's gotta get the bond on over to the criminal court clerk's office now. He loses his license if he waits until you've bolted the district. Filing your grandma's home title is why you're out already. José—just like your trucking business, everything in Boston's criminal process is *connected*. Once Falconi files his paperwork, word gets out that you'll have left this esteemed establishment. Speed a light kind of stuff. You know about the speed of light, José? Only constant in the whole universe. You can bend it, but you can't slow it down. Think about that as you ponder your future."

"Fitchburg Police Department, Sergeant Finch speaking, how may I..."

"Finch, its Johnson. Patch me through to McNamara. Asshole Boston judge just let José out with a next to nothing bail amount."

"Ah, Christ, we figured all those state police charges would save the day, Chris. I'm sorry to hear that. Routing you now."

As his intercom buzzed, Ron McNamara was sitting back in his piss poor office chair wondering when he'd get a crack at Ricardo and Pilar. "Yeah, McNamara here. OK, put him through."

"Ron, you there?"

"Yes, Chris, tell me the good news my man. And thanks by the way, for helping me Tuesday night wrap up those arrests. I owe you one."

"'Fraid I got some bad news Ronnie old boy. Some damned judge named Melanson let José walk. Set bail at $10,000 and José bonded out. I'm told he put up his grandmother's house title. Smart move, ya ask me—try to take us off the money trail. Keeps him looking unemployed and semi-destitute."

"Ya gotta be kidding me! José's *grand*mother bailed him out? That don't sound like the José I've grown to know and love. What's with this Melanson guy anyway? Didn't he get the connection to the Hergenroeder boy's kidnapping? Probably didn't make the Boston news."

"Nah, my contact down there, a DA named Fiandaca, Tammy Fiandaca, about my age, called me with the news. Way she tells it, the judge seemed to be playing fast and loose with the charges. She just couldn't figure it. Got to thinking no bail'd be a slam-dunk. Melanson threw her out on her ear. Seemed to take pity on José. Made hay out of her assertion that José might have been of suspect citizenship."

"Goddangit. You s'pose he's headed our way?"

"S'why I'm calling you now. Dude's smart, so I'm guessing he ain't headed for his grandma's home cooking, or to drop off a thank you note and flowers for the bond."

"Go on. Tell me the rest of it. Nuthin' surprises me about this case anymore," McNamara offered.

"I hear ya'. Apparently, his defense counsel, whom I've run into before, a Pablo Gomez, had his law clerk all ready at the grandmother's house at the crack of dawn with the bond paperwork. Seems like Gomez *knew in advance* that Melanson would go all soft. I smell a rat. Might have my boss call the big shot Boston District Attorney General his own self and get the lowdown on the judge."

McNamara sighed, then said, "Keep me posted. I'll have to get with command here and put out an APB. We've got a warrant, of course, for the kidnapping charge and, get this, contributing to the delinquency of a minor, several minors actually. I'm looking at money laundering—all related to his trucking operations. I know the state charges will take precedence but, Jesus, they basically let him go, and for what? He's back in business. I guess jail wouldn't have stopped his operations or him directing them. It shoulda slowed him down some. Shit."

"Couldn't have said it better myself."

McNamara slammed his hand on his desk in anger. "I'm going to Burbank to see what's up with our two Rican

Ranger associates. Can't imagine José will make a play for them, but heck, who knows. Thanks for the call, Chris. I'll be in touch."

McNamara's fears would prove revelatory.

CHAPTER 12

Thursday June 13, 1968—4:15 p.m.
José Slips Back Into Town

N ever anyone's fool, José caught a cab to Lynn, Massachusetts, home to his warehouse hideaway. The town had long been on the decline and a local landlord couldn't believe his luck when a "truck dispatching" operation signed a ten-year lease. It was some sort of holding company and its trustee, whom the landlord had never actually met, sent back the lease complete with a notarized signature and *one year's rent in advance.* José had long committed to memory the combination to the high security lock on the big garage door. It creaked when he lifted it, even though it had a special hydraulic assist to the spring mechanism. Once inside, José jogged over to a nondescript, 1963 Olds Dynamic 88, precursor to the more famous Delta 88. The car was the perfect foil and looked the part of the family sedan. He'd had it repainted battleship gray, thinking he might someday need a safe car the way intelligence operatives needed safe houses.

He bolted out of the garage making a beeline for Route 2 and Fitchburg, confident that the cops wouldn't be on the lookout for a sedan with New Jersey plates (stolen, of course, off of a parishioner's car parked next to a Catholic church during the Sunday services). In under two hours, he pulled into town, headed past the ball fields at Coolidge Park, and moved on up into apple orchard territory, just a half mile past the Hergenroeders' parsonage on Pearl Hill

Road. The Rangers had purchased an old Pearl Hill farmhouse from the estate of the former owner, a farmer who died of natural causes while still seated on his tractor. The tractor sat idling until its gasoline tank emptied. The neighbors finally noticed three days later. That same Rican Ranger trustee bought the property for cash at the estate sale. The executor of the farmer's will was only too happy to part with the property without having to bother with a lot of probate court nonsense.

José had recruited a tenant farmer to make legitimate use of the property, even making sure for good measure that his trustee purchased the former owner's John Deere tractor. No one else had wanted it at the estate sale, since word had gotten out that the former owner died in its seat.

The tenant couple, Juan Candelaria and his wife Mia, were only too happy to oblige the Rangers' needs. They kept the spare bedroom all fixed up, the bed ready-made, with a fresh set of towels in the adjoining bathroom. José and company had constructed a separate entrance and driveway for discrete ingress and egress. Juan and Mia heard José arrive and knew not to bother him with any questions or *in-choir-ees*.

As soon as he parked his butt on the bed, the princess phone sitting atop the bedside table rang. "Yo," José answered.

"Glad I caught you, José. This is Acosta. Listen, I saw that Jeremy kid going into the school this morning, under police guard mind you. Thought you'd want to know."

"Muchas gracias, Acosta. You've earned your keep for the week. Oh yeah, I wanted to know. How'd you see him?"

"I decided to keep my eyes peeled for the morning rush of kids. School was shut down tight as a drum yesterday, cops roaming everywhere. This morning I saw two cops patrolling, and one of them was greeting each of the kids as they arrived with their parents. Sort of checked them all out, scouting for you or Ricardo."

"Say, have you heard what's what with Ricardo and Pilar at Burbank?"

"Nah, I don't have much information other than what was in the paper. I tried to sneak a visit yesterday at Burbank, but once I saw those armed guards hanging outside their rooms, I hightailed it back to the dorm."

"What'd the paper say?"

"That's the thing, man. Reporter said witnesses saw two guys climbing down some building while shoving a big ass rifle in a duffle—all about the time the scene went down. Cops arrived right after the shooting stopped."

"Are you tellin' me it wasn't the cops that shot Pilar and Ricardo? Then who the hell did?"

"I don't know, paper didn't say."

"Listen, I need you to call the police station. I got a mole over there who can give us the lowdown. You mind?"

"Ah," Acosta hesitated.

José played him like a master. "No pressure, Dude. I'm just thinking you could do me a *second* favor today. Ya know, seeing as how I'm paying your tuition at Fitchburg State and all. Tell you what, just call and ask for Maria Catalina. She's a secretary there—real low level. It's not like you're calling an actual policeman. Get it?"

"Yeah, I guess. But if they…you know, the desk sergeant starts pelting me with questions…?"

"That ain't gonna happen. He's too busy fielding calls from grandmas whose cats are stuck up a tree. Just hang up if you get scared."

"It's not that..."

"I understand. Just do what you can and call me back quick," José urged, as he rang off.

Acosta dialed the operator and asked for the police.

"Hello, Sgt. Finch speaking, how may I help you?"

"Yes," Acosta burped out, "may I please speak to Maria, ahh, Ms. Catalina?"

"Sure young man, who should I tell her is calling? She's pretty busy with a case."

"Yes, Ac...Chase Matterhorn."

"Matterhorn, huh, you mean like that mountain in Switzerland?"

"Ah, yeah. Was my grandfather's name."

"Got it. You don't sound Swiss," Finch chuckled good naturedly, "Not that I'd know a Swiss accent if it came up and greeted me for Halloween. Patching you through now, Mr. *Matterhorn*."

"Maria Catalina speaking, who's calling please?"

"Well, ahh, Ma'am, you see, its, I'm calling for José. My name is Acosta, Acosta Gutiérrez."

"You got two first names or are you just nervous?" María teased.

"*Lo siento.* (I'm sorry.) I am nervous. Told the desk sergeant my last name was Matterhorn. I need you to call José right now. He's at 5216. He's expecting your call. Thank you!"

"Wait, Acosta..." Maria pleaded. But he'd already hung up, too skittish to continue after coming up with the Matterhorn lie. And getting away with it. Sort of.

Maria hung up the phone, then picked it back up and dialed José's number.

"Hola!"

"Hola yourself, you wiseass. I can't talk right now. Place is hoppin'. You're supposedly on your way back from Boston. They got a countywide APB out on you. Are you in town?" Maria asked in a hushed town. Like most police stations, the layout was pretty basic. No cubicles, offices only for the veteran detectives, and Maria's desk, such as it was, abutted two junior detectives' desks. Luckily, they all were out on calls.

"Yeah, I'm in town and hiding out. You don't need to know, got it?"

"Sure. What do you need?"

"OK, tell me the deal with Ricardo and Pilar."

"Best I can tell, Det. McNamara blew the case wide open. But he got to the scene...you know, Dr. Rebovitz's offices, about two minutes *after* all the gun play went down."

"So, he didn't shoot Ricardo and Pilar?"

"I don't think so. There was some badass military guy on a nearby roof. Had them both in his gun sights. When they came out of the car, he took them out. Surprised he didn't blow their damned heads clean off. Guess he just wanted to wound them. Pilar almost died from some sort of knife wound."

"Knife wound? I thought you said he got shot!"

"He did, but somehow he stabbed himself and the surgeons missed the wound when they were trying to save his leg. Guess they weren't looking at his chest. Wound got infected real bad. Knife must have been plenty dirty, I'll tell you."

"Shit!"

"You said that right."

José took a deep breath. "OK, what else can you tell me?"

"Have to call you back in a few. They're calling some sort of meeting, and I'm gonna try and get within earshot."

"OK, but call me back as soon as you can. I gotta come up with a plan," José pleaded to a dial tone. He leaned back on his bed, too tired to think. He hadn't really slept much in the last two nights. Way too stressed out. He fell asleep within minutes of hitting the pillow, his snores audible through the walls. Mia heard the snoring and a smirk formed on her face. She'd have felt differently if she'd only known that José had helped orchestrate the kidnapping of that precious five-year-old minister's child whom she'd heard about during the morning newscast on her kitchen radio.

Thirty minutes later, Mia again heard José's phone ring, and chuckled when she also heard José gagging awake right in the middle of a big, oxygen-starving snore.

"Hola!" José groaned.

"It's Maria. I only got a minute. I found out that they have a warrant for your arrest for conspiracy to commit kidnapping, and contributing to the delinquency of a minor, or several minors. I heard that they couldn't pile on the same charges that the state police warrant covered. They also figured you've snuck back into town, probably in a stolen vehicle. Where are you?"

"Safe and sound *mi amiga*, safe and sound!"

"OK, I got the name of the high octane shooter, some guy named Ed McPherson. He's apparently a decorated hero from the Korean War. Owns some property up in Ashburnham. Word is you don't want to tangle with him."

"Me, tangle with a war hero? Never. How much of a hero can he be if he didn't have the guts to face Ricardo and Pilar mano y mano? Didn't you tell me he shot them while perched on a roof? The hell kinda badass is that?"

"Look, I'm just telling you what Det. McNamara was saying in this meeting. It's all hush, hush. Jeremy and his family are staying with the McPhersons. Oh, he was a colonel. I forgot to mention that. Trains soldiers at Ft. Devens, even though he's retired. Apparently, he's some sort of crackerjack with sniper rifles. Practices all the time. What are you thinking José, or do I not want to know?"

"Just gathering info *mi amiga* (my friend). Ashburnham, you say? What's his address, *por favor*? Never mind. I'll look it up here in the phone book. Might have to mosey on by and get a look-see just for my own self. Any word on Ricardo and Pilar?"

"Yes, Pilar is finished with his surgeries. They saved him despite a massive infection in his gut. Doctors gave him some new-fangled antibiotic. They expect it to kill the bugs. They've got Ricardo started in physical therapy. Cop guards are watching his every move, but he ain't goin' anywhere any time soon. He's really laid up. They've got Pilar under heavy sedation. You better think about promoting some of your other RRs to fill in the gaps, José."

"Got it covered *mi amiga*, got it covered. You be good now. Sending your mamma some dinero as we speak. I always pay my debts," José bragged as he hung up.

CHAPTER 13

Friday June 14, 1968—7:00 a.m. [Flag Day!]
José Takes a Field Trip

The next day following a good night's sleep, and after a glorious breakfast spent bonding with his tenant farmers, Mia and Juan, José asked Mia for a quick haircut, short please. She got out her shears and went to work, her practiced hands trimming quickly. She used the same skill set with some of the annual migrant workers, not a one of whom had ever seen such service from an orchard owner. While she styled José's hair, he scanned the phone book for good ole McPherson's Ashburnham address. Sure enough, there it was, bright as the noonday sun, under "L. McPherson." Missing in the listing was any reference to Ed, the world-class sniper. *Guess Ma Bell don't know or the Colonel asked for some anonymity. That's gotta be his wife, since there's only one McPherson listed.*

New coiffure in place, José thanked Mia and headed out to the garage to fire up the big Olds. The car purred out of the garage and, as he floated down to the end of the driveway, a cop car passed by slowly, the officer scanning left and right. Thanks to the crisp haircut and the mirror shades he had donned, José no longer matched his 'be on the lookout' description, and the police car moved on. José looked at himself in the rearview mirror and laughed at his brilliance. *That copper would never dream I'd be the orchard owner! You think I'm too El Stupido, yes copper?*

Got some news for you. You just missed the arrest of your career!

José turned right, the same direction as the cop car, the more to reinforce in the officer's mind that whoever was driving the land yacht behind him was innocent as a baby lamb. José eventually turned off the orchard road and headed for Rindge Road, the most direct route to Ashburnham. He marveled at the same endless woods that Jeremy had admired just three days earlier. He flicked on the radio and heard Otis Redding's *Sittin' on the Dock of the Bay*. José sang along with Otis, never quite hitting the correct notes, but he didn't care, nor did the woodland creatures who heard him pass by with the windows down. *Si, si amigo, Jeremy, I be comin' for you while you sittin' on the dock of McPherson's bay.*

At that moment, a thought struck José like a whaler's harpoon from the last century. *I better shut off these thoughts and fast...else my little quarry will see me's a comin.* Not three seconds later Col. Ed, David and Jeremy passed by on their way to Fitchburg to drop Jeremy off at school. Neither David nor Ed noticed the big Olds pass by, but Jeremy felt José's head immediately.

"Dad, oh my..." Jeremy stuttered, almost speechless.

"What's wrong boy?" Ed turned around to look at Jeremy.

"That car that just went by. That was José driving."

"You sure? Didn't look like much of a bad guy to me, Jeremy," Ed announced with diminishing confidence. "I noticed him but he had almost a butch style haircut and had on a pair of them mirrored sunglasses."

David spoke up. "Jeremy, are you sure?"

"Yes. I think he's headed to your house, Col. McPherson. I felt his head for a second and then the thought disappeared."

"Ah, hell, boy," Ed complained as he reached for the CB. He clicked the button a couple of times and spoke into the mic, "Ma, ma…can you hear me?"

Lily and Alex were finishing cleaning up from breakfast, when Lily heard the CB blaring her husband's voice. She came running. "Yes, Ed, I hear you, what's going on?"

"Listen, Jeremy just gave me and Dave a warning. He swears he just saw José pass us headed to Ashburnham. Felt his head for a second and he's sure José's making his way to the house. You two get out to the gun range and lock the damned door behind you. Call the cops before you do. José's still 20 minutes out, you've got time. Wait, better yet, get out of there with the Hergenroeder's VW Bug and come into town the back way. Do some shopping or something and we can meet back up at the compound later. In the meantime, Pinky will scare that guy off if he makes a move. Don't call the cops, let's see if McNamara and his henchmen can lure him in. We don't want to let on that we know he's out and about."

At the McPherson residence, Alex and Lily raced around grabbing what they needed, purses and such and headed out to the VW Bug. Alex started it up as Pinky waited expectantly, and Lily jumped in the shotgun seat. They reached the servo gate, and Lily hopped out and punched in the security code. The trusty gate opened and they moved out while Pinky stood guard, tail wagging.

Several minutes later, José pulled up near the compound and looked out the passenger side window. He decided to get out of the car and stealthily walk up to the corner of the gate. Admiring the property, he didn't notice Pinky, who jumped up toward the top of the fence and nearly took off José's right hand as it hung over the top.

"Jesus H. Christ, dog! Well I'll be. Never seen no Doberman with its real ears and a long tail before!" José said, as he backed away from the fence. "Wish I had me a big ole T-bone steak to feed you. Heard once that you and your kin can't resist hot dogs soaked in arsenic. Get you right sick and fast. *Peligroso, muy peligroso* (dangerous) that is."

Pinky stood sentry, growling fiercely. José backed away not wanting to draw any more attention to himself. He lumbered back into the Oldsmobile and did a three point turn to head back to Fitchburg. *This is gonna take some planning. Big security gate and a bigger dog. Wonder if the war hero has any more surprises up his sleeve? And what the hell was that big long building off to the side? I don't like that security gate…looks pretty much state of the art. It's not too damned tall for me to just jump over, right into the jaws of that dog. Gotta be cameras around too. Wonder if they record! Shit. Don't need to be on any goddamned tape. I'd have to get a damned wig on. Shit, double shit. Maybe they don't look at the tapes unless there's some kind of trouble. That's me, though, trouble. I didn't see any cars around. Wonder if the Hergenroeders are even home? Maybe they're hiding out and put the cars in that long building?* José pressed hard on the gas pedal and the big V-

8 thrummed its approval. He cruised back down to Rindge Road, aiming for Fitchburg.

Lily and Alex had scooted away in the opposite direction a few minutes before José arrived. They missed seeing José's big Oldsmobile arrive beside the compound gate. No one had a picture of José as far as they knew, just a vague description and a police composite drawing.

Lily decided to play Colonel with her troop, Alex, and de-escalate all the tension. "Tell me, Alex, what was it like growing up in your family? I think I recall that your father worked on a road crew for the Massachusetts Department of Public Works. Did he drive one of those state issued, orange pickup trucks?"

"He sure did. He's a 'by the book' kind of guy. His whole career he followed every regulation and policy to the letter. I never got to ride in that truck, not once. He'd pass by me and my sisters in a blinding snowstorm as we trudged home from school, waving as he drove on. I'm far less rules oriented, thanks, I guess, to David. He sort of pulled me out of that trap. In some ways, my father is a lot like those Pharisees and Sadducees. You remember—the hard-nosed guys that used to hound Jesus—challenging him on how God's grace couldn't possibly trump the rules."

"Yeah, Ed can get that way sometimes. He thanks me every once in a while for giving him some grace. But the military has lots of rules for a reason—reduces variation. They have their systems in place—worked out over decades or centuries I suppose. He's a bit like my own father who liked to say, 'Everything in its place.'"

Alex nodded, "My father did teach me by example. Work hard and have a plan for your work. He never wastes time, except I suppose on Saturday nights when he watches the Jackie Gleason show. Gosh, he gets into fits of coughing, laughing so hard just trying to keep up with Jackie's sidekick, Art Carney. I get a chuckle just watching my dad enjoy that show. He also loves Pat Paulson, you know, that guy who is so deadpan. That's Saturday night for you. Dad's gotta have his franks and beans before those shows start. It's a tradition. My mother calls hot dogs 'tube steaks' as if that makes them more appealing. I like hot dogs, but not every weekend."

"Yup, they are a treat at a cook-out, but not as a staple. I met your dad and mom one time when they visited Rollstone. How's your dad's skin cancer doing?"

"Well, he got diagnosed really too late. I think he'll be OK. Goes into Mass General every few weeks. They've had to graft some of the skin from his leg onto the right side of his face. The surgeons did a good job, but he tells me the pain is almost unbearable. Doctors asked my mother one time if he was a swearing man. She said he never utters a swear word. They told her that's when they really knew he was hurting badly. Said he swore like a sailor. They're convinced that the sun did it to him—all those years working outside. You know he retired with almost 18 months of sick time. Can you imagine? Most guys he worked with took every sick day the state gave them, almost like it was a vacation. Not Dad. He'd go to work sick, figuring he was fortunate just to have a job, holding on to it like grim death."

"Ed's the same way. Couldn't hardly cotton the handful of men under him who behaved like that. He'd refuse to promote them just on general principles. Of course, those were the same guys who'd complain the loudest about every job Ed ordered them to do. Thankfully, they were few and far between."

The pair cruised on towards Fitchburg and enjoyed the silence for a few minutes, with Alex wondering if this was just the calm before yet another storm.

————

Ed, David and Jeremy pulled up in front of Edgerly, and Ed jogged on up to the police guard. Noting the name Ryan on the officer's badge, Ed said, "Listen, we just saw or Jeremy did, anyway, that José character you all are looking for. He was headed north towards Ashburnham in a big gray Olds Dynamic 88. We're dropping off Jeremy, but you all better be on the lookout and maybe put an officer outside Jeremy's classroom."

"OK, sir, thank you for the heads up. You s'pose José'll be coming this way? Why would he be going to Ashburnham?"

"He's going to look at Col. McPherson's house! Trying to find me!" Jeremy exclaimed.

"How in the blazes do you know that, son?" the befuddled cop asked.

"My son just likes to play detective, Officer…Ryan," David suggested, eyeballing Ryan's badge, "but he heard us talking and that's what we were guessing too."

"I see."

"We're headed now to see if we can meet up with Det. McNamara," Ed advised. "Are you gonna call it in?"

"Yeah," Ryan said, as he turned toward Jeremy. "Look, son, why don't you follow me into the school and then I'll run by the principal's office to use his office line." Jeremy understood that Ryan wasn't making a suggestion.

As Jeremy and Officer Ryan, all six foot two inches of him, headed into the school, Ed and David drove on to the church. "I think we ought to call Det. McNamara and see if he has any new information, don't you David?" Ed asked.

"Not a bad idea. I sure am glad the cops are guarding the school. This is so surreal."

Since Edgerly was barely a mile away, the pair made it to Rollstone in four minutes. The church felt vacuous as they entered, almost as if it held the ghosts of many a Christmas past, all of whom were awaiting escape orders from Charles Dickens himself. David unlocked the office and placed the call. Sgt. Finch answered, but advised that McNamara was working his way into the precinct. "I'll have him call you in a few minutes, Reverend."

As David hung up the phone, Ed said, "Why don't I make us some more coffee?" David nodded absentmindedly, lost in his thoughts about Jeremy's safety and Alex's. *This is so stupid. I really ought to call the UCC Conference HQ and see about a temporary fill-in here. I can't figure out how we reach 'safe,' whatever that is. José's still on the loose. What's with that guy?*

Ed noticed David had moved on to Chicago or Quebec City mentally. *Time to get his mind off all of this madness.* "David, I heard you let Roger Tomlinson work on your

124

lawnmower. You've got one heck of a hill in that backyard. How do you mow it without a tractor?"

"Huh? Oh, that. Yeah, I'm all thumbs when it comes to mechanical stuff. I picked up a used mower a few weeks back. Real antique, that thing. You have to wind a do-hickey rope around the starter and pull like heck. It's a reel mower, but with a motor on the top—sort of self-propelled. Roger got it started when I couldn't. Thing gave off a cloud of blue smoke and made a heck of a racket. It works, but doesn't like our back hill one bit."

"As you can imagine," Ed said, "I've *got* to use a tractor, else it'd take me a month to mow our back 40. I use my shooting earplugs when I ride that machine—so loud it is. The first few times I didn't use the plugs, I thought I'd lost my hearing. Took me a good 12 hours to get the ringing to go away. Real nuisance. Plus I have got to keep Pinky tied up; otherwise, he'd run beside the tractor and find himself a poisonous snake in the grass. You know he's a sight hunter, not anything like a bloodhound. He'd run right up on a snake unawares, and never sense it in time."

"Wow. Never occurred to me that beyond our hill lies a wide-open field with all sorts of tall grass. Bet there's snakes back there—great for getting rid of field mice, I suppose. Best keep Jeremy out of there, and Jimmy too. Those two are thick as thieves sometimes. Boys will be boys, as they say."

Just then, McNamara's call came through. David and his secretary, Linda Dunn, had set the Rollstone phone ringer way up high so that they could hear it from down the far hall, where committee meetings sometimes convened. The church was fortunate to have two phones, for this was back in the day when Ma Bell had an unfettered monopoly, meaning every additional phone came with a stack of fees, especially since the church had to have private lines.

David punched the speaker button and heard, "David, what's up? Are you calling about José? Finch said Officer Ryan called to say you all had seen José headed up to Ashburnham."

"Yes. Jeremy spotted him as we crossed paths, with José headed, as best we could figure, to Ed's house. Maybe he's wantin' to scope it out," David noted, partly embarrassed at his use of military jargon.

"Let me guess. Jeremy felt José's head and saw where he was headed?"

"Yes. How do we keep a lid on this gift of his? I'm figuring if you know it, the word is bound to get out to others on the force."

"Yes, I'd ordinarily agree. But I've not even told my captain, which is probably a breach of command protocol."

"I'm sorry about being so paranoid, but you've told no one and not put it in any report?"

"Yes, that's correct."

"What happens when we get these mobster types in front of a grand jury, or later at the actual trial? Aren't you going to have to tell the DA how you made the connections to get the arrest? Then it will be all over the press!"

"David, slow down for a minute. You are at step 27 and I'm only at step 5. We've got a long way to go..."

"Yea, I get that, and appreciate your discretion, but even if *you* can hold back, what's to stop José, Ricardo and Pilar from spouting it all over the courtroom...?"

"Again, now you are at step 52. Think about their interests. They aren't gonna get on the stand, if they testify at all, and launch into the particulars of why they kidnapped Jeremy. I get it that you're scared, but stick with Ed for now. Best I can tell he's a class act. Let's just go slowly. My first job is to get José in the slammer and fast."

"OK, that makes some sense."

"Look, I've already dispatched a squad car up to Ashburnham and put in a call to Sheriff Ringgold."

"Ringgold? What kind of name is that?"

McNamara took a breath before continuing. "Yeah, that's a pretty unusual name. You know his first name is Tilsbury. I think he hails from Ringgold, Georgia, right over the Tennessee line from Chattanooga. At least that's where his forebears came from after the Civil War. He's jumpin' on the case, and agreed to help us even before I could ask. The good news is that Ringgold had already read the article about José in the *Boston Globe*. He's taken quite an interest in the case. Have you seen the article? Short but sweet, and it didn't do any favors for Judge Melanson's political career. Made him look a bit weak on crime."

"No, I've not had a chance to look at the paper. Thanks for the tip..."

Ed, who'd been listening to the speaker, interrupted, "Detective, Ed here, and thanks for the compliment. So, can you clue us in on the plans—immediate and longer range?

"Not sure our plans have changed all that much since we arrested Pilar and Ricardo. Pilar nearly died the other day thanks to a knife wound."

"Knife wound?" Ed asked, incredulous. "Did he get stabbed on the way to the hospital or something? I sure as heck didn't knife him."

"No, nothing like that. The poor bastard had a knife tucked up under his belt, and stabbed himself in the upper groin area when he hit the pavement. Not sure how the surgeons missed it. They were pretty much focused on his upper right leg. As you'll recall, Ed, against my orders, you shot off most of his femur area. Not that I'm not grateful, mind you. You got there just in the nick of time.

"Anyway, we've got a dragnet operation going across Fitchburg trying to smoke out José. I'm on my way to Burbank Hospital to see if I can tease out any details from Ricardo, who has been screaming for his attorney. I doubt I'll get anywhere. Had an odd call with the chief nursing officer hinting that one of her newer ICU nurses might have gotten cuddly with Ricardo as if she knew him. I'll need to speak with her. Seems this nurse flat out ordered our officer, who was standing guard, to leave the room. His name's Testarossa, sort of a renegade, which is why we had him posted there. Nurse was someone named Benita Cruz..."

"Well don't that beat all, Detective. Handy that she was Latina!" Ed chuckled. "I bet she knew exactly who Ricardo was and Pilar, too."

"That's my hunch as well. I understand she got pretty much demoted on the spot—hadn't even finished her probation period on the ICU. She'd moved up from one of the surgical floors or something. I thought Testarossa was tough, but he tells me that nurse supervisor coulda kicked his ass! She got right in Ricardo's face, told him to back off and that she'd be putting a *reliable male nurse* on his case that very moment. Ventura's her name. Next time you're out doing pastoral rounds, David, you might want to look her up and thank her. Guess she learned that skill after taking abuse from those doctors. You're in the hospital, then the rule is, always, *always* befriend your nurse, no matter what."

David chimed in, "That's quite impressive. I've seen her around, just never crossed her path. Please continue to keep us posted. Jeremy's at Edgerly under the watchful eye of your officers. I'm grateful, as is Alex. We're trying real hard to give his life some semblance of normality, whatever that is at the moment. It didn't help that, no sooner had we set off for Edgerly from Ed's place, Jeremy smells a rat, no, *the boss rat*, and José's hot on our trail."

"We'll find him, just be patient. We've got feelers out with our confidential informants. Just stay tuned."

CHAPTER 14

In the Year of Our Lord 1943
Mia and Juan Come North Looking for Work

Mia had met her future husband Juan as they crossed the Rio Grande late one Sunday night 22 years before taking the orchard job José gave them. They both were a mere 15 years old. Juan could swim and she could not, so when she went under, he pulled her back to the surface and helped her across. Orphaned just two months earlier after her parents both died of tuberculosis, she'd stolen away late one night hoping to get to America, her promised land. He'd worked a Mexican plantation owned by the heirs of Spanish gentry, long since departed. The great, great, great grandchildren of those conquerors had never done a day's work in their lives and treated "the help" like the vermin they believed they were. Juan worked hard and to the bone, but never complained about the ill treatment. He schemed at night starting at age 10 when he finally understood that, like the ancient Israelite slaves, he, too, would need God's help and guidance to pull off an Exodus.

For all intents and purposes, Juan understood that he was enslaved. Both his parents had died in the same fields one particularly hot day when the overseers laughed at their requests for *"mas agua,"* more water, and were horse whipped for causing trouble. Giving water to them meant the *Los Jefes* (the bosses) would have to ride their burros back to the hacienda and pump some more. The bosses sat beneath two big shade trees and couldn't conceive of the workers' lack of production, or why, by high noon, the shiftless field workers had drunk all the water that usually lasted a full 15-hour day shift. Dizzy and out of their minds, his parents died under the whip while their fellow workers watched in abject horror. Somehow, the rest of the crew made it to sunset, including eight-year-old Juan. That night they all suffered from severe headaches thanks to their extensive dehydration. Unlike his older colleagues, Juan's headache included the toxic shock of witnessing his parents getting murdered.

Los Jefes weren't completely stupid. Fearing a small insurrection, the next day they put out the story that Juan Candelaria's parents were lazy and loathsome. Only now, could Juan forgive those monsters, having recognized through his bible readings that doing so meant he heaped red-hot coals on their heads. Unlike the plantation owners in the Antebellum South before the Civil War, these overseers hadn't thought to re-publish their workers' bibles with the slave passages removed. So the unabridged, liberating Word of God jumped out for all to see. Juan vowed never to let the grievance of his parents' murders eat him alive.

Juan believed with all his heart that taking revenge would serve only to cut his soul in half. His parents had drilled forgiveness into his being almost from the moment he could walk. He recalled his father squeaking out that same spirit of forgiveness between the cracks of the whip that killed him. It was this characteristic, more than any other trait, including his saving Mia from drowning, that

Mia found so endearing. She bonded with him, and he with her, for life.

The pair hunkered down after crossing the border and vowed to stick together no matter what. Years later, after working all manner of farms picking grapes, blueberries, fruit of every description and even potatoes, they ended up in Fitchburg to pick apples one fall in 1965, their lucky year. One of the Rangers, none other than Pilar Gutiérrez, happened by the apple orchard's worker housing one night on a recruitment run. Juan appeared to Pilar to be engaging, yet docile enough to keep his mouth shut. After the harvest, José came to visit Juan and Mia with his tenant farming offer. They couldn't believe their luck. He made them promise never to mention his name as the owner, only the name of the attorney trustee, a New Jersey lawyer named Kent Clark, Esq., a fictitious construction, courtesy of the firm of *Pellatino, Degrazio and Gomez*. José and Pablo Gomez laughed uproariously at the convention, which of course reversed the name of Superman's alter ego.

In what proved an ironic twist of fate, Juan and Mia now found themselves serving as the *Los Jefes*. With the tables turned and their own Exodus a cherished memory, they treated their migrant brethren with respect. Their workers wanted for nothing and, not only had *plenty of agua and nutritious meals*, but laundry facilities, clean cabañas and two teachers who educated their children while they themselves picked the fruit. José's orchards, thus, never went wanting for apple pickers.

Despite Juan and Mia's caution, however, the secret of José's orchard hideaway would not last much longer.

CHAPTER 15

José Heads Back to the Orchard to Reconnoiter

R ealizing he needed a better plan than just showing up at Col. McPherson's residence on the fly, José dashed back to his orchard base. He pulled up to the side garage, got out of the car, and pushed aside the thick door. He slid the car back in its place and padded into the apartment. As he lay down on the small bed, he thought about where things stood. Closing his eyes, he began meditating, just like he'd learned as a teenager. He controlled his breathing, settled down his pulse, and then let his thoughts flow right on by. Mediation had enabled him to let go of his deep desire for revenge against the mobster who'd killed his dad over that stupid debt. He didn't fight the thoughts, no matter how draining, bizarre or engrossing. He made sure he peeled his tongue off the roof of his mouth. As he deepened his breathing, he let out a groan with each breath. It sounded odd, and Mia next door heard the guttural effort, wondering what was going on, but knowing to let José have his privacy.

Finding quietude amidst the maelstrom of the last four days, José found a deep sense of peace. For the moment. Growing up in the shadow of the Puerto Rican ghetto off Green Street in downtown Fitchburg, seeing his father killed brazenly and without consequence, watching the cops haul away his father's body, only to have the medical examiner lose the body, and the family suspect city officials had donated the body to science or sold off the organs, all served to teach José that if he was going to make anything of himself, he'd have to do it by himself. He studied those mobsters, and they watched him, worried at first that this young boy would grow up to take revenge on them.

José found a new plan—one not based on revenge, which he had heard on some TV show was a dish best served cold. José marveled at these mobsters—how hard they worked at their craft, as hard as any Wall Street broker or Fifth Avenue ad man, working every hour of the day and well into the night, perfecting their products and distribution chains. Soon enough, he'd ingratiated himself into their businesses, kept up his studies, losing sleep in the process, but making his grandmother, who was raising him, proud, both for his grades and the extra income he brought home. He studied these guys, held them close, for they still were his enemies, not because of the murder of his father, but because soon he would be their competitor! *Never let them see me sweat*, he'd mouth to himself.

José's meditation guided him to new insights. His guttural breathing had given way to calming breath. His pulse now became tortoise like and his blood pressure dropped below sea level. Mia noticed the change, almost as if a calming wind had come through the kitchen window to cool one of her just baked apple pies. The plan came to him like a burning bush that was not consumed. He marveled at it, studied it from all angles to make sure there was no error or variation in how it would play out. Since he'd lost his lieutenants, Ricardo and Pilar, and they'd sacrificed for him time and again, this time nearly losing their lives, he felt a clear duty to take care of them. Roust them out of the hospital. All in good time, of course, after the medical professionals had done their magic work.

Hospitals and the nurses and doctors that work in them have one duty and one duty alone: protect their patients at all costs. Burbank is not a prison and is not set up to house prisoners. This is the primary weakness in the Fitchburg Police Department's plan to guard Ricardo and Pilar. I'm coming for you boys and the police won't notice until it's too late. Gotta get me to the library and study up on hospitals, natural disasters, and how governments and medical professionals respond. Maybe it's a problem with the air conditioning, or an explosion in the furnace area, or the lab. That'd be a place for a fire! Maybe the explosion destroys the integrity of some critical load-bearing wall. What I've got to understand is how they respond! I'm sure they've got plans and those plans are uniform in some respects. Whatever happens, Fitchburg's finest will be taken off guard duty to help respond, save the patients—so it'll have to be another floor, away from Ricardo and Pilar. Maybe it's a bomb threat that gets carried out just when everyone is starting to relax. No bomb-sniffing dogs can find this explosive device, comprende? I bet the library has whole volumes on this subject—disaster response. The cops. I gotta get them isolated from their chain of command, get them reacting to the event in such a way that they are totally focused on the hospital as a whole, not on my guys in those two adjacent rooms. What happens first, second, third, fourth? It's all pre-ordained. Hey, that's funny. Jeremy's father is ordained! I'm guessing when he was in divinity school he was pre-ordained.

José stood up, stretched and knocked on Mia and Juan's door, ever the polite landlord. When Mia answered the door, José asked, "Do you by any chance, or does Juan, have any kind of overalls, ya know, like farmers wear out in the fields? I need to look like a hayseed. Like they say, someone who just fell off the turnip truck. Fresh into town, but not a city boy, *comprende*?"

"*Si*, yes I mean," Mia responded. "Follow me please. I'm sure Juan has something along those lines."

José marveled at how well Mia and Juan kept the house. They clearly took pride in their work and in making sure the orchard produced a bountiful crop. He couldn't see a speck of dust anywhere, all the furniture spit polished, the rugs vacuumed and the dishes put away. *A house mouse would starve here as would a cook-a-racha,* José chuckled to himself. Their master bedroom was spartan, but dignified. Mia pulled open her closet door and pointed José to three sets of overalls.

"I'm thinking," Mia observed, "that you and Juan are nearly the same size. But you don't really have a neck, do you?"

José bowed his head somewhat out of embarrassment, "No, I guess not, Mia. One of the ways I kept awake at night to study when I was in school was to lift weights. My *familia* couldn't afford dumbbells or a weight bench, but I built a bench and put a steel rod I found in a scrap yard through some brick-o-blocks. When I'd get sleepy, I'd lift and get my heart pumping. Kept me awake to continue studying. Guess all that weight lifting worked, huh?"

"No, I mean yes, it worked. I didn't mean to embarrass you. Here, try this on," Mia said, holding up some farmer's duds. "I can hem them if we need to make a better fit."

José stepped into the odd garment. It fit quite well, as did Juan's work shirt that partnered with the overalls. He just couldn't button the shirt's top button. No way. But that was the style of the day and still is, so it didn't matter.

"Thank you, Ma'am!"

"*De nada* (you're welcome)," Mia chortled.

"Well then, I'm off and am in your debt."

"Don't be silly, José. We are forever in your debt and will always be grateful."

José departed through the side door and headed for the garage, with pen and pad in hand, all ready to take notes. The big Olds turned left out of the driveway and headed towards downtown. José found a neat-as-you please parking space right near the back door of the library and headed on in, confident that no one would be looking for him at the library. It was the same reason that his Rangers were always above suspicion and reproach—they studied hard and got good grades, ergo, they were not troublemakers. Library patrons as a rule did not commit crimes. Riding the escalator up to the main lobby, José homed in on the shelves holding the business periodicals. He was adept at research—having made good grades on all manner of term papers. He'd learned how to turn off the left side of his brain, the hemisphere that was orderly and judgmental. This gave him the capacity to write freely and quickly, after poring through all his research. He'd edit later, because it was always easier to reduce text than it was to create it.

Brazenly, he headed up to the librarian in the business section and feigned a hayseed accent. "Ah, Ma'am, I'm down from New Hampshire for the weekend and someone told me I should check out this here library, that it was brand new. It shore looks purty and lots of fine furnishings about the place. Books is everywhere I look, too. I'm trying to help my son, Isaac, whose got a term paper due Monday. It's supposed to be a report on disasters and how governments and hospitals respond. You know, like when a train derails, how does a small hospital get everyone checked out and healed up, like?"

Amused at what stood before her, Julia Condon nodded, "OK, I see what you are talking about. Please follow me. We have got books where authors analyzed that very topic—like with the flu pandemic of 1918, and some train derailments, just like you said. In fact, this whole shelf might be just what you need. Also, you may want to look through old newspaper articles from those times using our microfiche system. I can show you that system as well; all I need to know is the year and the publication that you want. I see you have a pen and a notepad, so just write anything down you find and we'll get right to it."

"Thanks so much, Ma'am. I shorely 'preciate it and so will Isaac. I'm sorry he couldn't come a-with me, but a-course he has schoolin' today. Didn't want to take him out for the day, so close to final exams and all."

Julia smiled a becoming smile and turned to walk back toward her desk. José scanned the volumes and found four tomes that would be useful, including one published by the American Hospital Association on emergency responders. *This is gold! Hell, it comes straight out of the mouths of hospital insiders.* Sure enough, the books gave José everything he needed including some ideas he'd never have thought of, especially the data on gases that hospitals piped throughout their buildings all the way into patient rooms. Nothing like a little oxygen to really cause a stir, especially when things get hot and there's plenty of fuel! *And, that nitrous oxide—what a unique opportunity that provides, get the cop/guard laughing as my boys, mis hermanos (brothers), haul off their prisoners.*

José took plenty of notes, tore off the pages and folded them in his pocket, leaving the first page of fake notes for show in case the librarian asked if he was successful. Little would she know how successful. Julia indeed came around her desk to ask that very question.

"Oh, yes, Ma'am. I dun found just what my boy will need. Lotsa good stuff. I jes hope he can read my writin' and such."

"It looked to me like you went through several books so I'm sure he'll get an A! Thanks for stopping by. Most folks, particularly out of towners, are too shy to ask for help. Maybe folks can learn from your example!"

José waved goodbye and actually took a bow, which made Julia blush. She found him handsome and, having recently been divorced, wondered if she might like to live in New Hampshire, married to a farmer who took such an active interest in his son's welfare. In many ways, that part of José's act was not an act at all, for it was just what he did for his Ranger corps. He drove back to the orchard cabin and, once in his apartment, headed to bed for a much needed nap. *That sure was stressful. Had to keep lookin' over my shoulder hoping no one would recognize me. Guess the disguise worked. Hayseed indeed.*

José dozed off and dreamed of a skyscraper in downtown Boston suddenly collapsing. Someone had detonated a bomb that they'd attached to one of structure's main support beams. He laughed in his sleep. It was such an odd sensation, especially since he knew he was sleeping, and, thus, could control the direction of his dreams. He aimed the dream reel towards Burbank and floated over Pilar's room, and then looked in on Ricardo, whispering in their ears that help was on the way. *I'll not only get you out of that hospital prison cell, I'll get you out of the country to Puerto Rico with enough spare cash to set up you and your long forgotten forebears for the next decade. I don't care how good that Gomez firm is, even with a store bought judge, you two would be toast otherwise.*

He didn't awaken until the next morning when his senses alerted him to a scrumptious breakfast. He caught a whiff of fried plantains that Mia had slathered with maple syrup. For good measure, she added real whipped cream on top. Juan, Mia and José ate together before José took his leave of them, not sure when he'd return. He'd also dreamed up a plan, literally, on how to snatch Jeremy and get his help with the shipping company. Execution would be *his* charge this time, not one for a lieutenant—or some junior birdman.

CHAPTER 16

Friday June 14, 1968—12:30 p.m.
Dr. R Pays a Visit to His Mother Eva

After finishing with his two young patients, 60-minute sessions each, Dr. R needed a break. The patient visits proved quite harrowing with the first boy a victim of sexual abuse by an uncle, and the second boy having witnessed his mother die as she saved *him* from a house fire. Dr. R hopped in his car with a sandwich to eat on the way, and headed toward Pinehurst Nursing Home to visit his mother. It had been three days since his mother, Eva, had called him with two pieces of news. The first was that his patient, Jeremy, was in serious trouble, else why would he be feeling her head(!). And the second news clip: she had the ability to feel when someone else was reading her thoughts. She just never told her son. *Might as well throw out all the psychiatry textbooks and research studies I've ever paid attention to! I don't even know how to explain this stuff, let alone how it all works.*

Dr. R stretched out his six foot, five inch frame as he unfolded from his Jaguar E-type. He loved the car, even though it spent more time in the fix-it shop than any reasonable man would have expected from a simple conveyance. He'd tried tinkering with it himself until one of his former patients, a Korean War veteran, advised him otherwise: "Doc, I love you man, but you have got to understand that only two kinds of people work on Jaguars: idiots and Jaguar mechanics. Now I know for sure I'm no

143

Jaguar mechanic, so if I were to work on one, I'd be an idiot, right?" Dr. R had laughed about that advice more often than he cared to remember, partly because it was so spot on, and partly because he'd never had any patients *while in their right and sane state of mind* diagnose him as an idiot. *Well, if the shoe fits.*

Ducking in under the low-hanging front entrance to Pinehurst, Dr. R saw Amy Quinn, the receptionist, working her magic on one of the more lonely residents, Jared Aloysius. "Now you know, Mr. Aloysius, I just don't have the cash *on hand* to buy you another Coke today. I gave you the last quarter I had early this morning. And, oh hi, Dr. Rebovitz!"

"And a good day to you, Ms. Quinn. Mr. Aloysius, are you bothering Ms. Quinn for money again? Why lookie here, there's a quarter right behind your ear!" Dr. R said, as he reached around Mr. A's head and produced the coin.

"Wow! Where did that come from?" Mr. Aloysius asked.

"I'll bet it's the same one Ms. Quinn gave you this morning. You just decided to hide it from us and pretend you were all poor and such, right?"

"No, sir, honest! I *spent* that quarter already!"

Amy didn't miss a punch, "Mr. Aloysius, why I can't believe you'd pull a fast one on me like that. You've been up here 10 whole minutes and all that time you were hiding the very quarter you said you needed right behind your ear!"

Mr. Aloysius started stammering, "Ah, but, you see…ahh." And that was all he could say. Words eluded him because he really had come, not for the quarter, but for

Amy's attention. *She's just so beautiful!* Deflecting the amorous intentions of male residents was not in Amy's job description, but it should have been. Her abject beauty had triggered the latent lust of lots of males over the years, but here, at Pinehurst, she was a sitting duck. She really was the front door of the facility, and even various workmen and service vendors lingered a few extra minutes hoping to win her favor. Single, she had an understanding boyfriend named Axel Block who, ironically, worked as a surgical tech at Burbank Hospital. She swooned the first time she saw Axel's brown eyes, aquiline nose and brown hair. As soon as their eyes met, he, too, fell for her. Always tanned, he got his auburn complexion from spending as much time outside as he could, even in the winter. Amy and Axel shared a love for the great outdoors, spending every spare weekend either on the slopes or area lakes. They joined the other New Englanders who got a tan while skiing—especially since the white snow bounced the sun rays right back on them just like those mirror boards beachgoers use to enhance and accelerate their tanning.

Still flummoxed about where that quarter came from, Mr. Aloysius turned and padded off. Amy winked at Dr. R and said, "I'm guessing you are here to see your mom, right Dr. Rebovitz? You know she caused quite a stir on Tuesday when she pushed her fellow resident, Mr. Jesse Stevens, away from the hall phone so she could call you!"

"Yes, Ms. Quinn, I'll speak to her about waiting her turn."

"Please do. I'm guessing the Administrator will want to speak with you. Ms. Barbara Bennett asked me to have you stop by her office the next time you came by. She doesn't want to have to write up a behavior contract on Mrs. Eva or put her on probation," Amy said with a kind wink. Nursing homes occasionally had to issue behavior contracts to errant residents who violated facility rules. It was the first stop on the way to an involuntary discharge. Patients had rights, and regulators were always on the watch for nursing homes who discharged patients merely for a sudden lack of funds, after having been only too happy to drain all of their patients' savings and assets.

"I'll pay Ms. Bennett a visit in a few minutes. In fact, is she in now?"

Amy leaned over conspiratorially, "No…you're in luck. If you can duck out before 2:00 p.m. when she's due back, I'll tell her she just missed you. It helps that you're a doctor and all. She's sort of scared of doctors, particularly psychiatrists. How about if I just tell her that I mentioned her concern about your mom violating Mr. Steven's rights, and that I warned you our next step would be to impose a behavior contract on Ms. Eva should she do something like that again? I'm thinking she had a pretty good reason to call you and I don't want to know the details. Mr. Stevens loves to make calls—he dominates that phone, so Ms. Eva doesn't come off looking too badly. Lots of our patients get fed up waiting for him to finish. Plus he's so danged loud, everyone can hear his conversations, but he can't really hear the person he's called. It does get ridiculous, and he refuses to wear his hearing aid."

"Ms. Quinn, I now understand why they place you as the greeting card for all the guests of this facility. You are a diplomat. Bet that wasn't part of the job ad you responded to, now was it?"

"No, sir!"

Dr. R took his leave of Amy and headed for his mother's room. He knocked and entered when she bade him to do so. "Hi, Mom. How are you this fine Friday?"

"It's Friday, huh? Guess that's why we are having fish for dinner and hush puppies. I do look forward to their fish dinners. The cook really has a great recipe. Now, give Momma a hug and let me look at you Azriel."

Dr. R obliged and bent over to kiss Eva on the cheek.

"I guess we have some things to discuss, right?"

"Mom, you've always been a better psychiatrist than me. Yes, I did want to speak with you. But I got some inside information from Amy Quinn."

"Do tell!"

"It seems that word of your aggressive efforts to get me on the phone last Tuesday reached Ms. Bennett, your Administrator. I just escaped her clutches—as she wanted a meeting with me to discuss your behavior. The inside scoop is that every employee here knows, as do many of your peers, that Mr. Stevens takes undue liberties over using that hall phone. So that's the good news. The odd news and I'm not sure it is bad, is that you have a secret psychic gift you never told me about. What's up with that?"

"Oh, it never seemed to matter when you were growing up. The only time I ever used it was when I was a little girl and my friend Helga had the same gift as Jeremy—she could read my mind and I could see her looking around in my brain. We were best friends up till about age seven or eight, before she and her family left for America. Her dad was some kind of engineer. He went to work for what later became IBM. I never heard from her again."

"How'd you two figure out all this stuff?"

"We didn't exactly. We just sort of stumbled on it when we played a version of charades. I think we called it 'guess what I'm thinking,' or something like that."

"Well, whatever it is, it's a unique gift, one I've never read about before, Mom."

"I really had forgotten all about it until Jeremy saw my *Kristallnact* memories."

"That's horrific, Mom."

"I know. That's why I insisted he never do that again, especially to me."

"Jeremy's incredibly gifted. He's got an eidetic memory. Instant recall of all events. He remembers what I say to him or anyone else says to him, word for word. Now that I think about it, people who have this gift really need help to avoid re-living traumas that the rest of us forget about over time. I will see him this Sunday and I'll need to help him with that issue. Sorry, didn't mean to get into patient confidences."

"That's OK. Who am I going to tell anyway?"

"Yup, you're right. In a sense, you're part of the therapeutic team. So walk me through what happened. How'd you realize it was Jeremy and more importantly how'd you know to make the call to my office?"

Eva moved gingerly from her bed to the easy chair across the room. David took up a seat next to her on the small couch. Eva's roommate had stepped out when David arrived to give them some privacy. Architects of the time designed nursing homes, including this one, on the hospital model: long hallways punctuated by a nurse's station in the middle. Pinehurst's investors, however, had refashioned the nurse's stations into sitting areas for the residents. This move prevented nurses from congregating like a gossip group and got them out interacting with the patients. They then did their charting in a small side office.

Eva took a deep breath and began her story. "David, err, Rev. Hergenroeder, brought Jeremy here on one of his visits. As we talked, I could tell Jeremy was quite sharp. All of a sudden, I felt him searching around in my mind and I had been thinking about Kristallnacht. Anyway, I was mortified. Here's this precious little boy in the middle of Nazi Germany. I put a stop to it immediately and I suppose I scared him a bit. I could tell he was a well-behaved young man and that he'd follow any rules I set, so I asked him never to read my mind again. I made him promise. Rev. Hergenroeder, of course, apologized immediately. So when I felt Jeremy getting back into my head on Tuesday, I just felt so sure he was in real trouble. I thought about pushing the call button but what was I going to say? That some five year old was rooting around in my memories looking at Kristallnact? Most of these nurses wouldn't have had a clue what I was talking about and the idea that I was hearing voices would have brought forth the medical director and a host of meds to calm me down."

"My, my. You really thought it through."

"That's one thing the Nazis did for me—taught me how to sneak around and avoid suspicion. I hoofed it down the hall to get to the phone, but that danged Mr. Stevens was rambling on and on to who knows whom. I could tell that he wasn't going to end the call anytime soon. I tried to bribe him when I heard the caller was sending him new underwear. I said I had received some by mistake and he was welcome to them if he'd just let me use the phone for two minutes. He screamed at me and I guess I lost it.

"I pushed him and his wheelchair out of the way, hung up on his caller and rang for you. I don't think I could do that again—he's a big old fellow don't you know. I suppose I scared him since he didn't rush back at me, just stared at me with an open mouth and a look of horror. When Velma gave me her sickly singsong hello, I knew I wasn't going to try to wade through her. I think I told her to shut up and get you on the phone. That's about it, other than having to admit to you that I had this *rooting around in my head gift*, such as it was."

"You know you saved the day Mom. Those two gangster types had Jeremy on the floorboard of a big car and they were coming after me figuring I could get him to help them with his mind reading gift. One of David's parishioners is some sort of Korean War veteran who used to send me lots of his soldiers as patients. Ed McPherson is his name. Well, he's an expert marksman. He and David sat perched atop a building adjacent to my office keeping watch. Sure enough, they got there just before the hoodlums arrived. Then Ed, err, Col. McPherson, saw one of them brandishing a gun as he headed for the backdoor of my office. Col. McPherson didn't hesitate. He shot the guy's hand clean off. The gun scattered away of course. Then his partner, who was holding Jeremy down in the back seat, hopped out and made a play for the gun. McPherson shot off most of his right femur. Doubt the guy will ever walk again. The police showed up 90 seconds later, but it was those 90 seconds that made all of the difference, otherwise I'd have been in a hostage situation."

Dr. R took a deep breath and leaned his head back on the rim of the couch. Eva mused for a few minutes thinking about some of their family's close calls in Germany when family friends hid them for several years in their attic. The Nazis finally found them and hauled the family off to Dachau. The Allied Army showed up before the Nazis could gas Dr. R and Eva. Dr. R's father had not been so lucky.

"I love you Mom. You've saved my life more times than I can count, and that was all before I turned 21! And here you did it again from the confines of this nursing home. You can't write this stuff."

"I love you, too, Azriel. Thank you for believing in me when I made the call. You ignored your professional training, didn't you?"

"Book learning didn't prepare me for any of this, Mom."

The pair hugged and Dr. R left to catch a few more afternoon appointments. Eva laid back down for a sound nap.

CHAPTER 17

Friday June 14, 1968—2:30 p.m.
School Lets Out; Time to Check the Pearl Hill Parsonage

The Edgerly School bell rang at precisely 2:30 p.m. Children screeched their excitement and scrambled out of the building as fast as their teachers would allow— double file. The kids remembered that there were two and a half days left of school, with next Wednesday the half day. Then, no more homework during the long blissful respite of summer vacation. No school till after Labor Day except, of course, for Jeremy's class. For most of the parading students, today felt like the last day. The promise of summer beckoned with all of its idyllic delights. As Jeremy came out the front door, Jimmy tagged along.

"Hey, Jeremy, are you getting in that fancy schmancy Lincoln that guy and your father are standing beside? Who is that guy anyway?"

"Oh, that's my dad's friend, Col. Ed McPherson. We're, ahh, going to his house for dinner."

"When are you guys coming back home? That big house of yours sure looks empty!"

"I know. I miss home, too. Heck, that's where all my toys are. Hey, you want a ride? I bet Col. McPherson will drive you home—it's on the way, sort of."

"Yeah, that'd be great. You think he'll mind?"

Just as all the other kids escaped in all directions, Acosta Gutiérrez, José's Fitchburg State henchman, lined up his binoculars from his dorm room perch across the street. Sure enough, he spied Jeremy yelling louder than he needed, "Col. McPherson. Could *we* give my friend Jimmy a ride home? Maybe we could take a look at our house while we drive by. Jimmy lives just next door!"

Ed looked up, "Why sure. You guys hop on in the back!"

Jimmy marveled at the back door that opened funny. "Jeremy—look at the way this door opens. It's so much easier to get into the back seat. You don't have to scrunch at all. And look at the push button windows! Wow."

David hopped back in the shotgun seat after making sure he thanked Officer Ryan for guarding the school *and* *Jeremy*. "We'll see you Monday. I might be able to get my wife to bake up some chocolate chip cookies to help steel you for this all day watch project."

"I never turn down chocolate in any form," Officer Ryan responded. "My wife ain't much of a cook, so the good stuff I get usually comes from the other guys' wives who take pity on us."

Ed steered the Lincoln towards Pearl Hill Road and David asked the inevitable adult question, "So, boys, what'd you learn in school today?"

Jimmy rolled his eyes and then explained, "Mrs. Murphy showed us a Jacques Cousteau T.V. show and we discussed the Galapagos Islands. You know, how there's all those funny looking animals there? There's one animal, real scary like, called a monitor. If he bites you, you'll die from his saliva—which is full of nasty back-tria."

Ed intervened, "Do you mean bacteria, Jimmy?"

"Yes sir."

David never found much use for the sciences, although he did like gardening and how hard honeybees worked to bring him his championship-sized tomatoes. Divinity school classes just presumed nature had taken its course all under the watchful eye of God. Zoology, and the rest of the physical sciences, failed to help David or the other students describe an unseeable God of the universe. The only monitor David had ever heard of was the jerk in the front of any classroom who made sure you weren't cheating on a test. "Why *do* they call it a monitor, Jimmy?" David inquired.

"I don't know, but the animal is pretty big and walks around like he's in charge of the whole island."

"That's pretty scary if all he has to do is take a bite of you and you die. Sounds almost as bad as a poisonous snake," Ed offered. He was thinking he'd never learned this kind of stuff in high school, let alone kindergarten.

Ed pulled up beside the parsonage, right at 123 Pearl Hill Road. David said, "Let's pull on in the driveway Ed. I'll take a gander inside. Jeremy—you want to grab any *two* of your toys?"

"Yes sir."

Jimmy thought, *Man, I'd die if I only had two toys to play with all weekend. What a gyp!* He then said, "Thanks Col. McPherson for the ride!"

"Yes sir, Jimmy. Glad to lend a hand," Ed responded.

David ran up the walk and unlocked the big front door. A whoosh of hot air greeted him. Back in 1968, very few New Englanders had air conditioning and the parsonage was not a trendsetter. The Hergenroeders kept the windows open and a couple of fans blowing to maintain a cooler inside temperature. Jeremy ran upstairs to his room and found the idea of grabbing just two toys perplexing. *Does that mean two Matchbox cars or do I get to grab my*

Erector Set and my Tinkertoys? Unfortunately, both play systems were sprawled out over his floor, one a city of aliens from Mars and the second a set of war machines all ready for battle. *I don't have time to take these apart!* Jeremy grabbed several Matchbox cars and his box of Lincoln Logs. *Maybe Col. McPherson or Mrs. Lily will show me some more of Truman's toys. That old trunk full of toys was amazing!*

Jeremy had always dreamed of having a train set like Truman had, complete with those funny pills you put into the top of the locomotive's smoke stack to get it to blow exhaust as it ran around the track. But he knew that his dad's salary would never enable the family to afford such high-end toys. He tromped down the stairs to find his dad looking out the front window forlornly. He felt his dad's head and saw that his father was worrying about what might happen next and when they could move back into their home.

"What's in the grocery bags, Dad?"

"The most important articles of clothing and supplies known to Man, Jeremy: underwear, deodorant, toothbrushes and clean socks! Your Mom had to buy us some new pairs just to get us through today, using money we really didn't have son."

"Guess that's more important than my toys, huh?"

"No, don't think that way. It's just part of home, it is. There's lots more we could grab, but this stuff will get us through the weekend. I'm hoping Det. McNamara will OK our coming back here after church. What do you think?" David asked, not realizing Jeremy would automatically look into the thoughts of the detective.

Jeremy's mind traveled to the police station, finding Det. McNamara seated at his desk. He'd just gotten back from Burbank Hospital not two hours earlier, having found Pilar still out of commission and heavily drugged, while Ricardo refused to speak at all. "Dad, I can't see where he's even thinking about our coming home yet. He's getting nowhere with Pilar and Ricardo."

"Really? Maybe I should call him and give him the hint."

"He's at the station sitting at his desk, Dad."

"I don't want to bother him. He's got enough on his mind. C'mon, we don't want to keep Ed waiting, I mean Col. McPherson."

The pair exited and headed for the Lincoln. Jimmy hollered from his front porch that his mother had made a batch of brownies. She'd doubled up on the recipe and wanted to hand half of the batch to David. Looking up from the car, David nodded and hopped across the front yard to meet Mrs. Evelyn Kendall. She was a stunner, David thought, and as with most beautiful women, he had trouble maintaining eye contact. It was an unconscious thing—sort of like the more he looked, the more they'd see his underlying lust. Not a good trait for a minister.

Jimmy's mother walked across the driveway and said, "Reverend! So good to see you. We've been worried sick since Tuesday. So glad to know you guys are OK. When you all didn't come home, we got scared, like maybe you all got hurt during that kidnapping. What a mess! How's Alex? Oh, and here, Lori and I made these. She's almost a better cook than me and she's only nine years old. In fact, it was her idea, but I warned her we might not see you all today. She was sure you'd be coming and Lord she was right."

David could smell the brownies even before he grabbed the Tupperware container. "Oh my, this is so sweet, no pun intended Evelyn. And please thank Lori for us."

"You can thank her yourself. Lori! C'mon out here," Evelyn roared for all the neighbors to hear. At the sound of Lori's name, Jeremy came running. He had a debilitating crush on Jimmy's sister. He found her drop dead gorgeous, and, worse, she always favored him in games of hide and seek and red light, green light. He found her brown eyes bewitching. She had helped teach Jeremy how to tie his shoes, but he had trouble paying attention because he was so smitten with her beauty. Young crushes are the worst and sometimes the hardest to get over.

"Hi Lori!" Jeremy exclaimed, as soon as Lori came off the Kendall's front porch. Lori blushed, but quickly recovered.

"Hi your own-self, Jeremy. Where have you been keeping yourself anyway?"

Jeremy's heart skipped a beat or three. He couldn't feel Lori's head, which confused him even more since that meant she felt LOVE for him! He suddenly had trouble breathing and answering her. Catching him in the act of ogling, Lori winked at him. Jeremy's knees nearly gave way, but he held on for dear life to keep his balance.

David handed the brownie container to Jeremy and said, "Thank you all so much. It's been heck trying to live in two places and with the police still on the lookout for that gang leader. We've all been on pins and needles. These brownies will be great solace for us. I'm sure we'll be home soon, or as soon as they'll let us, whichever comes first! You guys have a great weekend. Oh my, how rude of me. Let me introduce you to Col. Ed McPherson."

David turned to Ed who had wandered over to take in the view. "Nice to meet you all, and thanks for watching over the Reverend's home while they're staying with the Mrs. and me."

"The pleasure's all mine, Colonel," Evelyn said as she extended her hand.

David said, "We need to get back to Ashburnham. Evelyn, here's Ed's number should you need us or see any funny business."

David handed off his business card with the McPherson's number scribbled on the back. Lori grabbed it from him, saying, "We'll put this on our refrigerator Rev. Hergenroeder. You folks take care now. Jimmy and I will keep watch on your house."

Ed, David and Jeremy shuffled off to the waiting Lincoln, and David had an odd feeling that he'd missed something in the house that he was supposed to grab. He couldn't place the feeling, but since he didn't have with him his trusty 'Alex list,' he'd surely hear about the missing item(s) back at the McPherson's.

As the threesome drove up Pearl Hill Road, Jeremy looked out the back window and was heartened to see Jimmy and Lori standing out by the street, waving goodbye. He couldn't feel their heads and knew what that meant—only good things from the love of friendship.

Across town, Acosta called the orchard cabin only to learn that José was not to be disturbed. He'd get his message through soon enough. Then, José's Hergenroeder noose would stretch all the tighter.

CHAPTER 18

José Enlists New Lieutenants

A fter deciding a nap would be his best medicine, José snored himself awake. Nothing like a 20-minute siesta to get his mind sharp again after all the stress of the last three days. Sleep was the master you could not ignore. José knew you could put off the master's beckoning, for a price, sometimes a steep price, but eventually he'd get his due. After sliding out of bed, he showered and headed over to Mia's kitchen, hoping she'd left him a late lunch, maybe tortillas and eggs, some huevos rancheros. Sure enough, Mia had his plate waiting in the oven with a note that warned him to use an oven mitt and to grab the bowl of guacamole from the frig that she had prepared. He pulled on the nearby mitt and extracted the oven treasure that included homemade hash browns with hot peppers and a side of black beans, spiced up Cuban style. He put the mitt back in its drawer and looked out the kitchen window. He couldn't see his tenants. *Mia and Juan must be out working in the orchard.*

As he ate, he reviewed the notes he'd made earlier in the day, including looking through the list of his RR minions to appoint as replacements for Pilar and Ricardo. At the top, as part of his succession planning, he had listed somewhat more distant cousins, Luis Ortiz de la Renta and Hector Madera. Unfortunately, Pilar and Ricardo's siblings were not ready to move up since they'd barely broken into their teenage years. Luis and Hector would have to do.

José had admired Hector for some time and recalled that Hector's mother had named him for the Greek hero and former Prince of Troy. A big fan of Greek mythology and Homer's *The Iliad*, José knew that Hector was Troy's greatest warrior. Hector hadn't approved of the war between Greece and his native Troy, all of it brought on by his own brother, Paris, carrying off Helen, the very wife of the Greek ruler Menelaus. None other than Achilles, Greece's own war hero, had killed Hector. Then, Achilles died when his enemies shot a poisonous arrow into his heal, his one weak spot; thus placing the phrase Achilles' heel forever into the public lexicon. For José, blood lineage was the only thing to be trusted and both Hector and Luis qualified, thanks to their branch off of José's family tree. Blood kinship made it far less likely that they'd turn on their somewhat distant cousin.

José placed a call to Luis's house and Hector's, leaving messages for them to call him at Juan's place when they got back from their trucking firm jobs. Both men were short haul truckers, plying their wares across the six New England states. They'd graduated from Ray Peterson's shop classes at Fitchburg High with straight A's. They'd always toed the line on their runs, even making their deliveries early if not right on time, every time. Luis did have a neck, but still was tough as nails. Hector, neckless like Pilar and Ricardo, likewise had the courage of a shrew and the wit of the smoothest politician. Both sported black hair, and Hector had deep set, black eyes, while Luis, oddly, had one brown eye and one green.

As was required of all Rangers, they kept in great physical shape. José had set up an arrangement with a local boxing ring where any Ranger, male or female, could show up any time of the day or night and work out with weights, the punching bag, or get lessons in martial arts. Jumping rope was a must, and every Ranger could jump rope for an hour flat. José had set the expectation that all Ranger leaders maintain some semblance of physical fitness. Ricardo and Pilar, thanks to their veteran status, could choose how they kept in shape. Leadership and rank had to count for something, privilege wise. For his part, Pilar had taken up jogging, but still enjoyed sparring at the gym. Ricardo lifted weights and, incredibly, took up ballet, which a Ranger ballerina taught at the gym after hours and behind closed doors. The dance routines and discipline kept his body toned and no one dared make fun of him. He was, of course, too big to do all the moves, but his ballerina classmates loved that he joined them when he could. He could "throw" them a country mile, too, which helped ingratiatc him to the group.

José did his own dishes, something he knew would surprise Mia, who likely expected that she'd come in from the orchard to find a crusty mess left by a slob who didn't have the decency to at least put the plates in the sink to soak. Water had long ago been hailed as the universal solvent by chemists the world over, and for good reason. It started working the dirty dishes before any sponge could take command. José's grandmother had taught him this basic concept of self-reliance.

José saw the note from Acosta and rang his dorm hallway hoping to get an answer. "Hello," a young co-ed answered.

"Yes, could I speak to Acosta, if he is in by chance?"

The co-ed responded by letting the phone drop and it swung back and forth in pendulum fashion. José could hear her calling for Acosta. A minute later, he came on.

"Hello?

"Acosta! Good to hear your voice. Mia said you called. Whassup?"

"Yeah, I just wanted you to know I spied that Jeremy boy get in a big Lincoln Continental with his father, some friend of his, and some ramrod looking dude—after school today."

"Very good. That ramrod dude would be Col. Ed McPherson, the very man who shot off Ricardo's left hand…you know he's left handed, or used to be. And McPherson's the one who nearly shot off Pilar's leg—above the knee."

"Damn!"

"Damn indeed. I gotta get word to them in the hospital at some point that I'm going to take care of them. Benita Cruz, a nurse on the floor where they are, tried to help, but she got caught by the head nurse. Got demoted for her trouble. I've considered her a sleeper Ranger since she was 10 years old. I gotta figure out a way to help her. Like to have a word with that supervisor, help her understand there's consequences for screwing around with our Ranger corps. But that's a fight for another day, right?"

"Whatever you say José. You're the boss."

"I am, aren't I? Doesn't do me much good with the cops lookin' for me. You sure no one can hear you talkin' to me?"

"Don't worry. Folks around here are winding down for the semester. Exams are over—there's only a few of us left who are finishing up our student teaching assignments. We, of course, have to wait until the public schools let out. So, you were lucky actually to get someone to answer the hall phone. Sometimes it rings off the hook for 20 minutes."

"Well, thanks for your help and for staying in the background. Don't let that police guard figure out what you're up to. And, remember, those binoculars will broadcast a sunbeam back to your target!"

"Really? Well, shit."

"Yes, it's an old military rule. You gotta use binoculars back in cover, where the sun don't shine."

"Thanks for the tip. Guard might have thought I was some sort of perv or something."

"Yeah, that'd end your student teaching career real fast. Couldn't help you out with that problem, now could I?"

"No, I guess not."

"We'll talk again. Let me know if anything else happens at the school or with Jeremy. But be careful," José said as he rang off.

Not 30 second later, Mia's phone rang. José picked up, "Yo!"

"Yo, yourself José. This is Hector. How can I help?"

"Glad you called. I'm promoting you to first lieutenant. I need you to resign your trucking job just as soon as you can. Don't make it look too crazy, but I need your help ASAP. Whaddya think?"

"I've got some vacation due me. Boss'll hate it if I just up and leave. Howse about if I tell him my momma's real sick and I need to take a leave of absence? Saw a driver do that last year and it played right into the boss's sympathies."

"Great thinking. I knew you were smart. Listen, what I need—what the Rangers need, is some fast help that may not exactly fall within the bounds of the law. Are you OK with that?"

"Hey, I've always known which side of my bread gets buttered. Hauling those jobs and off-loading the precious metals at our sites without getting caught has been a real thrill."

"Yeah, we've been lucky to stay under the radar. All those loads of platinum, copper, tool steel, tungsten and such have brought in a lot of dough. The clowns on the receiving end never seem to notice the few pounds of the stuff we've shaved off. But I'm needing to reach out to international buyers and sellers now. These precious metal hauls are fine locally, making us some decent cash, but the world is shrinking and I'm needing us to expand to the shipping lanes that offload at Quincy and even L.A. on the west coast. This mind-reading Jeremy kid fell into my lap off of a stupid $500 loan to some jerk named Brodie. Works the General Dynamics yard as a welder."

"I'd heard part of the story, but not how you got hooked up with the kid. So, what's your plan now?" Hector asked.

"Working it out, but I need you up here as soon as you can make it. You remember the orchard place we own—tenants Juan and Mia runnin' the place? Brings in decent cash, plus the Rangers can wash money through the operation as well. So, it's a double boost to us all. I need your pal Luis Ortiz de la Renta to come on board at this level as well. He's with Overland Trucking. I'll be making the same pitch to him, but you've given me the mechanism he can use to slide out without creating a fuss."

"Alright, José, I'll be up later this afternoon."

"Bring your sleeping bag and bunk out here. Place is small but adequate, or you could take one of the smaller cabañas that Juan uses to house the apple pickers during harvest season. Your call. I can have Mia and Juan make up a couple of the places."

"OK, if it's a choice between sleeping on your floor and a cabaña, I'll take the cabaña."

"Consider it done. And if you somehow run in to Luis before I get to speak to him or he gets my message, ask him to call me."

"I know his dispatcher pretty well. You want I should call her?"

"No, again, let's keep this low key. But thanks for offering. See you in a bit."

José stretched out his five foot, eleven inch frame and did some yoga exercises to stay sharp and focused. He heard Juan or Mia come through to their part of the house from the orchards. He knocked on the access door, and Juan opened it.

"Say, Juan, need your help my man. Could you or Mia make up a couple of the cabañas before dinner? I got a couple of guests who are coming for the weekend and I don't want to have them sleeping on my floor."

"Excellente, El Jefe! Your wish is my command. The cabañas are pretty clean, but I'll make sure the plumbing is up to snuff and get some linen on the beds, with towels for showering in the group *baño* (bathroom)."

"Perfect and, hey..." José started to say as the phone rang. "Let me take this call, and I'll get with you shortly."

Juan closed the door as José answered, "Hello...*Hola!*"

"*Hola, José. Es Luis!* Good to hear your voice, boss man."

"Thanks for calling on such short notice. Listen, it's time I promoted you up the chain of command. I need you to quit your job at Overland, today in fact."

"Wow, pretty sudden man. I appreciate the promotion offer. Not sure what to say to the boss..."

"I got a great line which I got from your new partner in crime, Hector Madera. Tell your boss that your mother has taken ill, suddenly, with some terminal disease. Not long to live. You need a leave of absence. It'll let him down gently, ya know?"

"Yeah, I guess that'll work. What's the rush?"

"OK, so I'm having the Rangers move into international shipping. All the local skim loads we've been doing the last few years are great, but commerce is moving across oceans in ways it never used to before. We gotta get our piece, right? I'm thinking about getting in good with the dockworker's union, you know, they call themselves stevedores, not sure where that word came from. Neat as you like they simply move these trailers onto tractors and there's no chance for us to get in those damned things and hollow out a secret compartment. So I need a new strategy. I got this kid, or need to get him...he's a frickin' mind reader. Figure he can scope out the union boss, some guy named Rick Sullivan, and let me know how best to make the approach. We can discuss all this when you get here—

probably best not say anything else over this line. How soon can you get here?"

"I'll get off at 6:00 p.m., but I'm calling you about 30 miles south of the New Hampshire border. Dispatch said my mother was calling with some sort of emergency. That mighta been Hector, ya think?"

"Sounds like he took some initiative. Guess I'm OK with that. Anyway, plan on coming up here to the orchard house, stay the weekend. Bring a change of clothes and your toothbrush. I need your help mapping out a plan of action. You can bunk in one of the cabañas. Juan's getting it ready now for you. Nice and clean."

They rang off and José headed into his apartment to review his notes. His scheming electrified his whole body. *Fitchburg ain't never gonna see what's coming.*

CHAPTER 19

Saturday June 15, 1968—8:00 a.m.
Best Laid Rican Ranger Plans

Juan and Mia's orchard hermitage provided the perfect cover for José, Luis and Hector to map out their next tactical moves. Their overall goal remained accessing the international shipping lines to bring in even more exotic metals that their American clientele soon would need. Their thieving ways would ensure they could beat any legitimate competitor's pricing. After Hector and Luis arrived for dinner the previous evening, José kept the group banter light, not wanting anyone to lose sleep over his still evolving plans.

After sleeping in fits and starts, José awoke at 7:00 a.m. Hector and Luis slept like baby bear cubs in their own cabañas, lulled to sleep by the crickets chirping and tree frogs howling for mating opportunities. Around midnight, José had a rare nightmare. He stood on the gallows facing Jeremy, who sat as José's judge, jury and executioner. Jeremy asked, "Before I impose sentence Mr. Gutiérrez, is there anything you'd like to offer the court as mitigation for your string of heinous crimes?"

"Your honor, if it please the court, my father…when I was a young boy, well a loan shark murdered him right in front of my eyes. I later found out that the enforcer had instructions to only maim my father, not kill him. The loan was for peanuts—$150. And that turned into $2,500 in just a couple of weeks. No way my father could pay that off.

Worse still, my mother died when I was five years old. I grew up off of Green Street, ya know, the Puerto Rican ghetto. I saw my kinfolk killing each other without a second thought. At first I didn't care if I lived or died, man. But my grandmother, *mi abuela*, she saw *potential* in me. I skipped school one day and when I came home she grabbed me by the scruff of the neck, hauled me to my bedroom and pointed at my school books..."

Judge Jeremy interrupted José, "Is this going somewhere, Mr. Gutiérrez? Somewhere relevant to the charges the jury convicted you of? From where I sit, as a five year old, what do I care what you went through at 13, when you were eight years older than me? Your guys kidnapped me—how do you answer for that trauma? Seeing your dad get murdered did not give you *license* to kidnap me!"

"Yes, of course, you're right. Let me get to the point. I ask you to have faith in me, the faith my grandmother had for me when she helped me turn the corner from a life of murderous vengeance to becoming a productive businessman. I encourage and support scores of young people in Fitchburg, help them with their studies, guide them toward good paying jobs, give back to the community..."

"Again, how do these acts of kindness *mitigate* your crimes? You say these young people do great things, yet when I *feel your head*, I see a cauldron filled to the brim with lies. These same young people are like foreign agents, spies who have yet to be activated, most of them awaiting your call to commit crimes in your name and for the profit of the Rican Rangers. No, sir, you are the Tonto!"

Upon hearing the Rican Ranger slogan *tonto*, which was their common joke, because in Spanish tonto means stupid or moron, thus the Lone Ranger rode with a moron, José awoke in a cold sweat, screaming. Mia jumped out of bed and started banging on the access door, "Mr. José, please wake up…you are having a bad dream. Get up and open this door!"

José dragged himself out of the bed and opened the door to find Mia and Juan standing in the threshold holding a flashlight. *"Lo siento…(I'm sorry). Tuve un mal sueño."* (I had a bad dream.)

"Yes, you did. You gave us quite a scare José. Should I get you some warm milk to settle you down?"

"Ahh, yes, that would be nice," José replied, suddenly concerned about looking weak in the eyes of his tenants. *So I had a dream. It was just a dream, dangit. Not reality. I just need Jeremy's help. Then I'll let him be for the rest of eternity. I promise, God! Cut me some slack will ya? Just this once?*

A few minutes later, after turning the stove off, Mia handed José a mug of warm milk. "Since you are OK, Juan and I will head back to bed. Call us if you need anything, please."

"*Muchas gracias, Mia. Y usted, Juan* (you too). I'll be fine. If Luis, Hector and I could use your kitchen after breakfast, that would be great. We need to do some business planning and will need some privacy. Would that be OK?"

Juan responded, "Yes. Of course. After all, it is your kitchen, is it not?"

"Well…thank you, nonetheless."

At about 7:45 a.m., everyone sat down for breakfast. Mia had pulled out all the stops with bowls of deep fried hash browns, scrambled eggs and fried apples. She poured tomato juice into small glasses, had a mug of hot coffee at everyone's place setting and rye toast already buttered, sitting on everyone's platters. Before everyone dug in, Juan gave thanks.

After Juan's prayer, José began, "I need everyone's help. First, Mia and Juan, I need you two to take a short vacation. Get down to Cape Cod for a week. Here's $500 to cover your expenses. Luis, Hector and I will need the house for about five days. Everything will be back in order when you return. I will clean the kitchen after breakfast so you can pack. Is that OK?"

Juan looked surprised. "We have not had a vacation, like you say, ever. I'm not sure what we would do on such a vacation. I have seen advertisements, of course, where fat gringos lounge at the beach slathering themselves with baby oil. What kind of life is this?"

José chuckled, "Indeed, Juan, a great question, a *pregunta* as we say in Español! I want you to study the ways of these gringos and report back to me. Learn from them—what additional *inducements* might we add at your orchard shop to entice them to unload their money here? Huh? But I also want you to relax. Take a load off. Swim in the great pond...teach Mia to swim, yes? This is how you saved her life crossing the Rio, *si*? Bask in each other's company—you work all day and much of the night. God asks that you take a one week Sabbath, and so does your landlord, José, *comprende*?"

Everyone laughed at the theology reference. They all finished eating with muted, casual conversation. Mia and Juan knew better than to ask about the planning that was to come. They had their jobs running the orchard and that was bounty enough after having grown up in abject slavery.

Mia started to clear the dishes and José objected, "Mia, *por favor*, let *Tio* (uncle) José clean. My grandmother taught me well. This kitchen upon your return will look, how do they say on TV, *spic and span*, yes? Yes!"

With that, Juan and Mia took their leave of the threesome and headed to their bedroom to pack. They realized they did not have suitcases, so Mia returned to the kitchen to retrieve some grocery bags. Realizing what she needed, José peeled off another $100 bill and handed it to Mia.

"Mia, go buy yourself a couple of those American Tourister suitcases! I hear they're real tough. You could throw one out of a moving car and it would never even open. Ya know those Madison Avenue guys outta put one of those suitcases in a cage with a gorilla. Let the mad ape try to tear it apart. Good luck with that. I shoulda been a marketer. Anyway, you can take the grocery bags for now, but get rid of them when you get to the Cape. Stop at a rest area and re-pack your clothes into those new cases. Stop at Filene's Bargain Basement in Boston—I bet that store has good prices."

Mia blushed as she took the money and bowed to José in thanks.

After the threesome heard Juan and Mia drive off the property, José turned to Luis and Hector. "OK, I have big plans. I hope they are not too big. First, and I'll need your brainpower here, I want to get Pilar and Ricardo out of that hospital. I'm pretty sure we can get Ricardo out, but I do not know how badly Pilar is hurt. We have one shot at this. I realized that we would need to catch everyone off guard," José said, as he took in a deep breath and paused for effect.

Luis looked at José and said, "Wow, OK, what are you thinking? Those guys are under 24-hour police guard. Those hombres have guns and they stand watch like the hounds of hell. What do you think will get them off their game, as you say…?"

Hector interrupted, "I'm bound to you, José, for saving me from the brink of a life about to go bad, *malo*. *Pero* (but) there's a lot of eyes on the prize at that hospital. Everyone's paying attention all the time, *comprende*?"

"*Si*, yes they are, but I ask you Hector, what are they watching for?"

Luis interjected, "Ah, you think they are paying attention to patients and their vital signs. Lemme guess. You also think the cops are like fish out of water, *si*?"

José laughed as he pulled out his notes from the library. "Guess what hospitals have behind all their walls? Gas lines! Oxygen, nitrous oxide and such. You remember from your chemistry class what nitrous oxide is? You should! You both got straight As!"

"Laughing gas!"

"Correct-a-mundo! Now, can either of you tell me the name of the Ranger who delivers these gas supplies to Burbank?"

Hector and Luis shook their heads before Hector blurted out. "Yes, our good *compadre* Diego Toro!"

"Yes, Señor Diego and, built like a bull, just like his last name! I have his phone number right here, Luis. I want you to call him after our meeting. Tell him we'll need a special delivery. As I recall, he has kept back a nice supply of gas tanks in case we might ever need them. I never imagined we'd be doing something like this, but good things come to those who plan, *si*? We could keep the laughing gas in reserve for a back-up plan. Gotta figure out how to deploy it though. Anyway, we'll hit the hospital tomorrow afternoon. But I need to outline the rest of my plan," José said as he stood and headed for his bedroom through the access door.

José returned with a cloth bag filled with six smoke bombs. "We will dress as workman, or, rather, you two will dress as workmen. Ricardo and Pilar are on the fifth floor of the hospital. I studied up on the science of disaster response. Hospital staff members, you know, the nurses and doctors and the housekeepers, use the word R.A.C.E. to remind them about what to do. The R stands for Rescue, the A for Alert or Alarm, the C is for Contain, and the E, most important of all, stands for Evacuate. That letter is our key. The police will not know about RACE so, guess what, they'll be looking to the hospital staff for direction. We will divert their attention with our fake disaster. Everyone will be scurrying around in the chaos.

"I'll need that Rican Ranger, Ezequiel Camacho, who works as a hospital mechanic to place the bombs. Hector— he's close to you, I need you to help me make the ask when he shows up here in a few minutes. I called him yesterday. He agreed to come by this morning. It's his day off and he works tomorrow. Anyway, we gotta make sure he wears gloves when handling these bombs. I'm keeping two of them in reserve in case we need them later. I've wiped them off so there are no fingerprints. Ezequiel should have no trouble working his way into the basement to place these smoke bombs in the air vents. Best of all, these things burn up and disappear as ash—and guess what! The air venting system will just blow the ash throughout the venting system. It'll take them months to figure out where Ezequiel placed the bombs."

"Alright, that makes sense," Hector nodded.

"Yeah, it does, but then how do we get those guys out of the hospital, ya know, when the smoke is everywhere?" Luis interjected.

"Best I can figure, the hospital is going to set up some sort of command center. Likely the head nurse or head facility guy will be in charge. Sundays mean they have a limited staff—everyone likes to take Sunday off. I checked—Burbank only does emergency surgeries that day. Even the doctors are few and far between, meaning the cops will have to help out with disaster response. Those guards will figure that Ricardo and Pilar aren't going anywhere, right? They are bad hurt, especially Pilar. Now, we'll need Ricardo's help. I'm hoping he can hop along a little bit, maybe with crutches or something, because our man on the scene will be pushing Pilar's gurney out the back of the hospital and into our waiting ambulance!"

"You got us an ambulance? *Que bueno!*" Luis laughed.

"Ya gotta remember—we got Rangers in all sorts of jobs around this town."

Hector interrupted, "Who is this ambulance man on the scene that'll be airlifting Pilar from his gurney and making sure Ricardo jumps in?"

"Right, I got ahead of myself. I made two other calls late yesterday. The first, our ambulance driver, is Jayden Casiano. You remember him—graduated from Fitchburg High about four years ago and said he didn't want to drive trucks. So I asked him, how about you drive an ambulance? You should a seen his eyes light up. Man's a natural. Took all those medical classes and got himself certified. He's an 'EMS,' or something, I can't remember the exact title. He showed me his license the day he got it from the state. You know what I asked him? I said, 'Jayden, suppose you show up for a call at some fat lady's house. She weighs, oh, let's say 500 pounds. What are you going to do?' You know what he says? 'I'm gonna call for back-up!'" And with that José laughed so hard he started gagging.

Finally catching his breath, José continued, "Anyway, Jayden's on point. Talked with him last night and mum's the word as he says. Jayden also said the dispatcher on the weekends is usually a little inebriated. Real alchy that one. As soon as the disaster call comes in, he works solo by the way on Sundays, he'll race to the side door of Burbank—not out the back where ER deliveries arrive. So we got that part sewn up. Now, where do we all end up you might ask? That's Part 2. I gotta get to Quincy for a meet and greet with Rick Sullivan, the union boss of the longshoreman. Everything's arranged for Tuesday, early afternoon. Dominick got Rick to agree to a visit—we're meeting him at the union office. It'll be me and Jeremy."

Dominick Sangria was José's nephew who worked at the General Dynamics Shipyard. He had hooked up fellow welder Dan Brodie with José for the $500 loan that helped start all of Jeremy's troubles barely one week ago. Dan had promised José he needed the money for his mother in law, whom he claimed had some sort of cancerous growth in her "female" parts. José didn't buy the story, but lent him the cash anyway figuring he'd get one more welder on the hook for future use and quick cash.

"And how in blazes are we gonna snatch that kid again?" Luis asked incredulously.

"Calm down, *mi hermano* (my brother). I'm figuring we watch that Pearl Hill house and I just bet that Jeremy's parents can't stand to be away for too long. Monday's the Reverend's day off, so I doubt they'll be leaving the McPherson compound. Tuesday's the better bet for Mrs. H. While her husband's at work and Jeremy's at school, I'm thinking she'll want to check the place, pick up the mail. Luckily, this here orchard is only a half a mile from their house. Once we grab her, I'll fill you in on the Quincy plan. I don't want too many brains filled with our plans—where Jeremy can do his mind reading trick. So don't worry about that piece of the puzzle. Trust me."

There was a knock on the door and José said, "That'll be Ezequiel!" José got up and went to the front door. Luis and Hector heard laughter and greetings. Ezequiel entered the kitchen ahead of José and slapped the backs of the seated Hector and Luis.

"*Que pasa*, man, *que pasa* (what's happening) *mis amigos, mis hermanos* (my brothers)?" Ezequiel asked. The man died his hair blonde because he liked the color, but his brown eyes and brown eyebrows belied his Puerto Rican heritage. He also had a neck, unlike José, Pilar and Ricardo, but his RR brethren knew that extra bulk would only handicap him in the small confines of the hospital working amidst all those pipes and equipment. To say that Ezequiel was fastidious would be a grand understatement. His teeth were perfect; his hair was close cropped and neat as a pin. He got regular manicures and pedicures, always looking fashionable, since he spent most workdays in the blue garb of the working class. But after work, he was a ladies man par excellence.

"So, José, what do you need me to do, or rather how am I going to do it, since you told me the what, but not the how yesterday?"

José grinned. "We gotta get Ricardo and Pilar out—but we can't do it without a diversion. In this bag I've got six smoke bombs. I'll keep back two and leave you four. You are our inside man. I'm guessing all the heating and vent system units are housed in the hospital basement, *si*? I need you to get out a ladder and find one of the main ducts where there's an access point adjacent to several outbound vents. Place these four bombs in the vent door, replace the housing, and get down the ladder. Just push the timer button and you've got about 10 minutes before these things go off. That should give you plenty of time to get out on the floors so no one's the wiser. Get the ladder out of the vicinity, too. We don't need any sharp-eyed fire marshal putting two and two together. And oh, here, I almost forgot. I grabbed you a pair of Playtex gloves to use when holding the bombs—you know, no fingerprints, right? Wiped them off myself after I assembled them. Used to make these for fun and games at Fitchburg High. They give off a tremendous amount of smoke. Best of all, they burn up and the vent air pressure will blow the ashes all over the venting system. It'll take the fire department days to track this down. Or, hell, I suppose come Sunday late in the third shift or Monday morning, you could play the hero and "find" the source housing. Make you look good."

"I like the plan. Nice and simple. How do I know when to set the bombs off?"

"Right, good question. I say we do this right after the patients get their dinners. Maximum confusion—you know extra crap in the way in each patient room. How about we pull this off at 6:30 p.m. sharp? Everyone agree?"

Hector, Luis and Ezequiel all nodded.

"Thanks for stopping by Ezequiel. You've got your job so don't worry about anything else. Oh, make sure that side door is unlocked so we can get Pilar and Ricardo out that way. The ambulance will be waiting."

"OK, got my marching orders," Ezequiel replied. "I'm on my way. I think I'll stop by Burbank and scope out the basement for a minute. No one will pay me any mind. I think I know the best access point, but I want to make sure a ladder is set up nearby, make it look like someone is working up high on one of the vents anyway. No one will move the ladder. I might paint part of the wall and put up a sign that says wet paint, you know *pintura fresca*! All our warning signs are bilingual now!" With that joke, Ezequiel took his leave.

José turned back to the group, "Now the final part of my plan involves an old warehouse and an adjoining set of cabins up in Franconia Notch, New Hampshire. A few years ago, I bought a place up there as part of some sort of estate sale. Happened to be driving by one Friday evening and saw they had an auction set for the next day. I hung out overnight and that next day I got it for a song. Best of all it's right near three air strips. I'm figuring it's going to be my safe house for the next several months. I'm also thinking once we get up there with Ricardo and Pilar—we got to get them healed up, and then I'm shipping them back to Puerto Rico. They can live with their long lost families—it'll sure beat a couple of decades in the slammer."

"I get that we are able to escape with Pilar and Ricardo. But what, you're gonna fly them to Franconia? Pilar will have to be lying down—that flight will about kill him," Hector opined.

"I don't see that he's got much choice."

"But José, you got a nurse who can help him at the other end?"

"No, that's the one problem I haven't…," José stammered and stopped speaking when the phone rang.

Everyone looked at the phone. José spoke up, "Luis, you do impressions, answer the phone and make it sound like you are Juan!"

Luis got up and went to the phone, "*Hola, es Juan!*" He had to hold back a laugh when Hector started chuckling. He heard tears on the other end. The woman, whoever she was, started babbling about having been fired from her job and she really, really needed to speak with José.

"Yo, José, *es* some *chica*, wants to speak with you. I think she got fired or something."

José got up to the phone and said, "*Si?*"

"Oh, José, thank God. It's Benita Cruz. I just got fired from the hospital. Some UPS driver just delivered a letter to me signed by my supervisor, Ms. Ventura. The letter said I was fired immediately for gross insubordination and for violating hospital policies related to security. They sent me a check for two week's salary. What am I gonna do?"

"Ah, *mi amiga*. You have called me at a most opportune time. I need to show you my gratitude for trying to assist Ricardo in his hour of need. Because you tried to protect him, José now will extend his protection to you. Have you ever heard of…oh, never mind, can you come to 756 Pearl Hill Road? I have a big job for you. Come now. It's an old orchard farmstead. I'll be waiting."

"Who was that, José?" Luis asked.

"None other than an angel from heaven, Luis. Benita Cruz. Burbank just fired her for trying to help out Ricardo. She's just the ticket we need in Franconia. We can send her there now to get the warehouse and main cabin ready to receive our two patients. She'll be here in a few minutes."

"What a stroke of luck! Speaking of good fortune, who is our pilot and what kind of plane are we talking about?" Hector asked.

"Sitting in the hangar getting a quick tune-up is a Cessna twin engine *Rican Ranger* plane. It's got RR painted on the side, right next to the license number. The letters are small but if you were a Ranger, you wouldn't miss them. Our pilot? None other than my niece, Gianna Mercado, whom I sent to flight school a couple of years back. She's even got her instrument certification so she can fly in the dark, in fog, you name it. Spoke with her yesterday. She'll be hanging out near Fitchburg Municipal

Sunday night. I've told her to be back on Tuesday for a second flight because I'm thinking we're gonna need her help to get away after we finish our business in Quincy, or I finish my business. So that's about it, unless you have any questions. Good plan?"

"Yes, good plan," Luis chimed in. "Guess I won't be going back to my trucking job for quite a while—you know, that mother of mine is really sick, *malo*!"

José stood up and headed for the sink. "Bring me your dishes and I'll get this place ship shape. You all showered? If not, use Mia's upstairs."

"Nah, we got cleaned up before breakfast, José," Hector said.

"Good. Then just hang out for now and think through these plans I've laid out. Let me know what we are missing and what back up plans we should list."

Twenty minutes later, the doorbell rang. Hector ran to the door and welcomed Benita. She came into the kitchen sobbing, the tears running her mascara down her cheeks. Luis thought she was a real dish but, alas, was family, so he was out of luck. Hector thought the same thing. Benita's eyes dazzled even José, who prided himself at ignoring such predilections. She collapsed in the nearest kitchen chair. José came over and put his hand on her shoulder.

"You just have a good cry, Benita. You did the right thing, and now you are amongst friends. Just take your time. We've got a big project we need your help with, and Ricardo also needs your help. Let me get you a glass of water, or would you prefer warm milk in a mug?" José offered, thinking about the prior few hours when that same warm milk took the sting out of that bizarre nightmare.

"Warm, ahh, warm milk…would be good, thank you," Benita choked out.

José got the milk out of the frig, poured the right amount in a pot and turned the stove on medium heat. He stirred the milk as the heat increased and when it was ready, poured the liquid into a mug that was emblazoned with a picture of Snoopy lying atop his doghouse; a blue ribbon attached signifying first prize in the Christmas decorating contest. The same contest Charlie Brown had entered and lost. Benita drank the milk slowly and looked up after a minute to ask, "How can I help you?"

"Glad you asked, Benita, *mi amiga*. As you've figured out by now, Ricardo and Pilar are in big trouble. They likely, almost surely, are headed to prison after their hospital stay. So, being good Rican Rangers like yourself, and like Luis and Hector here, I gotta get them out of their…situation."

"You can't get them out of the hospital, José! The cops will never let you get near them!"

"You know, you may be right. But let's say I could get them out and maybe get the cops to help us do it. Sounds crazy, I know, but assuming we can get them out of there, what kind of medical care are they gonna need to get back on their feet?"

"Well, I don't know for sure. I think the surgeries are all finished. So they're both sewn up, and the stitches will have to come out in about a week. You know, Ricardo's left handed, so he's gonna need all sorts of help—occupational therapy to learn how to eat and write with his right hand. Pilar is going to need some sort of leg brace and physical therapy—once the big cast comes off. That will be a couple of months from now, though. Pilar ain't going anywhere fast, that's for sure."

"Good, good, *muy bueno* in fact. If we did get them out, could you help them, you know, with their stitches and such, not necessarily the therapy? How about crutches—could you go get some right now if I gave you some cash? How about one of those folding wheelchairs?"

"Really, right now?"

"Yes. Would you know what kind to buy?"

"Sure, crutches—they now carry adjustable ones—you just have to make sure they can carry the weight. Pilar weighs close to 200 pounds and he's a big guy."

"But you know where to go? I am guessing you don't just walk into the Five and Dime for crutches and a wheelchair?"

"No, I'd go to a specialty pharmacy. There's one just off of Main Street that has crutches, wheelchairs and other assistive devices right in the window." Benita looked around the kitchen finally realizing where she was and maybe what she was about to undertake. *My career is sunk. I'll never get another hospital job, especially in this town. Who'd hire me? All they have to do is call Burbank and find out I was insubordinate. I hate that word!*

José handed Benita $350 dollars and said, "Is this enough? Better get some bandages and bacitracin or something—to help fight off infection. Get some medical tape and any other kind of wraps you need. And pain meds. Can you get pain medicine?"

"Only aspirin. You need a doctor for the hard stuff."

"Well, load up on aspirin then. Just assume we'll be helping Pilar and Ricardo for *several weeks*."

"How are you going to hide them for that long?"

"Don't worry about that problem. Let's just say I can get them out. Could you help them heal over that period of time?"

"Yeah, I suppose."

"Will you?"

"Ahh, yes, of course I will. It seems I've got nothing better to do with my time."

"Good, I'll pay you $500 per week for every week you help them and me. How does that sound?"

"Amazing—that's quite a raise from what I'm getting now for my salary, err, was getting."

"Yup, and it's all under the table. You do understand how we Rangers stick together, right? I am trusting you here. Are you in it for the long haul? You'd be sort of a private duty nurse."

"Yes, sure, I'm in it for as long as you need me. Do you think you could work up some sort of reference when we're done?"

"Forgeries and the backup documentation to make the forgery bullet proof are one of my specialties, *mi amiga*. Just tell me what you need at the time you need it and José here will produce. Hector—give her your car keys please so she can head to town or, Benita, do you want to use that Datsun pick-up truck of yours? The pharmacist—he'll help you get the wheelchair in the back of the truck? Tie it down?"

"My truck is small but it should do just fine. Yes, I'll get the guy to help me lift the chair into the truck bed. Roundtrip'll take me about one hour. I'm guessing I should go home and pack and come back here, yes?"

"Good thinking. That part hadn't occurred to me. We'll have Juan and Mia, my tenant orchard farmers set up...oh heck, they've left for the Cape for a week. Damn. Luis—can you see if you can dig up the keys for another cabaña and get it cleaned up for Benita? I'm guessing there's some cleaning supplies in the barn. I saw a broom out there."

"Sure thing, *El Jefe*, sure thing!" Luis said as he snapped to attention and headed for the barn. Benita put José's cash in her purse and headed out.

Hector helped dry the dishes and then figured out where each piece went, neat as you please. José nodded his appreciation and thought ahead to Sunday's fun and games. The hospital would never know what hit it.

CHAPTER 20

Det. McNamara Pays a Visit to Burbank Hospital and Profits from the Experience.

After tinkering yet again with his towering Ford truck and its 534 cubic inch engine, all under the watchful eyes of sons Conor and Rod Jr., Det. McNamara finished the lunch his wife Agnes had made. The egg salad sandwich, toasted thank you very much, accompanied by a real dill pickle from the pickle factory in Maine, hit the spot. That pickle and sauerkraut factory held a special place in his heart because his father used to take him there as a boy. Gracing nearly every wall was a museum collection of girly calendars. The owners had hung them everywhere and every which way, not a one of them current, which fascinated him all the more. The workman would laugh at the joke about not getting a date with any of the pictorial women, all of whom seemed to smile back at Rod so sincerely. He now associated girly calendars like the ones in barbershops with the smell of pickles. Go figure.

"I'm headed to Burbank Hospital, darlin', in my big bad pickup truck. Got to speak with the arrestees from Tuesday's kidnapping. I should be back directly because I'm betting they ain't a one of them gonna want to talk to ole Rod."

"Hey," Conor said, "can I mosey along, too, you know, hang out by the nurse's station and listen in?" Conor dreamed of being a detective—so every chance he got to be near actual police work, he'd jump at it.

"I suppose. But you better not bother the nurses, you hear?"

Conor turned toward his twin brother Rod Jr. and asked, "Don't you want to tag along too, Rod? This'll be fun…"

Before Rod Jr. could answer, Rod Sr. swooped back into the conversation. "Now, see, this is what I'm talking about. This ain't gonna be fun and it's not like a roller coaster ride or something where you hold up your hands and show off for your girlfriends. I'm hoping the press won't be sitting around waiting for me to show up. The last thing I need is your photo splashed all over the police blotter in the *Sentinel*. You will have to hang back."

"Dad, don't worry for cripes' sake…"

"Hey, you owe me a quarter for using the Lord's name in vain, Conor!" Agnes interjected.

"But Mom, I didn't use Jesus' name. I said *cripes*!"

"It's all the same in God's eyes and you know it. Now fork it over."

Conor reached into his pocket for the two bits and sheepishly handed the quarter to Agnes. She opened the cabinet and the coin made quite a clink as it landed on top of the shame pile, which now filled a coffee mug, and that was just for the last three weeks. Rod Sr. was the biggest violator, so Conor knew no appeal writ would lie in his court. Agnes really killed the purpose of the fines because every few weeks she'd treat the family to ice cream at Gimble's Farms just east of Mt. Wachusett off of Route 2A. The Farm was famous for the amount of ice cream they dished out—just one of their sundaes would stuff a 20 pound Thanksgiving turkey. This meant their lines of customers always stretched out well past the parking lot, everyone waiting patiently for the gargantuan treats. Friday nights, in particular, were challenging—just to find parking. Conor loved the triple cones and always got a dish to catch the fall off. He ordered hot fudge to be placed in the bottom of the container so he'd have an instant sundae when gravity did its trick.

As Conor heard the clink of the coin, he asked, "Mom, how much is in there? I'm thinking that, when school lets out next week, we will have to head over to Gimble's, else you will have to get a second mug started, right Dad?

Rod Sr. shook his head and playfully grabbed Conor's left ear lobe to pull him gently along toward the door. Conor giggled the whole way, as did Agnes.

"C'mon Dad, I wanted to hear an answer to my question."

"Fine, then please stay and speak with your mother cause I'm headed out now."

Conor shook his head and followed along. "I get to start the truck Dad! And back it out of the garage. You let Rod Jr. do it last time!"

Bemused, Rod Sr. responded, "That's not my recollection. When did that happen?"

Caught in a trap of his own making, Conor said, "Well, maybe it didn't happen like that, but you gotta let me. I need to learn this stuff for when I take my driver's test."

"We'll be havin' none of that till your 18 son and a certified adult. I'll not have any 16 year old driving Betsy out on the hills and dales of Fitchburg!"

"When did you start calling her Betsy and, hey, why do I have to wait till I'm 18? That's crazy. You started driving the backroads of Fitchburg when you were 14!"

"I'm just a funnin' with ya, boy. Relax," said Rod Sr., as he threw Conor the keys.

Conor ran to the garage, opened the big door, and fired up the truck. He turned around to look out the rear window and placed his right hand along the seat back, just like he'd seen his dad do scores of times. He backed it out like a pro and then slid across the seat. Rod Sr. hopped in and aimed the truck for Burbank Hospital. The pair stewed silently in their own thoughts until they reached the parking lot.

"What floor are they on, Dad?"

"Five. It's the med-surg unit."

What's that mean?"

"I think it has something to do with patients who come out of surgery and are in recovery. You know that Col. McPherson did some real damage to the two arrestees. Shot off the left hand of Ricardo and nearly sliced through the femur of Pilar. That's the big leg bone."

"Dang…!"

"You said it. I'd not be messin' with that guy, I tell you. Perched up on that roof, he made for some kind of sniper I guess. Now that I think about it, I realize he had the sun to his back. Smart dude indeed."

"I get it. Crooks would have had a heck of a time seeing him."

"Basic sniper art, son, basic sniper art. Straight out of the book. Keep the sun at your back and guess what? Your opponent is blinded if he just happens to look your way."

The twosome sauntered past the Information Desk and the volunteer, Gloria Petri, recognized Rod Sr. "Hi, Detective! You here on a case? Love your work! You saved my mom all sorts of grief from those criminal roofers you nabbed. She was about to call her neighbor who'd just signed one of them criminal's contracts—was even admiring the pallet of roofing tiles sitting pretty as you like on her front lawn. That would have been $500 smackeroos down the drain I tell you. You ever come here around lunchtime you be sure to let me treat you to lunch in the hospital cafeteria. The food is actually pretty darned good."

Rod Sr. turned beat red since he hated any kind of public credit for his work. It just made it all the harder to use stealth on the next case. He couldn't hardly participate in a stakeout because, just as soon as he was ready to make a move, some passerby would go all crazy, jumping up and down and asking the same question Gloria just asked— "Hey, you're that famous detective. Are you on a stakeout? Which house is you watchin'? You need any help? I can watch 'em from my front window—real sneaky like."

McNamara looked at Gloria's name badge and said, "Nice to make your acquaintance, Mrs. Petri. This here's my son Conor. We're just a visitin', nothing special."

"Now don't you be a fussin' none, Detective. I won't tell a soul you're here on a case. I'm bettin' you're headed to the med-surg unit to check up on those ne'er do wells that they got under house arrest."

Rod Sr. just shook his head and smiled. Mrs. Petri had lost her husband of 35 years in an auto accident when he'd looked down to grab his cigarette that had fallen onto the floorboard. When he looked back up, he was facing oncoming traffic in a 50 mile per hour zone and couldn't swerve out of the way in time. No air bags back in 1968, because the automakers argued that they'd face liability if the bags *failed their essential purpose*. Mrs. Petri, age 59, had a fetching smile, and a diminutive countenance to accompany her just now graying hair. She'd gotten the life insurance her husband Wicksham had purchased years ago. He was astute enough to set up the monthly payout to a sum that would accommodate Gloria's insubstantial needs. It would last her the rest of her life and keep her in good stead. Not one to lay around idle, for that was the devil's temptation, she volunteered both at the hospital and the library, and anywhere else she could make a difference.

"Anyway, it's just nice to make your acquaintance and that of your son. Now, what did you say his name was? He's a looker!"

"My name is Conor, ma'am, and I get my looks from my mother!"

Rod Sr. laughed and Gloria just shook her head. The McNamaras headed to the bank of elevators and worked their way to the fifth floor, but not before a four-year-old boy and his mother got on the elevator. The child pushed all the buttons. The mother just shook her head as they stopped and got off on the second floor, having doomed Rod Sr. and Conor to two more unnecessary stops.

Getting off on five, they proceeded to the nurse's station and noticed Ms. Ventura playing out her role as the chief nursing officer while holding court with some new hires.

"Now, remember, doctors just think they run…Oh, hi, Detective. I'm sorry I was just training..."

Rod Sr. saw his opening and interrupted, "Yes, Nurse Ventura—I get it, you're in the middle of orientation," Rod Sr. looked both ways as if preparing to cross the street, "and you are letting the new hires know, as you rightly should, that nurses run the hospital. I learned that at the police academy. I'm not sure doctors ever learn that lesson, or do they? Pity the poor first year MD resident who thinks he or she is in charge the minute they walk onto your floor, right?"

"I couldn't have said it better myself. Allow me to introduce Det. McNamara ladies and, oh my, I should say, gentleman, for we have a rare bird indeed, Detective, a male nurse! His name is Rafael Figueroa."

Rod Sr. nodded at the new male RN recruit just as his detective radar registered a high alert. *Not again. Jesus H. I'll bet dollars to donuts that he is part of the RR gang. And on the very floor where we have stationed our guards.* Conor, too, picked up the scent and gave his father a knowing look, the kind that only works with family members that have been around each other for years. Rod Sr. nodded almost imperceptibly.

"Ms. Ventura—I don't suppose you'd be willing to do me a favor? I'm here to see the prisoners and I wondered if my son Conor could shadow you for a bit. Maybe we could get him thinking about a future in health care!"

"Of course. Step right up Conor and join our august group."

Conor, playing along, said, "Well, health care has been an interest of mine. Do you have to deal with blood and guts all the time? If so, I'm way OK with that. Got a strong stomach, yessiree."

Ventura eyed him and said, "Sure enough. You are thinking maybe about becoming a surgical nurse perhaps?"

"Yes, that's part of the reason I wanted to tag along with my father. Didn't know you'd be giving a tour."

As the nursing group continued their lessons with Conor listening in and keeping watch on Rafael, discretely of course, Rod Sr. headed over to speak to Officer Testarossa. "How's it hanging big guy? I sure do appreciate this service you're doing. I know it's a bit of a snoozer. Listen, I want you to look over my shoulder real subtle like and tell me if you can spot that male nurse, young guy, Hispanic looking."

Testarossa, cool as you like, leaned his head ever so slowly to see over Rod's shoulder, and nodded without saying a word.

"Good. Now I'm figuring that he's a Rican Ranger, what say you?"

"That's what I'm now thinking Detective. I'll keep an eye on him especially."

"You are my man. Understand you had another nurse give you fits the other day. What was her name…Cruise…Juanita something?"

"No, sir, it was Benita Cruz and, yes, she tried to keep me from my appointed duties. I understand the CNO, Ventura, demoted her on the spot. That'll learn her sir, that'll learn her."

"What I'm starting to understand, *Bill* (short for Testarossa's first name William), is that these Rican Ranger types are not just mechanics and such, they seem to be filtering or are filtered throughout several industries. Never would have guessed they'd infiltrated a health care setting like this here hospital, but there's a new surprise every day, right?"

"Right."

"I know Ventura pretty well, but I want your opinion. You think she can be discrete? What I'm thinking is that I put a bug in her ear—see if we can catch this Rafael fellow in the act, so to speak. You know, sort of give him some rope and let him hang himself with Ricardo, and same thing with Pilar if he ever comes out of his narcotized state. Maybe, in fact, we could jerry rig some sort of listening device in the adjoining room and catch some back talk."

"That'd work just fine, sir. But I gotta warn you, some attorney named Gomez is in with Ricardo as we speak, so we best keep our voices down."

"Shit," Rod Sr. whispered.

"Well said, sir, well said. He blew by me like I was a buoy in the bay and he was racing one of those 12 meter boats in the America's Cup."

"Ricardo wouldn't talk to me yesterday without his attorney present. Maybe this Gomez fellow will make a mistake and let something slip. Follow me then, Bill, and let's see what we can see," Rod Sr. said, as he opened Ricardo's door without knocking.

Gomez was leaning over Ricardo's bed talking conspiratorially with his client. "Yes, yes, do come in, officers. My name is Pablo Gomez, with the Boston firm of *Pellatino, Degrazio and Gomez*," he said with a smirk, barely concealed. "Of course, you are here to speak with my client, Mr. Gutiérrez, and I am here to tell you there'll be no such discussions."

"Pleasure to make your acquaintance, Mr. Gomez. I'm Det. Rod McNamara and I'm the one who I'm sure you know broke open this case. I'm guessing your client told you that he wouldn't speak to me yesterday. Least not without you being present. That's to be expected. Now, as I understand it from the state police, you also represent one José Gutiérrez, right?"

"Boy, word travels fast. Yes, he's my client also."

"And howse about Pilar, the other Mr. Gutiérrez? Funny how all your clients have the same last name. Does lend an air to this case about keeping things in the family, *la familia*, does it not?"

"I wouldn't know about that."

"Let me get this straight. You represent the three of them, right?" Before Gomez could answer, Rod continued, "So, when we all get to trial, there'll be *three* defendants and just *one little ole* criminal defense attorney, right?" McNamara emphasized the number for Ricardo's consideration. He noticed immediately that Ricardo sat up more erect in bed, his curiosity and angst getting the better of him. Just as Rod had hoped.

"Certainly. I've tried scores of cases and my won-loss record is heavily weighted in favor of my clients. I rarely lose as you will soon find out, Detective," Gomez added with a hint of derision.

Testarossa fumed behind Rod, and not inaudibly. Rod kept up his subtle attack. "Okey-dokey. So, Mr. Ricardo, just like yesterday you don't have to speak to me, but you sure as hell will hear what I have to say and Mr. *Pablo*, I'm sorry, Gomez, you'll please step aside."

Gomez complied, realizing he was outgunned and no saving judge was present to restore *his* order.

"So, here's the way I've got it figured *Ricardo*. This may all stay in the family, but the jig is up. I've got you all cornered at this point. Let me lay it out for you. You recruit your Rangers as young as you can. Support them and their families, get them working hard in school. Then, since they are straight A students, local trucking firms snap them up. Except these particular truck drivers not only are mechanically savvy, they've got some sort of welding skill to boot. Now why do we need to weld, when all we've hired them to do is drive a damned truck. And that's not a question. I heard about the driver you all beat to a pulp and within an inch of his life when he got too close to looking at the welded compartment in the nose of *his* trailer. Understand he got out of town at your invitation, or maybe it was José's. And, yes, we're on José's trail. Oh, yes, we are."

As Rod spoke, Ricardo skulked back under the covers. His face belied his anxiety and Rod moved in for the kill. "Right now you are looking at kidnapping, assault with a deadly weapon, auto theft, at least two vehicles by my count, attempted murder—since, weren't you trying to kill Dan Brodie for that loan he owed you on?"

Ricardo stared in disbelief. *How did this guy make the connection with Dan Brodie? How did he figure out the welding thing? Jesus Marimba. This Detective is pretty danged sharp. I figured he just ended up at the scene by that psychiatrist's office because he was nearby. He's been doing his homework, this one has.*

"I can tell by the look in your eyes that I'm on to something here."

"Now, look here, Detective, I won't have you badgering my client."

"You think this is badgering, Gomez? What are you used to in Boston anyway? This here's just little old Fitchburg and we are all still wet behind the ears, we are. You're right about one thing, though. I'm not going to lay out our case for you, not yet anyways. You can deal with Assistant D.A. Chris Johnson. What I still don't get is how you handle three defendants at once. Let's say *General Johnson* decides to offer just one of them a plea deal. How do you communicate that offer to just one of them? Do you then not have a duty to let the others know there's a plea offer on the table? Doesn't that affect the course of their defense—knowing that their third *compadre* will be turning state's evidence against them?

"What I'm thinking is that, between all of the state charges against José and, oh, by the way, I'm thinking some of those charges will reach into this hospital room, *Ricardo*, you all are going to have your hands full running back and forth between all the courthouses and jail cells. You didn't really think you'd be headed home after your hospital discharge, did you *Ricardo*? My, my. This is just entertaining isn't it, Officer Testarossa?"

"Yes, yes it is sir. I didn't make the connection with the charges in Boston reaching out here, but I suppose you are spot on. A conspiracy is not limited by local geography!"

Ricardo could not hold back the growing panic. *José better get me outta here and quick. I'm gonna need my own lawyer, that's for damned sure. Pilar, too, if he lives.*

Goddamnit. This case is multiplying before my eyes. I gotta...

Rod interrupted Ricardo's silent deliberations. "So, Gomez, welcome to Fitchburg. Chair capital of America. Electric chair that is. If we can tie this *evolving investigation* to any murders your client, no, your *clients* would be looking at having a seat in the chair. You know we started executing murderers in this state right after the Mayflower arrived. If memory serves, we executed a guy named John Billington—who had come over on the Mayflower. He murdered some guy named John Newcomen in Plymouth Colony. First white on white violence in America. And those folks came over for religious freedom, didn't they? Funny how their faith convinced them that the death penalty was a good thing to have—you know a great tool to ferret out the bad folks so the good folks could thrive. I'm thinking that is the opposite of what the Rican Rangers do—they ferret out the good folks so the bad folks can thrive."

Gomez tried in vain to intervene. "Now look here Detective. I don't want any Christian speeches here used against my client. He's made it clear *through me as his spokesman* that he will not speak to you, period. So let's all finish this up and fast."

"I've got all day Gomez. In fact, so does your client. He's not going anywhere, except maybe to physical therapy or is it occupational? I get those confused all the time. Officer Testarossa, what's the difference, please remind me?"

"Why, yes sir, occupational is what they train you to do from the hip upward. Physical therapy is below the waist—

you know, to help you re-learn to walk for example. Ricardo here is going to need all kinds of occupational therapy since he lost his left hand when he came to kidnap Dr. Rebovitz, and while he had young Jeremy slammed down in the back seat of that stolen Galaxie 500. Nice car that was, by the way. That CVS pharmacy owner came and got it back Thursday. He was real angry—cause he babies that car."

"Thank you, Officer Testarossa. Knew you were smart, I did. So that reminds me. All that money you've got saved up Ricardo...you know from all your criminal activity, your ill-gotten gains. Guess what? Not only might it end up as payment for criminal *fines*...Gomez did tell you that didn't he? But you are now subject to civil suit by all manner of folks. Those plaintiffs could walk away with all of your assets and then how are you going to pay your attorney here? Or is José paying? By the way, I bet there's a separate charge, an attorney's fee, for each criminal case and for each civil case, ain't that right Gomez?"

Gomez just shook his head and Ricardo could stand no more.

"You didn't tell me any of this shit, Gomez!" Ricardo blurted out.

"Shut up, Ricardo!" Gomez shot back. "He's baiting you! Wise up!"

Ricardo realized his mistake and cowered back into his mattress.

"Well, well, Ricardo. This is just what I'm talking about. One lawyer handling three different clients. All around the same set of events. If I were representing the three of you, hell, I'd have trouble giving you all the information you're going to need to defend yourself. This is one hot mess, I tell you. Officer Testarossa—anything I've forgotten?

"Why, yes, indeed sir. Let's not forget about Nurse Cruz."

"Oh, thank you very much Officer. Ricardo! Did you know you have now destroyed the career of the first nurse who came to your bedside to care for you after your surgery? Bet Ole Gomez here forgot to tell you that now didn't he?" McNamara said, as he looked at Gomez who dropped his head realizing there were significant details about this case that he had yet to sponge up.

Ricardo thought to himself, *Shit. That poor Cruz. She was so nice, too. Wonder what happened? Man that supervisor nurse, what was her name, Ventura—oh yeah, like the city in California, she caught us talking. Bad scene. God I hope Cruz don't turn on me. This thing is playing out in ways I'd never imagined. This Gomez clown ain't helpin' me, best I can tell. Who the hell does he represent anyway? I gotta ask him about what happened to José in that Boston court.*

"Ricardo, we're going to take our leave of you now," Rod continued. "I can tell I've got you thinking and that's a good thing. You really have a chance to save yourself. Even your lawyer will tell you, if he's worth the price of *admission* you're paying, or is it José who's paying, that getting out of a case early is the best thing. Waiting until the eve of trial to cut a deal is like waiting for your ship to come in when it's already left for the next port-of-call. It ain't comin' back for you. Once General Johnson starts building this case and combining efforts with the Boston District Attorney General, your goose is cooked, but good.

"You've not met General Johnson, have you? He's like a grizzly bear that one. Tough as nails, scares me even, and I'm on his side for Chrissakes. I make a mistake in a case and he's all over me like, how do they say it in the south, like a duck on a June bug. You don't want him working your case too much before you make your approach, ya hear? Think about it dude. Now you get some rest. I can tell we've agitated you a good bit, but you done did it to yourself, didn't you?"

With that, McNamara and Testarossa left without shaking Gomez's hand. As the door shut, Ricardo launched into Gomez. "What the hell are they talking about? What is this two trial thing—they go after me for a jail term and a fine, *and then there's a second case where they go after my money?* Who do you represent anyway, Gomez? What happened in Boston to José? He's out right, but on bail? What am I looking at?"

"Now just calm down. That McNamara is a master at getting guys like you all shook up, real bad. That's what he does all day long and you're just his latest target. Get it? So don't be talkin' to him or that Testarossa fella. Yeah, we got José out on $10,000 bail. Your great aunt, his grandmother, put up her house, so no real money changed hands. He ain't gonna come visit you here because the Fitchburg police and this McNamara badass are drag netting all over Route 2 trying to snare him. I figure they'll be bringing in the press soon enough to get José's high school picture out there for the masses to consume. I can get you your own attorney. José's got plenty of guacamole to bring in extra attorneys. Don't let McNamara get under your skin."

"Why didn't you kick him outta here?"

"Because it's just like you are in jail. He can talk at you all day long, but can't ask you any questions. Didn't you figure that out? He just makes statements that he knows will scare the crap out of you. And guess what? It worked. So just calm down. Focus on getting through your occupational therapy and let the doctors do their job. Let your lawyer do his job. I'll keep you posted, OK?"

"Yeah, I guess," Ricardo offered unconvincingly.

"Alright then."

"Listen, can we find out what happened to Benita?"

"Who is Benita?"

"You know that nurse that Ventura demoted or fired or something."

"You don't really want me asking out there what happened to her do you? They'll pass that little pearl on to the cops faster than I could get to the parking lot after asking. Let me ask you something. What the hell was your plan with that five year old anyway?"

Ricardo thought better than to answer, realizing this was McNamara's point. Share with Gomez, and everything he said would be used against him by José or Pilar, even if unintentionally. *Those guys would never turn on me, but what about this law firm? Gomez don't want to come off looking bad. How is he going to use what I say against me?*

"Listen, Gomez, dealing with that copper and his buddy took a lot out of me. I need to get some rest and my left hand still hurts like hell even though it ain't there no more. Go figure. I gotta get some rest and heal up. Go see if Pilar is awake or something and let me know."

"Alright, but I gotta get back to Boston. You know there's a chance General Johnson will bring the criminal court judge right out to your bedside for the arraignment. Pretty unusual, I know, but if there's even a hint that you're not cooperating with your therapy they might just do that. Seen it done in other settings. The court ain't a building you know, it's the judge himself. So, wherever he is, court's in session right there."

"Thanks for the law lesson and one more thing to worry about. I'm taking a nap."

With that, Ricardo turned on his side and closed his eyes, disgusted with this whole turn of events. McNamara had rattled him, but good. Gomez hadn't helped the situation, and really just piled more shit, more *caca*, on top of this monster sundae.

Out in the hallway, McNamara and Testarossa watched Gomez head for the elevators. He didn't bother to check out at the nurse's desk.

Testarossa leaned in toward McNamara and said, "Nice watching you work Detective. Thanks for letting me jump on in with some comments. We'd make a pretty good team, methinks."

"You're welcome. You'll make a great detective yourself someday. I don't really cotton to the good cop/bad cop approach, but with Gomez acting the part of the cool-headed lawyer, this played out in ways I would not have imagined. He really didn't have time to give Ricardo all the what-fors. I think I caught him off guard. Ricardo may not have seen me as his ally, but he sure figured out that what I was saying might just ring true. Poor sap. Almost feel sorry for him, at least until I remember this jerk kidnapped a five year old."

"What was he thinking, do you know? With the five year old, I mean?"

"Ahh," Rod hesitated, "that'll all come out at trial, if this ever gets to trial. Just stay tuned." Realizing he needed to change the subject, Rod said, "I wanna look into taking you on a couple of my investigations. Play your cards right and you might be able to help with this case. You seem pretty sharp and you played well in my sandbox, Officer."

Brightening, Testarossa exclaimed, "That sounds great, sir!"

CHAPTER 21

Alex drove with Jeremy up the Rebovitz's serpentine driveway. The flowers were out in full force, even more so than the previous week. Mrs. R was out weeding early, and had a cup of Joe at the ready sitting on a little cart that also held her tools. She waved as they passed and, before Jeremy could open his door, Philada, Dr. R's black lab, came sprinting over, tail wagging excitedly.

Jeremy hopped out of the VW and hugged Philada around the neck. The dog moaned her delight and Alex came over to pet her. Dr. R stepped out the front door and said, "My apologies, you've caught my wife weeding and my dog on sentry duty. Philada, you leave these fine folks alone now!"

Philada ignored her master and for good reason. New faces brought yet another opportunity for good lovin's. "She's hopeless, and you two are just encouraging her behavior. In the trade, we call that enabling!"

"Mom, can we get a dog? Pullleeeaassse!"

"Now Jeremy—you say you want a dog, but who will take it for walks, clean up its poo-poo and make sure it's doggie dish and water bowl are cleaned and filled every day?" Alex knew the answer to these questions because she had used the same tactic with her father when she was a little girl. He'd given in and, pretty soon to his consternation, she had missed one or two feedings. A dinner chat—quite stern as she remembered it, solved the problem. Either she stuck with her promise or dad would get rid of the dog once and for all. She had named the lab Rusty since it had a copper colored coat that glistened in the sun. Rusty could do no wrong in her mind and he never complained, even when his water dish ran dry. He just looked at her expectantly awaiting the inevitable refill. That was faith! *I've got to remind David of that story. It's a great image of what faith really means. He could use it with his confirmation class.*

Jeremy stood waiting for a better answer. He'd obviously been looking at her mind and knew what she was thinking. "Honey, maybe when everything settles down. Let's just wait and see. Can't ask the McPhersons to adopt us *and* a puppy."

"Why not? It'd give Pinky a playmate!"

Dr. R saw where this was headed and subtly intervened. "Alex, I think it's time for our therapy session, and I bet you need to hustle back to Ashburnham, or are you going somewhere else to hang out before church?"

"You know in all this hubbub I'd not thought about my next step. I'm all dressed for church with no place to go beforehand!"

"Well, why don't you come on in the house and make yourself at home? You can use my office, get a cup of coffee and read the Sunday Globe. How is that for hospitality?"

"Perfect. I'm humbled again by your generosity, Dr. R."

"Good. Don't forget to call me Azriel, please."

"Yes sir, I mean, yes Azriel."

Dr. R turned his tall frame toward Jeremy and Philada. "OK you two. Enough playing around. Jeremy I need you in my library and Philada, you stay outside and keep momma happy, you hear?"

Philada acted like she understood and wagged her tail as she headed toward where Mrs. R was weeding.

The two-person therapy group headed into the mansion with Alex in tow. Dr. R pointed Alex in the direction of his office. Dr. R and Jeremy headed into the library. Jeremy spied the freshly toasted bagels on the coffee table that Dr. R obviously had just laid out alongside a glass of orange juice. He grabbed his bagel and took a seat, all ready for his session. Dr. R did the same and they considered each other before Dr. R spoke.

"My, my, quite a week, eh Jeremy?"

"Yes sir."

"So tell me what's going on with your life today."

"OK, the last time I saw you I was at the hospital. That was right after Col. McPherson shot Pilar and Ricardo. You remember—outside your office?"

"Yes, well said. I've had a heck of a week, too. Had to fire Velma, my secretary, for telling your secret to José and company. I want to apologize to you for her mistake. That was unfair to you and your family, and almost a crime in my mind. I'm trying to be more careful with the next secretary I hire."

"Yes sir. Good to be careful my mom always says."

"So walk me through the rest of your week."

"When I arrived at the hospital, a nurse named Missy Klondike said, "Well, nice to meet you, Mr. Jeremy! And what brings you into *my* emergency room this fine Tuesday afternoon?" I told her, I said, "Ma'am, two men kidnapped me during recess today, and my dad and Colonel McPherson saved my life. They thought I should come to the hospital so you all could check me out. Make sure I'm OK." She then said, "Oh my God."

"Whoa, Nelly, Jeremy. I don't need you to tell me everything folks said that day in the hospital. Word for word. I forgot for a moment that you have that photographic memory. What I'm really interested in is how you are feeling about yourself."

"Oh. OK. Col. McPherson said I shouldn't blame myself for what happened."

"Huh. Did you tell him that you blamed yourself for the kidnapping?"

"Yes, sir. If I hadn't spoken up all those times at church and at school, Mom and Dad wouldn't have thought I was hearing voices in my head. I wouldn't have had to see you. And you wouldn't have told Velma that I could read people's heads."

"Ouch. Well said. All those facts are true. But wouldn't that have meant none of us, including your parents, ever would have gotten to know the real you?"

"Yeah. But I don't like the real me. I get people in trouble."

"What do you mean? Trouble?"

"OK, José's still after me. Mom, Dad, and me, we can't live at home. The Colonel has to put us up at his house. Velma's husband got beat up, didn't he? I saw it in Velma's head when I was at the hospital. Two bad guys got shot. One of them might never walk again. The other guy lost his left hand!"

"Much of what you say is true, Jeremy. Before we explore that notion of blame, tell me what Col. McPherson said—but not word for word, just the part you understood him to mean."

"Col. McPherson told me that those other people made choices. They have to take responsibility for what they did. I wasn't to blame."

"But are you telling me you disagree with Col. McPherson?"

"Yeah, I guess. I don't know. It's all so confusing. I try to filter like you said."

"That's good. Go on."

"But see I chose, too!"

"And what did you choose to do or say?"

"I told you I could feel your head and you told Velma."

"Well if the shoe fits. You are one of the smartest patients I've ever had and you're only five years old. You've got the wisdom of people much older than you. I'm not going to tell you you're wrong. In many ways you are right. I want to suggest a different way of thinking about the truths you have shared."

"OK."

"There's a big debate with doctors these days about how much we should tell patients. Used to be we wouldn't tell them much at all, just order them to get a test or take some medicine. We never really explained everything to them. That's called being paternalistic."

"Ternalistick?"

"Almost. It's a big word that starts with the idea of a father, an odd kind of father, who is more like a general. You know generals and even colonels like Ed McPherson have to tell soldiers to do things without explaining why. Soldiers just have to follow orders and trust that their generals know what's best. Sometimes those generals have to order their men onto the field of battle—knowing that they will die when they get out there. Can you imagine ordering your friends into a battle knowing they'd die?"

"No sir."

"Well, neither can I really. Anyway, the theory goes that doctors know best and so we don't need patients asking questions or not following our orders—like a soldier might do. So paternalistic means one-way communication—I tell you to do X and you do it. You don't really have a choice. In some ways it's like how we handle Philada. She just trusts us to make the right call. Never asks why and pretty much does what we ask, except of course when you show up and she wants your attention. But she's a dog and we're talking about people. Folks can always do what they want—but they have to face the consequences. You make choices and so do they. I think Col. McPherson is right— just because you make a choice and say something, doesn't mean people who hear what you say have to make a bad decision. Does that make sense? It's sort of a long explanation."

"Um..."

"Let's try it a different way. Your parents were worried you might be schizophrenic, remember? That's why they brought you to see me. What they didn't know was that schizophrenia is a disease that hits people only when they are much older than you. But they made a choice, correct? That they needed help and an explanation. Imagine if they'd just ignored you and didn't care what you had to say. That's a different set of choices right? And they can make that set of choices if they want, right? You couldn't really stop them, could you?"

"No, I guess not."

"So let's focus on the choice they made. They asked for help. Always a healthy thing in my view. You asked for help, too, didn't you? When you agreed to meet with me one on one? You could have pitched a fit or a tantrum and maybe we would not have been able to visit and I'd not have dictated the chart that Velma listened to. So, not only would your secret not have been disclosed, everyone in your family, your parents, would have thought you had some sickness or a dread disease. What kind of choices would they have made next?

"I don't know."

"I can guess. They'd have taken you to the hospital and hoped some other doctor would have stepped in. Maybe that doctor would have been paternalistic and given you drugs that would have dulled your mind. It would have solved the problem of your tantrum, right?"

"Yes sir."

"But your parents were smart. They made the right move. Yes, we ran into some criminals, didn't we? Weren't those criminals out there in the world already? They just found out about you because your family made the right choice to get help. You all trusted our relationship and that we'd keep your secret. We didn't. That was bad and I apologize to you."

"Um...," Jeremy tried to respond but started to cry instead. He could feel Dr. R's love for him and his family, all of a sudden and intensely. It was a new feeling in some ways, not through his feeling people's heads gift, but right smack in his heart.

"Come over here, Jeremy. Let me give you a hug."

Jeremy got up from his chair and went to Dr. R and they hugged. *I feel a little bit better. I hate it when I cry though. Bullies would laugh at me for being a big baby.* Jeremy headed back to his chair and climbed up on it.

"OK, you are a good man who made the tough call, Jeremy. Do you know what tears do?"

"No sir, other than make me look like I'm a big baby."

"A big baby, huh? Well I've seen soldiers cry just like that. Guys who were braver and tougher than I'll ever hope to be and when they got done crying they didn't think they were big babies. Why do you suppose that was?"

"I guess because they'd held back their pain."

"Bingo! So you've just been through a horrific experience. You've gone through more pain than lots of patients I've seen for years. All in a short period of time. You've experienced trauma. Your tears are your body, mind and soul's way of releasing that pain. You are giving that pain to God to deal with, aren't you?"

"I didn't think about God."

"Well you can bet your allowance for a whole year that God's been thinking about you. That's what your dad's job is all about—reminding folks that God loves them and hopes for the best for them *even when they make bad choices.* Right?"

"Alright. I need to think some more about my choices and God."

"Of course you do. Monks spend their whole adult lives thinking about this notion of God loving us no matter what—and especially when we least deserve that love. So what do you think *and feel* about the choices you and your parents made this past week?"

"I guess we did the right thing. Other people did the wrong thing."

"That's a start then, right? What would you have changed this past week if you could? Would you have avoided seeing me?"

"No. My parents couldn't have taught me how to filter. You know…my gift."

"True—or maybe they eventually would have figured it out or found someone like me who could have helped them figure it out. But time is precious, yes? So you want to make the right choice *at the right time*. Timing is almost as important as making the right choice. Do you understand?"

"Yeah. If we'd waited to come see you we might have missed our chance to get the help we needed."

"Yes. Good job. Now, there's one other thing I want to talk with you about before your mother comes a knockin' that it's time to go to church. We've talked about your memory. You remember everything as if it happened just a minute ago. That's another special gift you have, but it can cause you problems."

"How can remembering stuff hurt me?"

"OK, let's say a bully at school beat you up..."

"He'd have to be a big kid. I'm not afraid of anyone in my class."

"I understand, but there's kids at school who are much bigger than you, right?"

"Yes."

"OK, just follow along for a minute. Let's say you did get picked on, or someone bigger than you broke your nose in a fight. You're going to remember every part of that fight, aren't you? You'll recall what every other kid who saw that fight said, maybe even remember what they were thinking when you felt their heads during the fight. True?"

"Yup." Jeremy twitched nervously in his chair, wondering where Dr. R was headed.

"Eight years after the fight you'd *still* remember everything as if it happened a few minutes ago, right? That's part of your gift of instant recall. And getting in a fight will hurt, right? You'll feel physical pain—like your broken nose or maybe where the bully punched you in the stomach and you couldn't breathe for a while. And you'll remember how angry you were that someone bested you. And then you'll remember how you felt the next day and the next. It will be like you never are able to get over it. Do you know what I'm saying?"

"Ahh..."

"So, I want to teach you a new skill set. It's called meditation. You are unlike the rest of us who get in fights. We all slowly forget what happened to us, we forget some of the pain and later we forget most of the pain, physical, emotional, spiritual. We get over it more easily than you will. That's the tradeoff for the rest of us. We can't remember everything like you can, which also means we can't remember all the bad stuff just by thinking about it. It's sort of like a flashlight—you keep it on and eventually the battery runs out and you can see the light dimming. That's how memories work for me, and your mom and dad. But your flashlight has batteries that never run out. So, I want to give you a tool called mediation. Most people aren't ready for this tool until they reach adulthood. You don't have that kind of time or luxury."

"OK, I'm ready. I think."

"Good. Then sit back in your chair and close your eyes. Tell me what you are thinking about right now."

"I've got lots of thoughts."

"Of course. You've got a big mind with lots of stuff going on inside it. Pick any thought you want."

"I can feel my mom's head right now in the other room and she's worried that I'm going to get kidnapped again."

"Wow. OK, when you feel your mom's head, and see what she is thinking, what do *you* think about?"

"How can I help her?"

"Do you focus on that thought or just think it and move on to the next thought that pops into your mind?"

"Oh, that's easy. I think about how I can help her—a lot. I'll think about it the rest of today. See if I can come up with any ideas."

"That's good. In fact that's what a lot of us do. I want you to try saying something when you meditate. It's a word that doesn't mean anything. It's a chant really. So take a big deep breath and when you let out the air say, 'ohmmmmmmmm.'"

Jeremy took in a big, deep breath and let it out sighing, "ohmmmmm."

"That's just what I want you to start doing for 15 minutes each morning when you get up and each night before you go to bed. Meditation means letting your thoughts flow by you like you're a riverboat passing by all sorts of animals, cities and people on the shore. Those things on the shore are your thoughts. Since you are letting them pass, you don't have to concentrate on them. Just let them come and go as they please—all while you breath out, ohmmmmmm. Try it for a few minutes. I'm going outside for a second to see how my wife is doing with the weeding."

"Ohmmmmmmm..." Jeremy started his breathing exercise. As he did so, he felt calmer for some reason. All sorts of thoughts came and went and he sat back and watched them fly by. He saw Lori winking at him and he giggled. He felt Grandpa Phillip swearing like a sailor in his garage after he hit his thumb while hammering away. Mrs. Murphy came to mind as did the trick he and his dad played on her so she didn't know about his gift for feeling people's heads. Philada entered his mind and he smiled. Every time he pushed out an ohmmmm, thoughts would come and go and he realized he didn't *have to concentrate on anything*. All of a sudden, Philada was lapping his face and he opened his eyes. "That's a good girl. I'll pet you. I know you've been waiting patiently."

"Jeremy, time to go to church. Are you and Dr. R finished? Where is he by the way?" Alex asked.

"Oh, Mom, he just taught me how to meditate. Then he went outside to check on Mrs. Rebovitz. He must have left the front door open. Philada came running in so I could pet her."

"Ooops," said Dr. R. "Philada you are a sneaky dog, aren't you?"

Philada answered with a wagging tail and came running up to Alex instead of Dr. R. She could sense Dr. R scolding her just a bit, not to mention the psychiatrist's guilt laden gaze.

"Alex, we're done here. I think we made some progress, don't you Jeremy?"

"Yes, sir. Mom, we talked about choices. Good ones and bad ones. Dr. R thinks we made the right choice coming to see him even though Velma told my secret."

Dr. R interrupted, "True, Jeremy, but we also discussed how delaying seeing me might have had other consequences, right?"

Alex asked, "So, tell me about the meditation idea."

"I realized the other day that, since Jeremy has an eidetic memory, he'll always have instant recall of painful events, like his kidnapping. I wanted to give him a tool so he could de-focus from those painful thoughts, not give them power over him."

"Wow, that's great. I need to learn that skill."

"Mom, we can practice together. I'm supposed to meditate 15 minutes each morning and right before I go to bed. Before we say our prayers. Right Dr. R?"

"Yes, we'll have you ease into meditation. Oh, and don't forget to peel your tongue off the roof of your mouth when you meditate. The tongue can hold a lot of our stress!"

"Thank you again, Azriel. You've been a godsend to all of us, and David and I are most grateful. I don't think he's been out to see your mother lately. I know he wants to thank her for helping save our lives."

"I know she'll be happy to see him. You guys have a great day. Hope church goes well."

And church did go well, with David keeping his sermon short and sweet. The service, however, would not prepare the Hergenroeders for what José had in store for them on Tuesday.

CHAPTER 22

Sunday June 16, 1968—early afternoon
Hanging Out at the McPhersons

After church let out, the Hergenroeders joined the McPhersons for a feast. Everyone agreed that since God needed to rest on the seventh day, who were they to argue, so why not join in? David assured everyone around the dinner table that even Jesus obeyed the Sabbath, for how else could he have steeled himself to deal with all the requests for healings, preaching, protecting the poor, handing out loaves and fishes, making water into wine and calming the squalls at sea for the fishing boats (the ones that brought in those fishes that fed the 5,000)? Oh, and one more thing, David said, "It wasn't just Jesus and the Disciples walking around from town to town getting everything they needed, food, shelter, etc. Those guys had a whole support community that took care of all their needs. That little tidbit somehow turned up missing in the Gospels!"

After the meal, David and Ed adjourned to the den where each man had his own Barcalounger. Within minutes, their snoring filled the house and made Lily and Alex laugh. Everyone was bushed. Except in wartime, the McPhersons had not had to muster resources the way they had during the last several days. David and Ed both dreamed their dreams, some of which included a future of blissful living, and target practice under the watchful eye of Pinky, or in David's case, harvesting the red raspberry crop from behind the parsonage later that summer, with Alex and her girlfriends making jam.

Jeremy hated naps, and escaped to rediscover yet more toys in that cavernous trunk that he'd been unable to see the other night because he lacked a flashlight. This time it didn't matter. The trunk was like Disneyland and FAO Schwarz all built into one. Jeremy pulled out a vintage 1950s Pepsi Cola delivery truck that had bottles molded into the sides with miniature plastic cases. There were two, count them, two Tinker Toy sets! Even better, there was some sort of 'car of the future' or so it said on the box label. He pulled it out and slid it across the floor. Sparks came out of the exhaust! He did it again and put the sparks up to his face—they didn't hurt!

Digging even deeper, he found a Giant Pan American [Pan-Am] Clipper plane that had four propellers, all intact! It even sported a loading ramp for the passengers, but he couldn't squeeze in any of the Army guys he found scattered about the trunk. Then, the piece de resistance—a sure enough Dick Tracy Siren Squad Car. It looked like the red flashers on the light bar might just work, but there were no batteries handy. He put that aside in favor of some Caterpillar earthmoving equipment (three pieces!), including a scraper, a motor grader and a wagon with its own tractor! *Truman must have been rich! I bet he got $10 a week allowance. He could have bought, let's see, four quarters is two Matchboxes and, oh my, 20 Matchbox cars every week! How did he have time to play with all this stuff? Oh yeah, Mom, I'm volunteering to take a nap!*

For the next three hours until supper, Jeremy created whole cities, construction sites and an airport. *Maybe Mom and Dad could let me come here and the McPhersons could babysit me. Every weekend. Wow, Jimmy will never believe what's here. It's a whole universe.*

Jeremy felt his eyes getting heavy, so he laid down next to the Pan-Am plane and soon fell sound asleep. He dreamt that he was the pilot who flew that Pan-Am plane to Texas and beyond. The stewardesses would bring him coffee (they weren't called flight attendants yet!) so he could stay fresh and alert for the long trip. He looked down outside the cockpit and saw that the three Caterpillar toys had secured themselves on to the top of the wings. They were waving at him! He waved back and pressed on ahead with the flight plan. He snored a bit until he felt a gentle nudge on his shoulder. "Oh, hi Mom. I was just playing with Truman's toys. Look at all this stuff! The McPhersons are rich! Truman was, too. I bet his allowance was $10 a week. I added it up—that's enough to buy 20 Matchbox cars every week! Oh man."

"Yes, I do think the McPhersons are careful with their money."

Jeremy knew that was his mom's way of saying these folks were rich. *I'm careful with my money, too, but I'm not rich!*

"Let's us go downstairs. Mrs. McPherson made an apple pie and she's got vanilla ice cream to put on top. That's our dinner. Sound good?"

"All right! You betcha. This place is the best Mom. We should come here all the time!"

Alex and Jeremy headed downstairs and joined their hosts. Little did they know what lay in store for them the next two days. If they had, they surely would have stayed up in Truman's room to continue building an ideal community.

CHAPTER 23

Sunday June 16, 1968—3:00 p.m.
Disaster Descends on Burbank Hospital

"Ezequiel, aren't you ready to go home? You got here extra early this morning. I appreciate your diligence, but we can't afford the overtime!" warned Frank Hirschfeld, Burbank Hospital's Director of Facilities.

"Yes sir! I'm on my way home now, try to get in a nap and then barbecue me a steak before tonight's Movie of the Week. I've already punched out, Boss. Don't worry about the OT."

"Thanks. I don't need that CEO on my ass again. He's just a glorified bean counter is what he is," Frank replied, the fat under his chin jiggling, evidence of too many beers after work. For thirty years. The veins on his cheeks and nose showed their alcoholic consequence. He rarely came in on the weekends and caught Ezequiel by surprise. Ezequiel thought of him as a fat old fart, as did the other hospital mechanics. Mechanic was a funny term, jargon for all around maintenance man at a health care facility. Ezequiel and his peers could fix anything at any time, from a busted thermostat to a blown gasket in the furnace apparatus.

The only thing off limits to him and his colleagues were the elevators—those took the special expertise of an outside vendor, usually, and in this case, the same company that did the install years ago. Ezequiel knew that elevators ran on AC, alternating current, but he had heard stories about one real old elevator in a Boston building that still ran on DC current, the kind found in batteries. He could never figure how that elevator got power, but knew that none other than Thomas Edison himself favored DC power. Edison lost out to the likes of Mr. Westinghouse, who figured out how to run AC lines across miles of territory without any loss of power. DC's failure was that it lost its spark over longer distances, rendering it useless.

Ezequiel made as if to leave by starting to walk out with Hirschfeld, but then peeled off, telling Frank he "needed to make a piss stop." Hirschfeld laughed and was proud that he had reduced overtime yet again.

As Frank drove off, Ezequiel realized he now had the perfect alibi. His own supervisor would be his best witness: "No Officer, I saw Mr. Camacho leave the premises at the same time I did. Good man he is. I'd direct your inquiries elsewhere, sir."

Ezequiel headed for the basement and stood next to the big furnace. The air conditioners on top of the building still ended up routing down through the basement ventilation shafts, so it didn't matter which system was operational, the smoke would find its way to the patient centers no matter what. The hospital team had started using the AC a few weeks earlier when, one weekend, temperatures hit an unseasonably warm 90 degrees. Ezequiel found the ladder nearby just where he'd left it with the paint bucket and warning signs. Best of all, none other than Hirschfeld himself had issued a work order to have this very wall painted. Ezequiel was just getting to the job a couple days ahead of schedule, and Hirschfeld would never notice. He took a seat next to the ladder and waited for the 6:30 p.m. zero hour.

Outside the hospital, Hector and Luis drove up in their plumbing service van, borrowed from a Rican Ranger owned concern. The name on the side read "R&R Plumbing" with the motto, "We'll take care of your needs while you get some R&R." The hospital had kindly installed a parking sign that read, "Service Vendors Only" right next to all of the doctor spaces, which, of course, abutted the building close to the entrance. Hospitals did whatever they could to entice doctors to refer patients. No matter, Burbank was the only hospital for several miles.

Luis and Hector headed into the hospital with their tool belts fully loaded for any and all to see. No one noticed them, testament to the notion that service personnel are invisible and of no consequence, as long as they are doing their jobs. They made their way to the fifth floor, and headed straight for the nurse's station as they'd discussed with José on Saturday.

"Ma'am," Hector said to one of the nurses who was busy charting, "could you direct us to the plumbing closet. We're here to do your annual inspection."

Without looking up or really paying any attention at all, she pointed them toward the other side of the bank of elevators, "I believe what you need is right over there. I think the door is locked, though."

"No problem, ma'am, we've got our master key," Luis said, as they turned to go.

The "plumbers" noticed the two policemen out of the corner of their eyes. Both guards, as José predicted, didn't pay any attention or notice their presence. They fit in like they belonged there. Luis nodded at Hector, directing his attention to the spare gurney sitting next to the elevator. It was of sufficient size that it would easily accommodate Pilar's girth. Hector got out his burglary tools and bypassed the lock, which was a simple affair, so simple in fact, that anyone with a credit card could have slipped in.

The sophistication of the lock was proportional to the importance of the closet's contents: not very. The pair slipped into the closet and kept the door ajar. It was situated perfectly so they could see Pilar and Ricardo's rooms, obvious to anyone thanks to the sentries. The Rangers' only problem was figuring out which room was Pilar's. That was the big-ticket matter—getting the gurney in place and rolling Pilar onto it without making a big racket. They planned to muffle Pilar's mouth in case he needed to scream out in pain.

Like clockwork, a dietary technician was working her way down the unit delivering dinners, which, back in 1968, involved no patient choice, meaning congealed salad, lukewarm mashed potatoes (powdered box brand), watery green beans, and some sort of meat item, completely unrecognizable. Hector and Luis watched in amazement as the guards opened the doors of their friends' rooms to let in the tech without so much as an ID check or any kind of security screening. She came out a few seconds later and the Rangers couldn't decide if that meant Pilar, Ricardo, or both were asleep or just disinterested in eating the slop.

Hector looked down at his watch and saw the time approaching 6:30 p.m. Suddenly, at 6:29 p.m., he saw the first wisps of smoke. No one seemed to notice, not the guards or the nurses. Then came the full plume of blackness and the same nurse who had ignored them earlier yelled "RACE." The police guards looked completely befuddled, way out of their element. They ran over to the nurse to ask for directions. Hector and Luis heard her say, "I'm pulling the fire alarm NOW. I'll call facilities to find out what is going on. There's a fire somewhere."

The Ranger pair realized at that moment that José's initial idea of using nitrous oxide would have been a disaster because the two of them would have succumbed to it as well. The smoke bomb idea seemed to be working like a charm. Thanks to a skeletal staff of nurses, the few who were on duty were busy closing patient room doors. This step failed to protect the patients from the smoke because patient room ventilation matched that of the rest of the floor. Over the loudspeaker came an alert: "Evacuate all patients from all floors, now!" Pandemonium reigned supreme. Hector and Luis grabbed the lone gurney and slowly headed for the newly unguarded rooms. Now way out of their element, the police officers moved *together* down toward the other end of the long unit. The smoke spread fast and deep, making it hard for staff both to breathe and to see.

Luis entered Ricardo's room and Ricardo, wide-awake, immediately started getting out of his bed, thinking this "tech" was there to help him. Luis grabbed the two face cloths in the bathroom, wetting them for use as gas masks. He felt sure the cops wouldn't think of this measure.

"*Yo amigo! Es Luis.* Follow me and quickly, we gotta get Pilar onto a gurney before those cops notice. Here, put this over your mouth. Can you walk by yourself?"

"No, but they gave me these crutches to practice on. I got good at it. I'll follow, but I just can't go real fast."

Luis had already exited stage left and was in Pilar's room helping move him to the gurney. He stuffed the wet face cloth over Pilar's mouth. Pilar clearly was on a lot of pain meds and didn't understand what was happening. He groaned as Hector, who just arrived, helped Luis move him onto the gurney. As discussed and suggested by Benita, they lifted Pilar with his sheet and slid him from the bed to the conveyance. It went like clockwork. No sooner had they gotten Pilar onto the gurney when one of the police guards stumbled into the room.

"You guys need help?"

"No, man, we got this. That guy next door needs a gurney, looks like. Go find one, quick."

Now with a set of orders he could follow and that made immediate sense, the police guard ran off down the smoke filled unit. Ricardo had stayed back, but now joined the RR threesome, and the group hobbled their way to the elevators. A nurse yelled a warning that that they shouldn't use the elevators because the fire might trap them in the shaft. They ignored her and punched the first floor button. Pilar moaned in agony, the narcotics no match for all the pain the herky-jerky movement caused him. Ricardo, ever the trooper, followed along into the elevator just as the door started closing. Because every hospital staffer knew not to use the elevators in the event of fire, the foursome caught an "express" to the first floor.

As the door opened, smoke poured into the elevator space. They turned right, away from the front entrance, and found their way to the agreed upon exit. Sure enough, as they opened the door, they spied Jayden awaiting them with a grin and an open rear door to his ambulance. Expertly Jayden directed Hector and Luis on how to move Pilar onto his ambulance gurney. Once the transition was complete, Jayden pushed Pilar into the ambulance and locked him into place much like a new set of cars latched onto a transport truck. Jayden jumped back out and helped Ricardo up and in. Hector and Luis left the hospital gurney where it was and ran for their plumbing truck. As they drove down Burbank hill, several police cars and three fire trucks passed them going up the hill. Jayden's ambulance followed close behind, without its lights or sirens running. Minutes later, Jayden backed into the orchard driveway and found José at the ready. They slid Pilar out first and then helped Ricardo, who stood for a minute in abject disbelief at his newfound freedom.

"How in the blue frick did you pull this off, José? I thought my ass was grass, permanently," Ricardo marveled.

"We can go over the what fors later..." José started to say as Benita came out the side of the house to look at her new patients.

Ricardo said, "Benita, oh my God. I thought you were toast! What happened and why are you here, not that I'm not happy to see you?"

"Burbank fired me so I thought I could lend a hand by working as a private duty nurse. Right here at the Rican Ranger orchard facility," she giggled in delight. "Our big problem is that all I have for Pilar's pain is aspirin. Nothing stronger. But there's nothing to be done for now except to get him into the bed in José's room."

Benita helped Jayden lift Pilar off the gurney and slowly moved him into the house. Pilar now realized what was happening and suppressed a scream, biting down on the washcloth he still had clenched between his jaws. Despite the agonizing pain, he had a twinkle in his eye from the realization he wasn't under guard anymore.

Back at Burbank, the smoke finally cleared. The fire department could not locate the source and the facility's mechanics had shut down the air conditioning system, which seemed to stop the flow of smoke. The men were on the roof taking off the panels to the compressors to check for damage or obvious signs of a short circuit. Fitchburg's Fire Chief, Ben Knight, stood next to them, flummoxed. He'd been a veteran of the Fire Department for nearly 40 years and had seen every kind of conflagration, but none where the source couldn't be located fairly quickly.

"What do you all think?"

Artie Smithson, one of the mechanics, scratched his head and responded, "Ya got me Chief. Everything we're seeing looks honky dory. It had to be one of these compressors since the smoke was everywhere. It was a hell of a lot of smoke, too, so you'd think the thing musta exploded or something. My hunch was that one of the units went bad, real bad, and the other kept working, moving the bad air around through all of the floors. Whaddya figure, John?" Artie nodded to John Miller, his fellow second shift mechanic.

"It's just too weird for words, Artie," John confirmed. "I'm seeing no damage whatsoever. I guess we can go floor to floor and check all the access panels. Maybe that will give us a clue."

"So, you guys are telling me," continued the Chief, "that these units are just fine? I'm concerned that the heat of the day will build up quickly. Should we be opening windows to get some fresh air into the building? Jesus, look at all the patients out on the grounds! They are our first priority. I can't let the patients back in their rooms until we all can certify that the systems are safe and in proper working order. Are you saying in your expert opinions that these compressors are just fine? Hell, even I can see there's no obvious fire damage. What caused the goddamned smoke?"

Just then Police Chief Tim Tolliver came up behind the group and said, "My prisoners escaped in all the chaos. I had guards on their rooms, but when all the smoke hit, the officers started helping the nurses evacuate the patients."

"I understand, Chief. I'm grateful that your officers helped with the patients," Knight offered as consolation. "Didn't realize you had prisoners here. Who were or are they?"

"They were those guys that kidnapped that five-year-old kid the other day. One of them got his left hand shot off in the showdown, and the other about got his leg blown off."

Knight exclaimed, "I read something about all that. Man, when your guys go after the criminal classes they don't hold back!"

"I'd love to take credit for the smack down, but it was none other than Col. Ed McPherson who took those boys out from his perch on an adjacent rooftop."

"No shit? He was my commanding officer in Korea. Sharp dude, always fair. If he took those shots, then those guys musta had it coming to them. In the worst way. I get in a situation like that, I'm wanting Col. Ed fighting on my side. His word is gold. And he always hits what he aims for."

"Yeah, so I've come to find out. Class act. I'm thinking I ought to warn him that the Gutiérrez boys just flew the coop. They might be lookin' to get some payback, although I can't imagine how they'd do it since Ed took the fight right out of them."

Knight and Tolliver heard the roof door slam and shot a glance in that direction. Tolliver chuckled and said, "I shoulda figured you'd get word of the escape, McNamara. I was just telling our esteemed Fire Chief here, Ben Knight, by the way, have you two met before…that we ought to get word to Ed McPherson, you know, since he's the guy that put the Gutiérrez boys in the hospital."

"Yes, Chief Knight, good to see you again, although I hate the circumstances. Thank you Chief Tolliver, I'll be calling Ed directly. So I'm just guessing here, but looking at how clean the guts of these AC units are, you all figure this for a staged event?"

Tolliver looked at McNamara with a hint of surprise, and then said, "Of course, you are probably right. That's why you are the detective and all I am is a paper pusher. Good insight as usual, Rod. Boys, I think we can call the all clear, don't you Chief Knight? Get these patients back to their beds before they have an accident or go into cardiac arrest?"

Knight nodded. "That's my assessment, too. My boys will collaborate with the hospital mechanics here and figure out what happened and where it started. Probably some sort of smoke creating device. Must have been quite a payload to hit all the floors like that and so completely."

John and Artie muscled the panels back on the units, and then the group headed for the stairs. The real trouble started brewing across town at the orchard hideaway.

CHAPTER 24

Monday June 17, 1968—Early Morning
Convalescing at the Orchard Abode; and Time to Check in with Fitchburg's Finest

With Mia and Juan on vacation, Benita Cruz took over the administration of the orchard house. She stayed up most of the night trying to comfort Pilar. The aspirin were no help at all and, of course, increased the risk of bleeding at the point of his sutures. So far, so good. No blood. *I always wanted to run an ICU and here I am doing it, as a private duty nurse. I think Pilar's past the point of no return. His knife wound is still draining puss and I can only hope he'll get to keep that leg after those guys hustled him out of Burbank. Suboptimal that was. Not sure how they got away. News of the daring escape has been all over the radio.*

Ricardo called out to Benita as he awoke, "How's Pilar doing, Benita?"

"He should have stayed in the hospital. I've got no tools to help him and am no better than a witch doctor whose only medicine is aspirin, a blood thinner for cripes' sake."

"I'm sure when Pilar comes around he'll thank you for saving him from the prison doctors."

"Maybe. If he lives. That gunshot to the leg, as best I can tell and from reading his chart, took out the main artery that feeds the bottom of his leg. We have to watch for gangrene—and I don't know how to check for blood flow since he's got that cast on the leg. Our first indicator will be a bad smell."

"Dang."

"Well said. I'm sure José didn't think about that likelihood, you know, of Pilar dying of infection or losing the rest of his leg."

"Did I hear my name mentioned?" José asked, entering the hospital "suite."

"You did indeed sir. I was just telling Ricardo that I'm not real sure how to examine Pilar's leg for infection and all we may have to go on is the smell. So far, it smells like antiseptic, which is a good thing. Have you thought through any additional medical care options that might be available in Franconia?"

"No, you are my main plan, Benita. May I suggest that you get all the textbooks you need? Go to the library, why don't you—see if there is some wound care advice in any of the stacks. Believe it or not, I noticed that they carry a subscription to the New England Journal of Medicine."

"That's actually not a bad idea. First, I've got to get some sleep. I stayed up all night standing vigil with Pilar. I'm starting to hallucinate, dreaming as we sit here."

"Take my bed—or Juan's across the hall and upstairs. Get some rest. We need you fresh, especially for the next couple of days when our next transport call comes through."

"Will we use Jayden's ambulance to get Pilar to the Fitchburg airport?"

"Nope, too obvious. An ambulance headed to a small private plane, even a twin-engine job, will look suspicious to the controllers in the tower. They'll want answers and a footnote in the flight plan, if I was to guess."

"Then we'll need some sort of station wagon—so we can lay Pilar down. Speaking of laying him down, what's the seating arrangement in your plane?"

"Hadn't thought that through. I'll have my hangar guy take out one of the rows and jerry-rig in some sort of bunk arrangement. I'm guessing we'll need to strap him in to keep him stable?"

"Absolutely."

"I'll make the call in a few. First, I gotta call Acosta to get through to our friendly neighborhood mole in the police department. I think you know her, Maria Catalina. Named just like that fancy salad dressing. So get some rest before you go to the library. I'll take a whiff of Pilar's cast area so I can help you identify infection."

"Thanks. I'm off."

José dialed Acosta's dorm hall number. Amazingly, someone answered, and got Acosta on the line.

"Hello?"

"Yo, Acosta. It's your uncle José."

"Oh God."

"Is that anyway to greet your benefactor?"

"No, sorry sir, it's just that I got pretty stressed out lying to that desk sergeant the other day."

"Really? I thought it went off rather well. Speaking of which, I need you to do it again and get Maria to call me at 4638. Like now."

"Shit. OK, I'll give it a whirl."

Acosta hung up the hall phone, looked around and, seeing no one, dialed the police station. Easy to do since the number was burned into his brain like a cattle brand.

"Fitchburg Police, Sgt. Finch speaking. How may we be of service?"

"Ah, yeah, this is Matterhorn calling back."

"You mean the one and only *Chase* Matterhorn?"

Oh shit. This guy is so on to me it's not even funny. And he remembered my made up first name—which I'd forgotten! Goddamnit.

"Son, you still on the line?"

"Ah, yes, yes sir. Could I please speak to…?"

Finch interrupted, "Let me guess, Maria—you need Maria. You know I hope you stop down here soon cause I'd like to meet a Swiss expat. Didn't know we had one in all of Worcester County. Just kidding kid. I can hear you breathing through the phone. Just relax, old Finchie's just giving you down the road. I like you, I really do. Patching you through."

Shit, now this guy likes me and wants to meet...

"Police, Catalina speaking."

"Yo, Maria. It's Acosta."

"Ah, my favorite Swiss Miss fake. Whassup?"

"José needs to speak with you. Please call him as soon as you can at 4638."

"OK, do you know what he wants?"

"You're shitting me, right? He never tells me nothin'."

"OK, talk to you next time Acosta, I mean, *Chase Matterhorn*."

Back at the orchard house, the phone rang and José picked up. "Yessssss???"

"José? Maria here. What do you need?"

"Just wanting to check in with my favorite employee at the police department."

"Quit bullshitting me. Don't be an asshole."

Det. McNamara was passing Maria's desk and heard the cow dung reference. "Who's that ya got on the line Maria? No one can bullshit you. Give me that phone and I'll take the caller to task!"

José could hear McNamara in the background and vowed to hang up if he came on the line.

"No, ahh, it's just my, ahh, uncle. He's just being an asshole. Wants me to clean his house while he's at the Cape next weekend. And, of course, is offering no remuneration for my troubles!" Maria couldn't believe how fast and efficiently she could lie. Just like that, but then she saw a twinkle in McNamara's eyes and realized that this guy makes his living identifying liars.

"OK, Maria. You tell that uncle of yours that if he gives you any more grief I'll send a patrol car over there to investigate a call that we got saying he's a Peeping Tom. That'll clean his house real fast, won't it?'

"Ah, yeah. Thanks for the offer," Maria said to Rod's back as he glided away.

"Back."

"You handled that like a pro, Maria. I'm impressed."

"Shut up. Not even sure he bought it. That guy's the best in the department at interrogations. Last thing I need is him focusing his radar on my sorry little ass."

"You got a great ass, Maria. I bet he's focused on it already."

"So, what do you want? Let me guess. You were behind the Sunday smoke job, right?" Maria asked as she suddenly realized the squad room was mostly empty, to her relief.

"Not me. No way. But I do want to know what your colleagues is sayin'."

"OK, they figured out in about 10 minutes it was you guys. I don't think they've found whatever device you all used to 'smoke out' all those patients. Even McNamara got up on the Burbank roof and the Chief, both Chiefs, fire and police, got the insight from him that you did something. He looked over the AC units his own self. No burn marks anywhere."

"Got it. Ruse worked though."

"For now. That's a whole different set of crimes by the way. You endangered patients. One lady even had a heart attack right there in the lobby as they rushed her out the front door. She lived, but just barely."

"Shit."

"You got that right."

"Anything else?"

"Yeah, no one here can figure out what you all are doing with the prisoner patients. Apparently, Pilar was at the point of death. You may have killed him just by taking him out of there."

"We're watching him close."

"Yup, but do you know *what* you're watching for? I heard tell that his infection might come roaring back and, if it does, he'll die for sure unless you get him back in the ICU."

"Thanks for the warning. I'll advise our on-site medical team. Changing the subject. Any news on the Edgerly front?"

"Well, we still got those two guards on site, Ryan and Callahan. What are your plans...oh never mind, I don't want to know."

"Best you don't. I might be leaving the jurisdiction soon and on a rather semi-permanent basis. I'm just too hot to handle. You guys would find me soon enough. Thanks for taking the call."

"Did I have a choice?"

"Always, but then again I have a long memory of the support our Ranger Corps has provided to you and your family. Since before you were born. I am grateful."

The pair hung up. Ever suspicious, McNamara had headed to the front desk to visit with his pal Finch, while Maria took José's call.

"So, Mon-sewer Finch, how art thou?"

"Great, my Irish friend, great. Don't you owe me a pint of Guinness and soon?"

"Why, I believe I do, and I am grateful for the reminder. Say, did a call come in for Maria a few minutes ago?"

"Sure did. Some Swiss boy, maybe in his 20's by the sound of his voice. Claims his name is Matterhorn, Chase Matterhorn!"

"You're kidding? You mean like that big ass mountain in Switzerland?"

"One and the same, my man, one and the same."

"Well, I'll be a monkey's uncle."

"Why you askin'?"

"Oh, between you and me, Finch, she just lied to me. Said it was her uncle, she did. Claimed he was calling to get her over to clean his house, gratis, while he went on a vacation."

"That weren't no uncle, ya ask me, Rod."

"What caught my attention was her raising her voice and calling the guy an asshole. My ears pricked right up, Finch. Ya know—asshole is the one universal word used by every civilization, ceptin' of course lines like, 'I'm hungry' and, 'howse about a little hoochie-koo darlin'.' Say, why don't we put Mr. Matterhorn through to me next time? I'll make out like I'm Maria's backup for the department. Ya know we always help each other out now, don't we?"

"You got it, Rod. That kid was nervous as a delinquent taxpayer on the 16th of April. He just stutters away when I try to engage him in a little chit chat. Poor sap. Come to think of it, you know he never talks to her for very long. Like 35 seconds max. As soon as her call light goes off, she's right back on the phone again. Might be he calls her to get her to call some third party, don't you know."

"Finch, you're a damned good detective in your own right."

"We try to please, yes we do."

"Guinness on me then—tonight, 6:00 p.m. sharp, usual place. Good for you Finch?"

"Good for me, Rod. Love ya, I do."

CHAPTER 25

Monday June 17, 1968—Early Morning
Pilar Takes a Turn for the Worse

As José finished his call with Maria, thankful for the intelligence, he heard Pilar howl in the adjoining room. He ran over to check on him.

"Pilar, José here. How you doin'?"

Still delirious, Pilar could only moan.

"Dude, I got to take a whiff of your cast. So my head's going to be down by your crotch." José took a whiff of Jif and was not pleased. *I ain't sure what infection smells like, but this ain't the antiseptic that Benita said she smelled. Probably nothin'. Just have to keep watch.* "Ricardo? Luis? Hector? C'mon in here for a minute. Smell down by Pilar's cast—at the top of his leg."

"Why?" asked Ricardo.

"Cause we gotta be on the lookout for infection. When I spoke to Maria at the police station, she told me Pilar had a knife stuck under his belt—ended up stabbing himself when he fell after Col. Ed shot him. Surgeons didn't see it when they were rooting around in his leg."

"Shit, it smells a bit, José," Hector offered, while Luis and Ricardo stood back.

"That's what I thought. We gotta let Benita sleep for a bit. She's dog-tired. But I don't know what you do for infection. Pilar is not exactly able to speak to us. Is that like shock?"

"Hell if I know, José, hell if I know," Ricardo exclaimed.

"We'll just check on him every hour," José said as he felt Pilar's forehead. "Jesus, the guy's burning up!" José leaned over Pilar's face—listening to his breathing. "Shit, he's hardly breathing at all. When I tried to talk to him a few minutes ago, he didn't even know who I was. Couldn't even speak, really. Go get Benita."

Hector ran into the main house and up the stairs. He woke up Benita and the pair ran back to José's apartment.

"What's going on?" Benita whispered groggily.

"Pilar's hotter than Hades and he's not breathing real well."

"OK, let's not get excited," Benita said with false confidence. She leaned over towards Pilar, felt his forehead. "Shit. He's in shock—and has a high fever. I don't know if his system can beat this infection. Something *malo* (bad) must a been smeared on that knife."

Benita peeled back the bandages covering the knife wound, which his surgeons had debrided and sutured closed. The wound had now turned gangrenous, giving off a horrific smell, a scent that had been masked by the bandages. "God, this is bad. I can do nothing for him. I can try to clean the wound out, but this infection likely is ripping through all his organs and chest cavity."

"What the hell does that mean?" José demanded.

"It means if you want him to live, you better call an ambulance right frickin' now."

"We can't. He'll go to prison, so will Ricardo and so will I."

"Then you've condemned him to death."

"Hector, Luis—you think there's any way we can drop him off somewhere and then call for an ambulance?"

"You mean in broad daylight?" Hector asked. "We're gonna do that we might as well take him right to the hospital and apologize for nearly killing him."

"That ain't funny!" José yelled.

"I wasn't trying to be funny," Hector mouthed back.

"What's this bride stuff you were saying, Benita?" José asked.

"De-bride, de-bride. It's where surgeons cut away the dying tissue—peel it off the body. It's nothing I know how to do, but it's textbook stuff. This is gross, but the only other treatment I have heard of is maggots."

"You mean like flies? Their eggs?"

"Yes. Maggots. They only eat dead tissue."

"Well, shit, where are we going to get maggots?"

"You just said it José. Off a dog shit."

Everyone looked at each other, desperate for some saving solution. Pilar gagged and coughed. Benita leaned over to see if she could feel his breath on her cheek. "It's probably too late. He's dying and fast."

"Oh God!" Ricardo yelled. "Pilar, don't die, please don't die! I love you man!"

Benita put new bandages on the wound site, if only to cover up the widening stench. As she touched Pilar's chest to tape on the bandages, he winced visibly, and then coughed faintly. He died in that minute, softly breathing his last.

"Oh shit, he just died," Benita wailed. "I didn't sign up for this!"

José collapsed on the floor weeping. Ricardo fought back his tears. Hector and Luis, meanwhile, just looked at each other wondering at the same time just what they had smoked out of the hospital.

"We're gonna have to bury him and soon," Benita pointed out. "At least he died among friends and family, instead of prison."

"Instead of prison," Ricardo mumbled, "instead of prison."

CHAPTER 26

Monday June 17, 1968—7:55 a.m.
Jeremy Heads to Edgerly

"Nice to see you this fine June day, Jeremy. And how was your weekend?" Officer Ryan asked.

"It was nice, Officer Ryan. Thank you for keeping us safe."

"My pleasure, my pleasure. You let me or Officer Callahan know if you see anything," turning to Ed and David as he spoke. "Gentlemen, we've been on high alert since we lost those two Rangers who were in the hospital. Not sure how they are caring for that Pilar fellow. He's gotta be hurting real bad I suspect."

"Yeah, pretty brazen shutting down the hospital and absconding with those two fellers," Ed pointed out.

"Not sure José did Pilar any favors," David said. "You know you don't want to mess with infection. In hospitals, they call it sepsis. Gets bad enough and on comes gangrene!"

The three men all bowed their heads unconsciously at the realization. Ed looked up and saw Jeremy waving goodbye to them. Ed admired Jeremy for his fortitude as he watched the boy tromp up the front steps of the school.

Jeremy found Jimmy kneeling down beside the classroom door waiting for him. Most of the rest of the class had arrived as well, with several parents bidding their children goodbye. Mrs. Murphy greeted each parent cordially and assured them things would be OK and that this was just a phase.

Earlier at breakfast, Alex had discovered that David had not, in fact, thrown out the roast beef she had laid out on the kitchen table to thaw on the day of the kidnapping. "I should have brought your list, I just plum forgot," David had said apologetically. Then added, "You know, there *was* a funny smell—I just never thought to double check the kitchen. Had no real reason to go there—other than that was the main point of my stopping by. At least I got us a bunch of clean underwear!"

Alex had nodded, not wanting to pile on and said, "I'll stop by there later tomorrow and I can take the Bug since Ed's driving you boys into town again. My gut tells me that waiting another day will be safer—and maybe the police will catch José."

CHAPTER 27

Tuesday June 18, 1968—7:55 a.m.
Pilar's Burial; Alex Checks out the Parsonage

B ack at the orchard hideout, José, Hector, Luis, Ricardo and Benita had spent part of Monday afternoon preparing a gravesite for Pilar. They agreed it would be fitting to place him as close as they could to the oldest apple tree in the orchard. Everyone was solemn as they buried their relative and friend. After the make-do ceremony, they agreed to get back together the next morning to begin planning for Ricardo's eventual escape to Puerto Rico, and how to expand the Ranger's venture into international shipping. They now realized how precious life was and how quickly a strapping young man like Pilar could be returned to dust. For that's all they were, too, dust, enlivened for a time on earth, but to dust they would return.

With everyone gathered around Mia's kitchen table, Benita and Ricardo listened as José, Hector and Luis hatched two alternative plans. Since Jeremy didn't know Hector or Luis, Plan A had them creating a smoke-bomb-diversion at Edgerly that would draw away the attention of the two police guards. Best of all, several grades were still in session including those of the adjacent junior high school. The Ranger group knew that the resulting chaos would create the perfect escape. They had two extra smoke bombs, not to mention air conditioning repairman uniforms that would complete the one act play, making them seem invisible.

Plan B involved the Ranger elite somehow capturing either David or Alex and forcing one of them to place a call to Jeremy at the school office. When Jeremy answered, José would come on the line and tell Jeremy that his parents needed him to keep his mouth shut and to come across town as quickly as possible, preferably with a bicycle. They'd not worried about how Jeremy might get a bike. Finding a bike would be his problem.

While Jeremy and his classmates listened intently as Mrs. Murphy taught them about the nine planets, Hector dressed for his morning run. He decided to head up Pearl Hill Road from the orchard and then, after hitting the summit, he'd turn back down towards Putts Pond. As he ran, he took in the scenery, the rolling hills, the other apple orchards on nearby hilltops, and the sun just starting to blaze its early summer heat. After three miles up to the summit and back, he passed the hideout and kept striding. In a few minutes he came up on the parsonage and was stunned to see Alex heading into the house, unguarded and unawares. Hector snapped to attention and bolted in the back door after her, almost before the screen door slammed shut. He caught her completely by surprise, knocked her down as she entered the dining room from the kitchen, and tied her up with an extension cord that was lying out. He then found a potholder and stuffed it into her mouth. He took a minute to catch his breath.

After he calmed down, Hector said, "Look, lady, you may think the cops got your son safe, but I'm telling you that, unless you cooperate right frickin' now and do exactly what I say, he'll be in a world of hurt. We only need him for one job—it's the same goddamn job as last week, and so we're baaackkkk! Cooperate and everything will be fine. Fight me and I'll start breaking your fingers one at a time, got it?"

Through tears of rage, Alex nodded. She couldn't speak, of course, thanks to the potholder, a present from a church member whose fourth-grade son had made several last fall as Christmas gifts during study periods at Edgerly. Nor had she taken enough martial arts lessons to fight off Hector. She could taste squash on the potholder and realized she'd not washed any of them in quite a while. *Idiotic thought. Why didn't David just check the kitchen, dangit? Stupid roast beef!*

"Lady, what in the blue blazes is that godforsaken smell? Stinks like a dead thing."

Alex moaned through the potholder. Then nodded toward the kitchen.

"OK, you stay put. I'm calling José and I'll check out what died in your kitchen."

Hector padded off the 10 feet from the dining room to the kitchen, leaving Alex hogtied and stewing in her own juices. He found the family phone attached to the wall and finally noticed the putrefying beef festering on the table. Alex tried desperately to untie the cord, but Hector had weaved a double square knot and she was going nowhere fast. *These Rican Rangers breed like rabbits. Where do they mint them all? You take out two of them and another three take their place. We are seriously outmanned and outgunned. Wonder what this clown's name is?* She calmed down so she could hear Hector place the call and pick up some information.

"Yeah, Benita, it's me Hector. Could you put José on the line?" Hector waited a few seconds. "José, you ain't gonna believe my luck. Guess who I ran into and tackled just five minutes ago? Nope. I got the minister's wife herself—right her in her own damn house, and man does this place stink to high heaven. Looks like the missus left out a roast to thaw. And man did it thaw and then some. What's that? No, I got her tied up with an extension cord and I advised her of her rights. She's cooperating. Yeah, you better get down here. I'll open the garage and you can get the Olds in real sneaky like—the left side, since her VW is in the other bay."

Alex thought, *OK, I know José is nearby, and this guy's name is Hector. Like that Greek warrior, or was he a Trojan? Shit fire, it don't matter. And who in blazes is Benita? Some sort of Rican Ranger secretary? Maybe I can figure out how close they are by counting alligators until they get here. One alligator, two alligators, three..."*

She heard the screen door slam twice and then found Hector standing above her. "Lady, you're in luck today. Posse's on its way. I threw the meat out in your garbage pail in the garage. José will be here directly. We'll need you to call the school for us and ask to speak to your son. Tell whoever answers that your mom, Jeremy's grandmother, is real sick and that you'll need to update him on how she's doin'. They'll understand I'm sure, this being a high security situation and all. Now, any hint that you're trying to pass a message to the school otherwise and we'll just execute Plan B. Need I say Plan B involves a lot more danger than this plan—danger for your sweet little child? Got it? Nod if you understand."

Alex nodded. She'd stopped counting alligators. *That was a stupid idea anyway. It wasn't like figuring out how close lightning was—you saw the lighting and then counted alligators until you heard the thunder. Every five count represented a mile's distance from where the lightning hit, or was it a seven count? This was just like lightning—an unpredictable danger and one that could spell doom for you or, if you were lucky, your neighbor.*

Just then, Alex heard the rumble of a big V-8 engine, clearly a car entering their garage. She heard *two* car doors close. Was that José and Benita? Three seconds later, she heard the squeak of the garage door closing and then heard a man's voice.

"Yo, Hector my man, executing a plan on the fly. I am impressed!" exclaimed José as he entered the dining room. Seeing Alex tied up on what appeared to be a fine oriental rug, he exclaimed, "Why this just has to be Mrs. David Hergenroeder! I'm José and we could have done this a few days ago and you'd ah been right back to your silly little life as a minister's wife. And Jeremy would have been back in his bedroom playing with his toys. But then the Colonel intervened, now didn't he? Did you expect that we'd just dry up and blow away? We have issues and Jeremy can resolve them all with his neat little gift. So, Hector may have told you our plan. This is improvised, but falls well within what we hoped might happen.

"Now, should you refuse to help us, we'll use our back-up plan. That means we unleash smoke bombs and all manner of diversionary mayhem at the school. But if Jeremy and you cooperate, we'll be all set and we don't need to do the Burbank Hospital routine at Edgerly. If things go well with our next set of business prospects, thanks to Jeremy's eye in the sky, we'll be out of Fitchburg for good. You see we won't even have to stay in Massachusetts," José paused for effect. "I see the look of shock and relief in your eyes. No, we are not murderers. We are exceptional thieves, just like those Wall Street boys who feed off of company pensions and all those little investors for whom they care not a wit."

José stretched his arms toward the ceiling and then said, "OK, here we go. I'm going to take that, what the hell is that in your mouth? Oh, a potholder. Hector—great job improvising—using whatever tools are at hand. Again, I'm impressed. But guess what! Hector may have told you we need you to call Edgerly and get Jeremy on the line. When he answers, you just hand the phone over to me, got it?"

Alex nodded. She'd never felt such hatred for anyone in her whole life. She'd kill José herself if she got the chance and happily spend eternity in hell serving the devil.

"Hector, let's get that potholder out of the Mrs.' mouth."

Hector complied and Alex gasped. She spit out some hair that had been on the potholder or maybe it was frayed fabric. She spied some third guy, whose name she didn't yet know, dial Edgerly. He handed her the phone as José passed her a sheet with the text to read.

"Hello, Edgerly Elementary School, Mrs. Taylor speaking. How may I help you?"

"Ahh, hello Mrs. Taylor. This is Alex Hergenroeder. My mom, Jeremy's grandmother, has taken ill. Jeremy had asked me to call him with an update. What's that? No, I know, he's quite the sensitive boy. He may get upset when

I tell him. Maybe you could give him a wee bit of privacy just for a minute?"

Alex turned to José, "She's going to get him."

"You played that real well, Mrs. H. Nice touch getting her to agree to let him have some privacy when I speak to him."

It took five minutes for Jeremy to come to the phone, but seemed like a lifetime. Alex looked at Hector and José, studying them discretely so she could help with a police composite if things ever got that far. Alex heard Jeremy's voice and said, "Honey, I need you to be brave…" She dropped the phone unwittingly and started balling.

José picked up the phone and said sweetly, "Jeremy, this is José. I know you want to help your mom and that you can feel my head right now. I don't mean to do her any harm, but I need your help. So I need you to…huh, what's that?"

Jeremy said, "You better not hurt my mom!"

"No sir," José said. "Listen, the sooner you get here the faster this will all be over. So, tell the secretary who answered the phone that your grandma is real sick and that you are going to see her *after school lets out*. Got it? Then, instead of going back to class, I need you to sneak past the police guards and come home as fast as you can. Go ahead and steal a bike. Do what I tell you and your mom will be safe."

"OK," was all Jeremy said as he hung up the phone. He could feel José's head and saw that the goons had tied up his mom with some sort of brown rope thing. He felt his mom's head and knew she was real angry and scared, both. He knew that neither Col. McPherson nor his dad had a clue what was going on, and worse, he had no way of telling them. He advised the secretary exactly what José had told him to say, word for word. Eidetic memory a handy thing in this instance. He pretended to head back to class and then ran out the basement door of the school toward the junior high parking lot where a bike rack stood. He scanned the set of bikes and saw a new Schwinn stingray bike with a banana seat. The bike was blue, girls' style, with a lock on it. He touched the lock and concentrated. Finally, he saw the girl who owned it. Her name was Becky Filcher and she was in 7th grade and, lucky for him, small for her age.

The lock had three dials on it. Jeremy felt Becky's head and saw three numbers floating around: 3, 4, 2. He turned the dials to the numbers in that order, but it wouldn't open. Then he tried it the other way, 2-4-3 and it snapped loose. He got on the bike as best he could, thanking his lucky stars that his dad had just recently taught him how to ride. Wobbly at first, he started peddling and then got going faster and faster.

Once he hit the street, tears started flowing from his eyes making it hard to see ahead. He heard the flapping of the plastic tassels on the ends of the handlebar. As he whisked down Highland Avenue behind the junior high, the wind whistled past his ears. Jeremy blasted past a stop sign and a car swerved to miss him, the driver angrily honking at the delinquent youth. He felt the driver's head, a woman on her way to a book club at the Catholic church by Burbank Hospital, and realized she was wondering why he was out of school. He pressed on, finally crossing Route 2. He raced up Pearl Hill, defying gravity, not tiring at all, full of adrenalin and all the rage a five year old could muster. In minutes, he pulled into *his* driveway and dropped the bike like it had cooties. He ran into the kitchen to find José, Hector and his mom all sitting at the kitchen table as if it was a church meeting and all was well. All was not well. A third guy, *his name is Luis(!)* eyed Jeremy from the archway leading into the dining room.

"My, my, we finally meet, Jeremy. I'm José. I'm not going to give you any lines of bullshit, so here's the play: Hector and Luis here are going to take your mother to our little hideout right up Pearl Hill Road. You and I are going to join them to make sure your mother doesn't try to pull any fast ones. Then we, you and I, are going to Quincy to meet a guy whose head I need you to feel and let me know what he's thinking. Got it?" José paused and Jeremy nodded, but said nothing.

"Good. Then we can talk on the way and maybe you can give me a reading on what he's thinking already. Assuming our meeting goes well, I'll bring you back to meet your mom. We'll then go to the airport and fly off, leaving you two in a locker that we'll have someone open later when we're good and far away. You'll then never see me again. I know you can tell if I'm lying, so tell me what you see in my head."

Jeremy looked at José with more hatred than the devil himself could have mustered on his best day. "Yes, you are telling the truth," Jeremy responded and then looked at his mother. "He's telling the truth Mom."

José looked at Jeremy and said, "That's what I need to hear. Then we all understand we can do this the hard way, or the easy way. Hard way, Hector and Luis here, keep your mom tied up and that potholder stuffed in her mouth. They then leave her in the barn at our orchard property. In the dark, no water, no nothing. Easy way, she just sits in my living room and bides her time until you and I get back from Quincy. We'll feed her and she can relax, so to speak. Your call Jeremy."

Alex intervened, realizing this was not her son's decision to make, "I'll cooperate, but if you hurt my son I'll kill you myself."

"Perfect-a-mundo. That tells me you are highly motivated to protect Jeremy. Your best protection is to cooperate. Now, we are all going to head out to the garage real quiet like, but not out the back door here. I bet you have a basement, and I'm guessing it accesses the garage, correct?"

"Yes."

"Convenient. Let's all proceed quietly."

The group headed through the dining room to the basement access door, and then threaded down the stairs. They exited out of the other basement door that fed into the garage, and everyone hopped in José's big Olds. José started backing out of the driveway, but hit something and stopped. He piled out of the car to find Jeremy's stolen bike. He hopped back in and moved the car forward back over the bike. José turned off the car engine, took the key out of the ignition, used it to open the trunk, and threw the bike into the cavernous space with an audible thud. "Sorry gang. Didn't see the bike."

He finished backing out of the driveway, but didn't see Mrs. Kendall next door eyeballing the group. She had promised David that she'd keep an eye on the house and, true to her word, she watched the group like a hawk. She couldn't help but notice that everyone in the car seemed calm, even though the car had run over the bike. *That's odd. Real odd. Who were those men? Why was Jeremy out of school? That sure looked like Alex sitting in the back seat. Whose bike was that? It looked new—brand new, but it was a girl's bike! That man treated it like a piece of trash. Maybe I'll just call Rollstone and ask David.*

The big Olds headed up Pearl Hill at a moderate pace. Kneeling up on the back seat, Jeremy looked out the back window and saw Mrs. Kendall looking right at him. He hoped she saw him shake his head ever so subtly. Turning around he watched the houses pass and saw into each one, who might be home, and what they were thinking. After driving a half-mile past the parsonage, José turned right into the long driveway of the orchard house. Jeremy thought, *This is where they'll keep mom!*

"Alright, everyone out and let's go into the house," José bellowed.

The five-person group moved like a caterpillar, all segments in tandem, single file. José held the door for everyone and as soon as Jeremy entered the domain, he saw Ricardo, and got a catch in his throat. Ricardo looked back at him with venom in his eyes, but said nothing. Jeremy returned the look in kind and likewise stayed silent.

"OK, Ricardo here will watch your mother. Jeremy let's you and I head out. Benita here made us some sandwiches I see. Mrs. H eat up. You'll need your strength later on for your time in the airport box."

Alex took a seat in the living room and bowed her head so that no one noticed the look of fury on her face. Without saying another word, Jeremy and José headed out to the car and left for Quincy. As the pair eased down Pearl Hill Road, Mrs. Kendall was still standing out front of her purple house. She saw the Olds coming and ducked behind one of the big fir trees that ran along her driveway. She saw Jeremy, who looked at her, shaking his head again. Unawares, José continued down the big hill, over the Putts Pond bridge and stopped at the Route 2 stop sign. He waited for the traffic to ease up and then turned left, aiming for Quincy.

José decided to break the ice with his young charge. "So, Jeremy, I'm guessing you know some of my story, but not all. I'll fill you in. My dad was killed when I was a little older than you. He'd borrowed money from a loan shark who came to beat him up because he was behind in his payments. He'd borrowed $150, and within a couple of weeks owed $2,500. Not a sum my dad could pay. The beating didn't work out so well, and the guy killed my dad, accidentally I suppose, but murder it was, nonetheless. You might expect that I would have wanted to kill that goon—when I got older. I did at first, but later I decided to study him and the other thugs in my neighborhood. You know, Green Street, down by your dad's church. Did you know any of this?

"No, sir. I knew you came from a bad part of town."

"Bad indeed. Anyway, I learned the ways of the street, and built up a little loan service of my own, selling the free lunch tickets us poor kids got, and then getting a bit of interest back from my borrowers. For a short while, I even sold drugs. I stopped when I saw two of my friends overdose on the product. When I sold them drugs, they were happy and so was I, everyone won, right? Wrong. So I stopped drugging—saw what it did to people. After my grandmother rung my neck one day when she caught me skipping school, I hunkered down and worked hard. I got straight A's after that. Got my cousins to do the same and we built up a business. That's what this trip is about. So here's what I need. Are you ready?"

"Yes sir," Jeremy lied. He hated José more than anything he'd ever experienced. He felt José's head and saw Pilar dying in the house they'd just left. Saw José scheming on how to get Ricardo out of the hospital, saw all the smoke and saw in Det. McNamara's head the moments when he'd been standing on the hospital's roof figuring out the smoke bomb ruse.

"Good," Jeremy heard José say, and then Jeremy stopped listening and traveled back to the murder scene with José's father. It was more gruesome than José described and Jeremy started to understand this man. This enemy. He wondered how he would feel seeing his own father murdered. Dr. R's warning filled his mind. He heard again what Dr. R was saying to his mother as they prepared to head to church after his therapy session: "I realized the other day that, since Jeremy has an eidetic memory, he'll always have instant recall of painful events, like his kidnapping. I wanted to give him a tool so he could de-focus from those painful thoughts, not give them power over him." *How do I not give José power over me? I need to listen to José's thoughts and feel his head more.*

"…the union," José stopped talking after realizing he'd lost Jeremy. "Kid, I need you to listen to me. I need your help, OK? We'll make sure your mother is OK. I ain't a murderer anyway. You gonna listen or ignore me?"

"I'm sorry, sir. I was daydreaming. I'll listen better, I promise."

"Good. There's a man named Rick Sullivan. He's the union boss for all the guys that take the loads off the ships that come into Boston. He's called a stevedore or his union guys are called that. Sometimes we all just call them longshoremen. They work real hard in difficult conditions, but they can help me. You know all those big wigs on Wall Street, the real moneymen, they're no better than me. They steal from little guys and pad their own bank accounts. Me? I steal from the rich and give to poor kids in my neighborhood. So this here trip is just about me expanding my market, got it?"

"I think so. It's like my allowance. My Dad gives me a quarter every week. But when he was my age his father, my Grandpa Phillip, gave him $5.00 a week!"

"Right. It's like we took you back in time and you got that $5.00 every week instead of a quarter. When I increase my take, ya know, my allowance, then I can increase all the other Rangers' allowances at the same time. Rising tide floats all boats. So, what can you tell me about Rick Sullivan?"

"I don't know him. Please tell me about him."

"My nephew, Dominick Sangria, works at the yard, for General Dynamics. He's in the union. He says this Rick guy is pretty serious, all business—really tries to stick up for the guys with the company."

"What's a union?"

"Whoa, OK. A union just means a bunch of guys who work for a company and they get together to stick up for their rights."

"What rights?"

"Dang Jeremy, I don't know. I suppose how long they have to work every day, how many breaks they get, stuff like that. If they don't get what they want they go on strike."

"You mean like in baseball?"

José laughed and laughed hard, "Oh yeah, that's a good one. No, a strike means they stop working and picket the company. And before you ask what picket means…"

"Is it like the fence my Grandpa Cotter has in front of his house?"

"Ah, not quite, but sort of. When union guys picket, it means they stand out front of the shipyard and prevent anyone from going through to work. Any guys that get past the picket line—you know where they're holding up signs, they call those guys scabs. And no, not like you get when you get a bruise. It's just a bad name they use. They try to embarrass those guys who still work, get 'em to stop."

"So, why do you care about the union? How do they get you more money?"

"This guy Rick, see, he has an in with the company—he knows ahead of time what ships are coming in to port and what they're carrying. My Rangers are often driving the trucks that take the loads off the ships. But we don't always know what we're carrying and don't have the time to look over the load to see what we could take. Rick can get me the list…"

Jeremy closed his eyes and stopped listening to José. He traveled to Quincy and saw the shipyard through none other than Dan Brodie's eyes. Dan was the welder who had made the mistake of borrowing money from José. His wife Velma stole Jeremy's secret and tried to sell it to José. Jeremy saw Dan welding a ship and realized *that the Dominick guy was the one who got Dan to borrow money from* José! Jeremy then bounced to the foreman's trailer, felt the head of the foreman, Connie Calhoun, and saw him laughing with…Rick Sullivan. Jeremy moved to Rick's head, to get a feel for the man.

"Mr. Sullivan," Jeremy began, before José interrupted.

"What—you've got a bead on the guy?"

"Yes. He's in some metal building. Sitting in a squeaky chair. He's talking to some guy named Connie Calhoun. I guess he is the four guy."

"Foreman, you mean foreman. Calhoun's everyone's boss."

"OK. Foreman. Mr. Sullivan sure is a serious guy. He's joking around with Mr. Calhoun, but he's worried about the company. Who is the General you keep talking about? I know a colonel."

"That's just the name of the big ship building company—General Dynamics. It's not a guy."

"Oh. Mr. Sullivan is worried about how General Dynamics is treating his buddies. He wants the company to be fair—not work everyone too hard. So he's trying to be nice to Mr. Calhoun."

"That's good stuff. Anything else?"

"He's got a daughter whose eight years old. There's something wrong with her, her mind. She isn't smart. Has trouble just brushing her teeth and stuff. Mr. Sullivan is real worried about her—like she'll never get married or have kids of her own. Mrs. Sullivan, she's worried, too, but she works hard teaching the daughter, I think her name is Rebecca, teaching her stuff like how to make her bed, and to be good in church."

"OK, so the guy and his family go to church."

"Yes, but they worry they can't give the church money. They have a lot of bills. Mr. Sullivan is scared that his wife will have to go to work to pay the bills. But she can't, because Rebecca is home all the time and can't take care of herself. Mrs. Sullivan left her for a few minutes one time. Just to go run an errand. When she came back, the toilet was overflowing and Rebecca had left the back door open. A squirrel had come into the house, ran around the kitchen. It scared Rebecca. She chased it with a broom before her mom got back. Broke a bunch of stuff in the kitchen. It was a real mess."

"Wow. So the guy needs extra money. Do you think he'd work with me?"

"I don't think so. He's honest. He would be afraid of losing his job. He likes how all the guys like him. They trust him, he figures. He always does the right thing."

"Well, shit. Ain't that a bite in the shorts."

"Who would bite your shorts?"

"Huh? It's just a saying. Maybe what I can do, see, is offer to help him out, you know, with his daughter's medical bills. I gotta think about this."

Jeremy looked out the Olds' window, listened to the breeze flowing through the vent window, and felt his mom's head. He saw that she was calm and was hoping he'd be OK. *She's wondering how to get word to Dad.* He felt the head of Mrs. Kendall who was baking in her kitchen. *Mrs. Kendall hopes nothing bad is happening to me and Mom. She doesn't want to call the church because she thinks Dad's been through enough without creating a false alarm. She's can't figure out why I was shaking my head when we drove by her house.*

The pair drove on toward Quincy, with José scheming how to manipulate Rick and Jeremy lost in his thoughts about how to save his parents, even if he might not live through this nightmare.

CHAPTER 28

Tuesday June 18, 1968—2:32 p.m.
The School Bell Rings at Edgerly; Mrs. Kendall Makes the Call

As the closing bell rang, Sondra Taylor, the secretary for the main office, skipped down the hall past the accelerated kindergarten classroom. She saw Mrs. Murphy, Dr. Murphy thank you very much, erasing the blackboard with one of those fancy, triple sized erasers that worked so well.

"Dr. Murphy! Hello. I was wondering if Jeremy seemed upset after the phone call he got from his mother?"

"Excuse me? I thought she must have come and gotten him. He didn't return to class after you all got him to go to the office. Oh, my God! Where's Officer Callahan or Ryan?" Murphy shouted as she flew past Taylor.

Dr. Murphy ran out the front of the school building and saw Officer Callahan waving to various parents, assuring them that everything was OK.

"Officer Callahan! Have you seen Jeremy?"

"Why, no, Ma'am, come to think of it, I have not. I assumed he was still in the building, you know, maybe getting stuff out of his locker."

"The students don't get lockers until they're in the 4th grade! He doesn't have a locker. Oh my."

"When's the last time you saw him?"

"Three hours ago at least or more. He got called down to the office. His mother was on the phone with an urgent call."

"Alright, let's work backward from that...Oh God, here's his father and that Colonel coming to pick him up."

As Murphy and Callahan looked urgently at the Lincoln slowly pulling up, across town on Pearl Hill Road, the Hergenroeder's neighbor, Mrs. Kendall had a belly full of worrying about whether or not to call Rev. Hergenroeder. *Hells bells, I'll make the call and consequences be damned.* Rollstone secretary Linda Dunn answered on the first ring.

"Ah, hello, my name is Kendall. I live next door to the Hergenroeders or, rather, my family does."

"OK, nice to meet you over the phone. What did you say your first name was? I'm Linda Dunn, David's secretary."

"I'm sorry, my name is Evelyn. I need to speak with David, err, Rev. Hergenroeder. I think it's urgent."

"He's not here right now. I don't expect him back to the office today. Could I take a message?"

"Gosh, I suppose. When will he get it?"

"He might call in later today to check messages."

"Dangit! Look I don't know you from Adam but I think something bad has happened to Jeremy..." Evelyn relayed the whole story to Linda, including the smashed bicycle, a description of the car and driver, the bad look on Jeremy's face when he drove by with that strange man, why Alex was even at the house, and how Alex didn't look too sprightly either.

"Look, Evelyn, I'll call Lily McPherson. David, Alex and Jeremy are staying with them in Ashburnham—till all this blows over. From what I understand, Lily can get word to her husband via his CB radio—the one from the house connects to Ed's car. David and Col. McPherson are probably at Edgerly right now to pick up Jeremy."

"Oh yes, they picked up my son yesterday. Very kind of them. Please keep me posted and call me back with any news. I'll continue keeping an eye on their house. Oh, this is so worrisome," Evelyn said as she rang off, forgetting to give Linda her phone number.

Linda phoned the McPherson residence almost before Evelyn had hung up. Lily answered right away. Linda passed along the message and Lily got on the CB immediately.

"Ed, can you read me, Ed?"

Ed and David were standing next to the Lincoln wondering why Officer Callahan and Jeremy's teacher had a scared look on their faces. The pair walked towards Ed and David with Jeremy nowhere in sight.

Ed boomed into the mic, "Just a minute Momma...I think we got us a situation here."

"You're damned right we do, you listen here old man."

"Go ahead, what've you got?" Ed said, as David moved closer to the driver door so he could hear the speaker.

"Earlier today, the Hergenroeder's neighbor saw some big car pulling out of their driveway, with Alex and Jeremy in the back seat. Two hooligans sat next to them. The driver ran over some fancy new bicycle lying in the driveway and crushed it. He got out, apparently Hispanic looking, and threw it in the trunk like so much garbage. *It was a girl's bike.* Later the neighbor, I think her name is Evelyn something, saw the man and Jeremy driving down Pearl Hill Road. Same car!"

"Momma—did she get the license plate?"

"No, she was hiding behind a tree so the man wouldn't see her. By the time she ran to the end of the drive it was too far to see. She said it was a big old car, a Buick or an Oldsmobile. Four door. She said it looked like a battleship—gray in color. I've not seen Alex for several hours. She had wanted to run by the parsonage to clean it up a bit. Said David forgot to throw out a roast beef she had thawing the day Jeremy got kidnapped."

"Good work, Lily. This is a situation. Shit. Keep me posted," Ed advised as he hung up the mic. "David, you catch all that?"

"Sure did. Let's see what Callahan has to say," as the pair moved to meet the guard and Jeremy's teacher.

Callahan spoke right up, "Rev. Hergenroeder! It looks like Jeremy may have left school. Not sure how, but he got a call from your wife in the school office what, Dr. Murphy, around 10:30 a.m. or so?"

"Yes, yes that's right. I just assumed he'd had to go home, given the call. He never came back to class and I just found out that your wife didn't pick him up after all. The front office secretary, Mrs. Sondra Taylor, stopped by my classroom after the bell rang and asked me how Jeremy was faring. Apparently the call involved some news about how sick his grandmother had taken."

"Oh God," David shuddered. "Neither Alex's nor my mother are ill at all. That call was a ruse, I bet."

"Sondra said she spoke with your wife directly and everything seemed normal."

"Normal with a gun to her head, I'll bet," Col. McPherson offered, as he watched Callahan turn tail and run to the school office, surely to call the station.

"David," Ed said, "Best thing you and I can do is head over to Det. McNamara's office and set up a command center."

David felt his knees starting to buckle. "Yes, sir. Let's get on it."

They hopped in the Lincoln and gunned it toward the police station. Little did they know what was about to happen at the shipyard.

CHAPTER 29

Dan Brodie Thrives in his 12 Step Meetings and Picks up the Pace at Work; Jeremy and José Arrive at the Shipyard

As the shipyard's whistle warned the workers that their lunch break was over, Dan Brodie welded with a growing sense of recovery from his gambling addiction. During his lunch break, he'd just finished attending his third Gamblers Anonymous meeting in as many days. He felt grateful he still had a job at all, and welded quickly and efficiently on the side of a massive submarine. When finished, General Dynamics would drop the ship into the bay where it would join its sister subs on Cold War patrols in the Pacific. Dan mused, *I bet that José was behind the smoke screen at Burbank on Sunday. That guy! What I wouldn't give to get my hands on him without all those felons around to protect him. Velma getting fired and all, I suppose, like my sponsor says, this was all a consequence of my gambling addiction. I've polluted her life and she still forgives me. There really is a God somewhere!*

As he finished his welding bead, he stood back up and took off his welding helmet so he could wipe the sweat off his brow. Whenever the salty sweat droplets seeped into his eyes, they'd sting and he'd have to stop welding, otherwise his bead would go off kilter. As he removed his mask, he looked up to see José and some little kid walking toward the union office. And none other than Dominick Sangria was leading the threesome.

Well I'll be damned! How'd that criminal get here on the shipyard? I figured he'd be holed up somewhere seeing as how all of Fitchburg's finest is out looking for him. Who is the kid? No matter, this is my chance...!

Since Connie, the foreman, was working on the other side of the sub, Dan saw his opportunity. He grabbed a monkey wrench and angled over to the side of the union office, awaiting his prey. He could hear muffled voices inside.

"Thank you for seeing us, Rick," Dominick began. "This here's my Uncle, José Gutiérrez. I appreciate your time, uh, we appreciate your making time."

"Certainly," Rick said, as he looked over the threesome. *Have to play this one close to the vest. José, your reputation precedes you. I wouldn't hop in the last life raft from a sinking ship with your sorry ass. Rather drown instead.* "Who is this youngster, Dominick? You know the rules. No children allowed on site."

José intervened, "Ahh, sorry, that's my fault. We'll be out of your hair in a minute Mr. Sullivan. Yessirree. This here's Jeremy—a friend of the family. I'm stuck on babysitting duty...ahh, sorry Jeremy, I mean sitter duty."

"OK, let's get to it. I gotta get back on the yard. Being union boss doesn't exempt me from working like the rest of the guys."

Jeremy felt Rick's head and knew this meeting would not go the way José had hoped. Rick knew all about José's loan sharking with his union members.

"Well, you see," José began, "I represent, or my firm represents, confidentially speaking, in a marketing capacity, several national and local trucking companies. Some of these companies work closely with the stevedores, you know, offloading material from around the globe. I'd like to increase the capacity, or our trucking firms' members would, the ability of the shipping companies to route their goods across the United States. This is my first stop and next I'll be in Los Angeles making the same effort."

"You do realize," Rick responded, "that this here's a ship *building* yard, not a shipping yard. I'm just the steward for the shipbuilder's union here, the IUMSWA Local 8650. We don't handle any freight."

"Yes, yes of course. What I was wanting to ask was if you could make me an introduction to the port authority leadership?"

"Well our unions are yoked, if that's what you mean. Do you have a business card I could pass along?"

"Ahh, no, in my rush to make sure I picked up Jeremy after school, I forgot to grab some."

"Then just write down your name, address and contact information on this sheet here and I'll see what I can do."

"OK, that would be great. Listen, I heard that you have a disabled daughter. So, my prayers for her future."

"Who told you that?" Rick said with barely suppressed anger.

"Ahh, well, I just heard it around. If there's ever anything our marketing firm can do for you and your family please ask. You know scholarships for special schools, medical bills, etc."

"Are you trying to bribe me Mister?"

Dominick stepped in to try to salvage the situation, "No, Rick, José here just helps out with some of the guys' bills now and then."

"Yeah, I heard about that. I think it's best you three leave and leave now."

José realized he'd have to take a different approach—a different day. *I'll find ways of getting to and through you, asshole. You shouldn't bite the hand that might someday feed you and your daughter.*

"Sure, we'll leave. Sorry to take up your valuable time," José said as he moved to leave with Dominick and Jeremy following close behind. As he started down the stairs, José held open the office door for Jeremy and Dominick.

José hardly heard Dominick's warning, "Watch out Jos..." before Dan Brodie stormed José slamming the monkey wrench on José's left knee.

"You sonofabitch José! You've ruined my life!" Before Dominick could grab Dan, Dan swung the wrench high and hit José's right knee, revenge for the beating he took in Boston at Antonio's.

The office door swung open and on came Rick. "Dan, calm down..."

"Calm down your own damn self, Rick. This here's a wanted man. Fitchburg Police are looking for him."

As Dan finished speaking, he looked at Jeremy and said, "You have got to be Jeremy! Are you OK, son?

"Yes sir. José kidnapped me and some of his guys got my mom tied up at home."

"You hear that Rick! You hear that!" Dan shouted to Rick's back as Rick climbed back into the office to call the police.

Dan followed. "You tell Connie what happened and that I'm taking this kid home now. You all can dock my pay, but I owe this kid, I do."

Rick nodded as he waited for the police dispatcher to come on the line. He watched out the open door to make sure José didn't try to run off. Dan walked back out of the office and admired José lying on the ground alone, moaning. Dominick had made a fast exit, bolting back to his welding area. Dan looked up to see Jeremy standing off to the side about 10 yards away watching everything.

"C'mon Jeremy. I'll take you home."

"Shouldn't we call my dad, first, let him know where I am? I'm supposed to let my folks know."

"Good thinking. Follow me into Rick's office. He'll place the call."

José had promised he'd call the orchard house gang *no later* than 4:00 p.m., one way or the other, success or failure. As the clock approached 3:45 p.m. and no word from José, Benita and her 'patient,' Ricardo, felt panic setting in. Exhausted and with Alex now bound and gagged on the living room floor (despite José's promise to the contrary), they'd dozed in fits and starts, ever vigilant for *The Call*. The phone hadn't rung yet, its silence deafening. They started to realize that José's second kidnapping scheme likely had ended in disaster or his arrest or both. He'd left strict instructions about Alex: "Keep her hogtied and if you don't hear from me by 4:00 p.m. get the hell outta Dodge and head for the safe house."

"This is loco, man," Luis argued to the silent room. Alex stared at him wondering if they'd take her to the safe house with them.

"Yeah, I got a real bad feeling," Hector offered. "We should bolt. Now!"

Putting up a brave front, Ricardo said, "José knows what he's doing. Let's give him the 12 remaining minutes. He'll call. I just know it. So sit down and shaddup!"

Luis and Hector looked at each other.

"I'm outta here. Hector, this is stupid," Luis exclaimed as he got up from his perch on one of the kitchen chairs they'd brought in from Juan's kitchen.

"I'm with you!" Hector responded.

The pair bolted, but not for the safe house. Luis had other plans and Hector followed him down Pearl Hill Road.

As soon as they dashed off, Benita decided she'd had enough. "Ricardo, let's go. Just leave the woman. The cops'll find her soon enough. Jeremy will tell them where this place is. José's failed. Face facts!"

"OK, but you gotta help me to get into your car. Leaving that hospital was stupid for Pilar and now I'm wondering if it was stupid of me, too. My wrist hurts like Hades. It still feels like I'm moving my fingers even though they ain't there!" Ricardo's left wrist, still wrapped after surgeons closed up the maw that had been his left hand, needed a fresh dressing.

"That's phantom limb syndrome," Benita advised. "I remember reading about how they started diagnosing it during the Civil War, you know, with all those leg and arm amputations the field surgeons did."

"Ah, shit. What's the cure?"

"There isn't one that I've heard of. Hopefully it will go away on its own. We've got bigger problems to worry about. I'm sorry."

As Benita helped him to his feet, she thought, *he's gotta get a prosthetic—but from where? I gotta make sure his wound doesn't get infected like Pilar's or he, too, will die. Nursing school didn't train me for this—I'm supposed to be part of a treating health care TEAM, dangit.*

They both eyeballed Alex and never thought twice about untying her. As they headed out the door, Ricardo whispered to Benita, "We should head to the *other* safe house in Lynn. José told me the code to the combination locks that are on the entry door. There's more stuff there like a change of clothes for me, money and a couple of guns."

Benita said, "I could just go out and buy us some stuff, ya know, provisions. That little Datsun truck won't hide us very well when the sun comes up."

"Don't worry. We've got a spare car at the place in Lynn—for just this kind of occasion."

In the distance, the pair heard a faint series of police sirens and they hurried to the truck. Benita started it up and they roared in reverse out of the driveway.

"Head up Pearl Hill. I know the back way to Route 2. The cops won't be coming that way since it's too far away from the downtown precinct."

As soon as Alex heard the Datsun shoot out the driveway, she wriggled against her rope with all her might. After several minutes, she finally broke free of the knot. She scampered out the door and started running down Pearl Hill Road for all her life. As her feet pounded the pavement, she didn't tire at all. She could hear sirens, but they sounded far off. As she ran into her driveway, she saw the first of the police cars zoom past the parsonage. She tried to wave down the patrol car, but the officer just ignored her, never realizing she was the kidnap victim he was called to save. Alex ran into the house and called the police station.

Sergeant Finch Hudson answered and, once he got her calmed down, said, "Oh yeah. Your son called us from Quincy, ma'am. Told us right where José's orchard hideout was. I dispatched three patrol cars there not ten minutes ago."

"Is Jeremy OK?"

"Yes, yes he is. Brave young man he is. I don't know how to tell you this, but Dan Brodie is driving him here from Quincy."

"Brodie? He's the one that started all this trouble!"

"Yes, I understand. Apparently he's gotten religion. Wants to make things right. Talked to him myself, I did. Jeremy said it was Dan that cut down José with a monkey wrench to both knees. He's sort of a hero for the moment. Got his foreman on the phone. Some guy named Sullivan. He vouched for him and I figured it would be faster than us sending a patrol car down to Quincy."

"Alright, I guess that makes sense. Does my husband know what's going on?"

"Yes. I called up to the McPherson's. Got the missus on the line and she got us hooked up through the Colonel's CB. I think they are headed to the orchard house as we speak. You want I should call them back and tell them to meet you at your house?"

"Please. And, geez, I guess our family owes you a second round of thank yous, Sergeant!"

"Well, you are most welcome and I'd sure appreciate the chance to meet your son sometime after all the dust settles."

"I'll bring him in to visit you and we'll have a picnic basket for you and the other officers. I think I know some ladies at Rollstone who'd be glad to pitch in with a feast. They're all great cooks. Oh, wait! I hear a car in the driveway."

"Keep me on the line, Mrs. Hergenroeder, while you check. If you don't pick back up, I'll send a car your way pronto."

Alex walked across the kitchen stretching the phone cord to its limit. "No, we are OK. It's my husband David and Col. McPherson. I'm going to ring off. Thanks for everything."

"Yes ma'am."

Alex ran out to the driveway and the threesome hugged. She got David and Ed up to speed and they agreed to wait at the house for Dan's truck to appear with their son. As they entered the kitchen, Alex finally got to clean the stain on the kitchen table that the festering roast beef had leached out.

Back in Quincy, the local police had arrested José and hauled him off to Quincy General Hospital. They'd posted a triple guard on his room. Finch had called ahead and warned his desk sergeant peer to expect another smoke out routine like the Rangers had pulled at Burbank.

Several miles south towards Boston, Judge Melanson soon would be obliged to revoke José's bail and Fitchburg soon would get its fill of justice due, all under the watchful eyes of Assistant District Attorney General Chris Johnson and Det. Rod McNamara.

EPILOGUE

Tuesday June 18, 1968—6:30 p.m.
Fitchburg Sentinel—Late Special Edition

Police Thwart Juvenile's Second Kidnapping

By Kristen Brigham

L ate this afternoon, Quincy police arrested Fitchburg
resident José Gutiérrez at the General Dynamics
shipyard charging him in the kidnapping of a five-year-old
boy. Police made the arrest at Quincy General Hospital
after an ambulance rushed him to the ER. A fellow
shipyard worker had assaulted Gutiérrez, smashing both his
knees with a monkey wrench. Police did not arrest the yard
worker and refused to release his name.

Just last week, Fitchburg Police arrested Gutierrez's
cousins, Pilar and Ricardo Gutierrez, after they had
kidnapped a five-year-old boy during the lunch recess
period at Edgerly Elementary School. On Sunday, the latter
two Gutierrez men escaped from police custody while they
were under armed guard at Burbank Hospital. Police
theorize that they had inside help because someone planted
smoke bombs in the hospital's ventilation units, setting off
alarms and forcing the evacuation of most of the hospital's
patients. One patient nearly died from a heart attack
during the evacuation. Quincy and Fitchburg police
representatives refused to say whether the boy was the

same child kidnapped in the earlier incident at Edgerly. Both departments have withheld the boys' names along with the names of their parents.

Det. Rod McNamara, who led the hunt for the first kidnapping victim and his abductors last week also refused comment. During the first kidnapping last Tuesday, an unnamed gunmen sat atop a nearby roof and shot Pilar and Ricardo Gutiérrez, severely injuring both men. Fire Department ambulances rushed both men to Burbank. The pair had brought the kidnap victim with them as they parked behind a local psychiatrist's office. School officials did confirm earlier today that Fitchburg Police have stationed armed guards on duty while school is in session.

Edgerly Principal Dr. Joseph Chandler denied that any child had been kidnapped from school today. "Our children are all safe and we are thankful for the police presence as we wind down the school year." School Superintendent Alfred Gonyer recently appointed Chandler to the position, making him the district's first African American principal. Edgerly is the main teaching facility for students on the campus of Fitchburg State Teacher's College.

Additional unnamed sources confirmed that, earlier today, a five-year-old boy left school without permission and eluded police guards. It is unclear if this unnamed child was the kidnapping victim.

Massachusetts State Police arrested Mr. José Gutiérrez last Tuesday, charging him with loan sharking, extortion, conspiracy to transport stolen goods across state lines and criminal assault. During his June 13 arraignment and bail hearing in Boston Superior Court, Judge Chuck Melanson released Gutiérrez on $10,000 bail. A search of the bond records revealed that his grandmother, Daniella Gutiérrez, posted the deed to her Fitchburg home to guarantee the bail amount. When reached earlier this afternoon, Mrs. Gutiérrez refused to comment on the bail matter.

Fitchburg Police sources acknowledged off the record that Mr. José Gutiérrez is their prime suspect in arranging the escape of his cousins from their guarded rooms at Burbank Hospital last Sunday. The pair left in an ambulance after the smoke bombs diverted their guards' attention. The whereabouts of Pilar and Ricardo Gutierrez are still unknown.

As this breaking story unfolds, The Sentinel will publish further details in tomorrow's edition.

The End...

ACKNOWLEDGEMENTS

Self-publishing a book is the penultimate do-it-yourself job. If you are lucky, you get help as I did from friends and family. It is sort of like a neighborhood yard sale where everyone contributes to the enterprise ideas, suggestions and criticisms. I have found that it is easy to write a book and get the story down on paper. The hard parts that take ten times as long are the editing, revising and making sure I catch all of the *thousands* of mistakes I made with each successive draft.

I learned the hard way with my first novel to be critical not only of my own work, but that of paid editors. Some edits are accurate and spot on, and some not so much. The trick is to separate wheat from chafe, otherwise my readers will sheepishly email me to say that I missed a word or left a character hanging on page X. At the end of the day, I have to fend for myself and decide which changes to make. Therefore, if you find mistakes and I know you might, I'm to blame! Those who are not to blame and for whom I am ever so grateful include the following:

Wendy Overlock, my wife and confidante. Wendy implored me *for decades* to put pen to paper and write a novel. Her frequent refrain on our morning walks was, "When are you going to write your novel?" To which I could only respond, "Soon." Wendy is my best editor, partly because she can call me on my B.S., and does not hesitate to tell me a chapter transition does not make sense. Thank you Dee!

To my colleague Nancy McCullough, RN, an oncology nurse and researcher at Nashville General Hospital where we both work: Thank you! Nancy edited my first novel and thank heavens had the temerity to point out internal inconsistencies in several chapters. She did it again with this novel, handing me back 177 pages with purple slips showing where the errors sat on each page.

I have to thank Mom, too. Mrs. Sally Overlock read the first three chapters and called me immediately after finishing to say, "What happens next? Is Jeremy going to be OK?"

Finally, to the Rev. Enoch Fuzz to whom I owe some accolades. Rev. Fuzz, who ministers at Corinthian Baptist Church in Nashville, TN, has been an inspiration to me. He will be embarrassed that I mentioned him in this book. For two whole minutes.